SINISTER SPRINKLES

A DONUT SHOP MYSTERY

SINISTER SPRINKLES

JESSICA BECK

**WHEELER
CHIVERS**

This Large Print edition is published by Wheeler Publishing, Waterville, Maine, USA and by AudioGO Ltd, Bath, England.
Wheeler Publishing, a part of Gale, Cengage Learning.
Copyright © 2010 by Jessica Beck.
The moral right of the author has been asserted.

ALL RIGHTS RESERVED

The text of this Large Print edition is unabridged.
Other aspects of the book may vary from the original edition.
Set in 16 pt. Plantin.

LIBRARY OF CONGRESS CATALOGING-IN-PUBLICATION DATA

Beck, Jessica.
    Sinister sprinkles : a donut shop mystery / by Jessica Beck.
        p. cm. — (Wheeler Publishing large print cozy mystery)
    ISBN-13: 978-1-4104-3467-8 (softcover)
    ISBN-10: 1-4104-3467-2 (softcover)
    1. Coffee shops—North Carolina—Fiction. 2. Private investigators—Fiction. 3. North Carolina—Fiction. 4. Large type books. I. Title.
    PS3602.E2693.S56 2010
    813'.6—dc22   2010049212

BRITISH LIBRARY CATALOGUING-IN-PUBLICATION DATA AVAILABLE

Published in 2011 in the U.S. by arrangement with St. Martin's Press, LLC.
Published in 2011 in the U.K. by arrangement with the author.

U.K. Hardcover: 978 1 445 83684 3 (Chivers Large Print)
U.K. Softcover: 978 1 445 83685 0 (Camden Large Print)

Printed in the United States of America
2 3 4 5 6   15 14 13 12 11

ED130

For T,
You know who you are,
and why this book is dedicated to you!

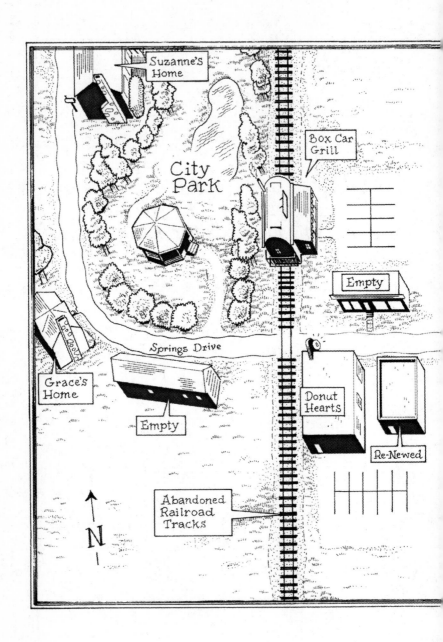

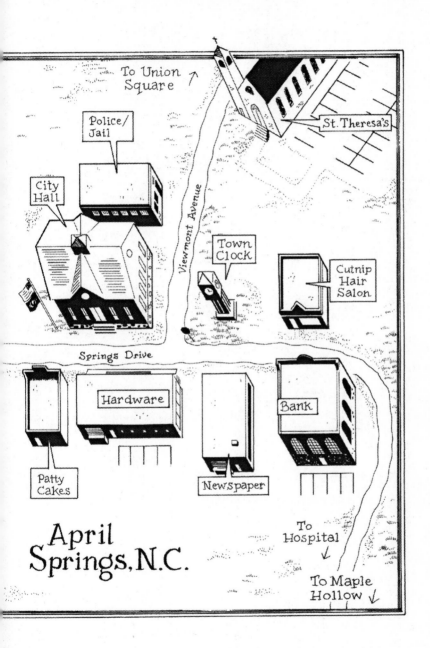

"I bought a donut and they gave me a receipt. When will I ever need to prove that I bought a donut?"

— Mitch Hedberg

CHAPTER 1

I heard the first scream just as I gave a warm apple-spice donut and change to Phyllis Higgins from the booth outside my shop, Donut Hearts, during the nineteenth annual April Springs Winter Carnival. There had been whoops of great merriment long before then coming from the crowd of folks out enjoying the displays and vendors' offerings, but there was a quality to this particular shriek that chilled me to my toes, despite my wearing two layers of thick woolen socks and my most sensible shoes. I wondered for a second if it had been some kind of aberration, but then there was another scream, and yet another.

When I heard someone in front of the courthouse shout, "Muriel Stevens has been murdered," I knew the Winter Carnival — and Muriel — had come to a sudden and abrupt end.

■ ■ ■ ■

Christmas is my favorite time of year. I love the way my neighbors decorate their homes with icicles of light and erect trees overloaded with ornaments and tinsel inside. It's no accident that my attitude is reflected in the selection of donuts at my shop, offering treats adorned with red and green icing and glistening sprinkles that overload the display cases in honor of the holidays.

Our Winter Carnival — balanced precariously around Thanksgiving, Hanukkah, and Christmas — offers the residents of my small town in the North Carolina foothills of the Blue Ridge Mountains the opportunity, even the excuse, to go outside and enjoy the brisk weather. During most years of the festival, we hadn't experienced our first snow of the season yet, but at the moment, the streets of our quaint little town were covered in a glistening layer of white. It was like everything was topped with icy frosting, a place nearly everybody in the world would visit if they could.

But now all that was ruined.

Phyllis dropped her donut in the snow when she heard Muriel's name.

"Suzanne, could it be true?" she asked me.

"I was standing right here beside you when we heard the first scream," I said. "Let me get you another donut, and then we'll go see what's going on."

"Don't bother," she said. "I couldn't bear to eat it now. Poor Muriel." I knew Phyllis was shaken. She'd never passed up the chance at a donut in her life.

As she waddled away toward the courthouse, I turned around and rushed into Donut Hearts. It was handy having my booth right in front of my business, and I'd asked my friend and the carnival coordinator, Trish Granger — owner of the Boxcar grill just across the street from my donut shop — for the favor, which she'd gladly granted me. There had been some grumbling from a few of the other vendors when they learned of my coup, so to be fair, Trish decided to scrap the previous year's plan and start completely over. Business owners in April Springs got their first choice of spots, and vendors from out of town had to make do with what was left. It made sense, especially for me. If I was going to supply my customers with fresh, hot donuts, I needed to be as close to the source as I could manage. I had my assistant, Emma Blake, inside, ready to add hot glaze to some of the extra donuts we'd made that morning as we needed fresh supplies. I would have loved to make the donuts themselves as they were needed, but the process didn't lend itself to sudden orders, and the warm glaze still managed to give the donuts an air of instant creation.

"What's going on?" Emma asked as she peered outside at the people hurrying by the shop window. Barely out of her teens, Emma had a petite figure I envied and flaming red hair.

We watched what was going on from where we stood inside the shop. My donut shop was housed in an old railroad depot, and it afforded plenty of views of the abandoned tracks beside us as well as Springs Drive through the front windows, the main road in our little town.

"I need you to watch the booth," I said. "Somebody just screamed that Muriel Stevens is dead, and I need to check it out."

Emma reached for the telephone. "Should I call 911?"

"No, from the sound of it, it came from in front of City Hall. I'm sure Chief Martin is already there."

Emma frowned at me as she asked, "Suzanne, you're not investigating another murder, are you?"

I shook my head. "No way. I've had my fill of that. I just want to go check on poor Muriel."

"Fine, but come back as soon as you hear anything. Promise?"

"I'll get back as fast as I can," I said as I left the shop.

The snow was falling again, picking up its intensity, and I wondered if that would affect the crime scene. I'd been thrown into an investigation or two in the past, and I'd been forced to learn a little about police techniques, if for no other reason than to keep myself out of jail as I dug around the edges of cases that impacted my life.

Muriel's murder wasn't going to be one of them, though. She was a regular customer of mine, but nearly every other business owner in April Springs could make that claim as well. Muriel Stevens was the grandmother figure everyone loved, and I couldn't imagine what would drive anyone to kill her.

As I started toward the courthouse, I felt a hand grab my shoulder from behind, and I wondered for a split second if I was next on the killer's list.

Then I heard Gabby Williams speak, and almost found myself wishing it was the murderer instead. At least then I could be openly hostile, something that I could never afford to do with Gabby. She was the town wag, spreading stories and rumors at a speed that put satellite relays to shame, and worse yet, her used clothing shop was right next to mine. Getting on her bad side was a form of character suicide, and I always tried to tread on her good side, though at times it was a tough line to toe.

"Suzanne, where are you going in such a hurry?"

I tried to brush her hand loose, but she had the grip of a longshoreman, despite her prim and petite appearance. It would be easy to underestimate the woman, but I'd made that mistake before, and wasn't about to make it again.

"It's Muriel Stevens," I said.

Gabby's face went ashen. "What about her?"

"I heard someone say she was dead. Murdered," I added softly.

Gabby frowned. "Why are we standing here, then? Let's go."

Her grip barely eased as we hurried up the sidewalk toward the courthouse. There was a crowd gathered around the town clock mounted on an ancient cast-iron pole, but it was clear no one was all that interested in the time. As Gabby and I fought our way through the mass of people to get a better look, her grip on my shoulder finally eased, and I broke away from her before she could reattach it.

I saw George Morris, a loyal customer and retired cop who helped me with inquiries from time to time, so I pushed through the crowd toward him.

"What's going on?" I asked as I finally reached him.

"Hey, Suzanne," George said. "At this point it's still too hard to tell, but someone shouted that Muriel Stevens had been murdered, so of course everybody in town rushed right over here. I tried to help with crowd control, but the chief sent me over here." He looked miffed by the thought of his dismissal, and I didn't blame him. "I thought I might be of some use is all."

"It's tough being a retired cop, isn't it?" I said as I patted his shoulder.

"I admit it, 'Serve and Protect' kind of gets in your blood." As George spoke, his gaze stayed firmly on the body in the snow. When folks nearby shifted from foot to foot, I caught a glimpse or two of Muriel's coat, and I knew that there'd been no mistaking her, even from that distance. The jacket was a patchwork whirlwind of reds, yellows, oranges, and blues, something as distinctive as the woman herself had been.

Then I saw a touch of gray in the murder victim's hair — which made me look closer — and said softly, "That's not Muriel."

"What are you talking about, Suzanne," George said. "No one else in the world has a coat like that."

"I'm telling you, it's not her," I repeated, staring again at what had to be a wig. The black and gray hair had skewed a little — maybe in the attack — and I could see blonde hair beneath it pinned down. If there was one thing Muriel was prouder of than her coat, it had to be her lustrous black hair. Whenever a gray hair dared to appear, it was quickly either plucked or dyed out of existence.

Before he could ask me more, we were interrupted by a voice behind me.

"There you are," Gabby said as she joined us. I moved instinctively away from her, but if she noticed, she kept it to herself.

After a moment, Gabby said flatly, "That's not Muriel," leaving no room for debate.

For once, and maybe the first time in my life, I was startled to realize that I agreed with her. "That's what I've been trying to tell George. It's the hair, isn't it?"

Gabby didn't even look back at the body as she spoke. "No, that's not it. She brought

18

a bag of clothes into the shop yesterday, and three hours later she was pounding on my door, a good thirty minutes after I was closed for the day. It seemed that she was under the impression that she had put her favorite coat," she paused and glanced briefly at the body, "that coat, in the bag by mistake. She wanted it back, and I mean instantly. The problem was, though, when we went through the bag, the coat wasn't there. She claimed someone stole it from my backroom, but I've never had anyone ever take any of my merchandise."

"At least not that you're aware of," George said.

She put her ferret-eyed gaze on him. "Sir, I know my business, and I know my inventory. If I say something about my shop, you can believe it."

George was suppressing a smile, but he somehow managed to keep her from noticing. "My apologies, ma'am." I swear, if he'd had a hat, he would have tipped it to her.

"Can you even be sure the coat was there in the first place? Did you go through the bag the second it arrived?" I asked.

"Suzanne, I don't have time to evaluate the things I'm offered immediately," Gabby said. "I categorize and price the items at my leisure, not my clients'."

"So you can't be sure the coat ever made it to ReNewed," I said.

Gabby frowned. "I just told you, it was never there." She paused, then added, "Though Muriel was absolutely certain of it. She accused me of keeping it for myself, as if I'd ever wear something as garish as that, much less display it in my store." Gabby Williams made a nice living reselling some of the nicer clothing items in our part of North Carolina. I'd bought a suit there once myself, and with our shops next door to each other, I saw her inventory more often than I liked. She was right, too. I couldn't imagine Gabby ever selling something as, well, for lack of a better word, colorful as Muriel's coat in her shop.

Chief Martin was shouting for everyone's attention, and we quieted down to listen to what he had to say.

"Folks, it's pretty obvious this year's Carnival is over. We'd appreciate it if you'd give your names and addresses to one of the deputies standing by as you leave. Have a driver's license ready to show them, or some kind of photo identification so they can confirm your information."

"Who killed Muriel?" a voice from the back shouted.

"We're not ready to disclose what happened here yet," he said. "And I'm not going to answer any questions until I've got a better handle on what's going on."

I couldn't help myself. "How about a statement, then? It's pretty obvious that's not Muriel Stevens. Why don't you tell us who it really is under that wig?"

Chief Martin met my gaze, then said icily, "Suzanne Hart, get up here. Right now. Everybody else, do as I said. Now." The last word was delivered with an explosive forcefulness that got the crowd moving, albeit reluctantly. Deputies were posted on both sides of Springs Drive with clipboards, and I noticed folks digging for their IDs as I walked up to the police chief.

That's when I realized that George was right behind me.

I stopped in my tracks and said, "I appreciate the show of support, but I don't want to make him any madder than I already have."

"Don't sweat it," George said. "I'm not going to let him bully you."

I shook my head, but I didn't say anything else as I walked toward the chief. If he wanted to get rid of George, let him try. Honestly, I was kind of glad he was there beside me, despite my effort to convince him otherwise.

"Just Suzanne," the chief said when he saw him.

"Sorry, that's not happening," George said.

He and the chief locked glares, then Martin waved a hand in the air. "Don't push me, George."

"I won't any more than I have to," my friend said, and I had to wonder how much of his bridge to the April Springs Police Department he was burning on my account. As a retired cop, George enjoyed nearly free access to his old workplace, but we all knew that it was at the whim and will of the chief.

Chief Martin seemed to forget all about him as he focused back on me. "Suzanne, how did you know it wasn't Muriel, especially from that far away?"

"Gabby Williams told me Muriel lost her coat yesterday, so I figured it couldn't be her. Plus, I saw that black-haired wig with touches of gray on that poor woman's head, and I knew it without a doubt. You know how proud Muriel was of her black hair. She never wore a wig in her life, especially not one with gray hair in it. Whoever was killed was a blonde, you can see that, if you look closely enough. So, who was it?"

"You seem to know a lot about this," the chief of police said, still refusing to answer my question.

"She's observant," George said.

"Who was it, Chief?" I asked again, hoping he'd tell me, though I knew he had every reason in the world not to.

"We're not releasing that information at the moment," he said as he turned his back on me and dismissed me.

I tried to get another look at the body, but there was still a cluster of police blocking the way, so that was pointless. I turned to George and said, "Let's go."

As we walked toward one of the deputies, I told George, "I didn't mean for you to get into trouble because of me."

He shrugged. "If it wasn't you, it would be something else. I seem to have a knack for it lately." As our gazes met, George added, "You need to stay out of this investigation."

"I'm not disagreeing with you," I said. "I just wanted to know what happened, so I asked."

George didn't respond to that, and after we gave our names to one of the deputies and showed our IDs, we went our separate ways.

I walked back to my booth, thinking about what I had to do to shut it down for another season. The Carnival still had a few hours until its official closing time, but I had to agree with Chief Martin. It was no longer a time for fun and frivolity.

When I got back to Donut Hearts, I found Emma peering out the front window toward me.

She said, "What's going on? Is it true? Is Muriel dead?"

"No, it was someone else," I said as I took off my jacket and hung it on the coat rack. I looked around, happy to be back in my shop where I felt safe and happy. The front dining area was filled with couches and comfortable chairs, while the walls and harsh concrete floors were painted with a pretty plum faux finish. All in all, it was a lovely place to spend my life.

Emma asked, "Who was it, then?"

"The police aren't saying," I said.

"And you're going to let it go at that?" she asked. "That's not like you, Suzanne. What's happened to you?"

"I've decided to keep my nose out of it, for once," I said. "Do you want to help break down the booth, or would you like to stay inside where it's warm?"

"Thanks, but the snow's still coming down pretty hard. I think I'll cover the front," she said.

Emma wasn't a big fan of the cold, and

one of her constant threats was to move as far south as she could until she could see the outline of Cuba in the distance. I'd been to Key West once — had even rubbed the colorful marker at the southernmost point of the U.S. for good luck — and I didn't have the heart to tell her that Cuba was invisible from there, still nearly ninety miles away. Emma perused college brochures of schools in warmer climates whenever the temperature dropped below forty degrees. I knew my assistant would go off to study somewhere soon enough — and I dreaded that day like a root canal — but I couldn't expect her to be my helper for the rest of her life.

"I'll take care of the booth, then," I said as I grabbed my jacket and headed back outside. The sooner I got to work, the faster I could hope to forget seeing that body lying on the cold, snow-covered ground. I loved the snow, relished the way it decorated the world with a fresh, new coat of promise. Even the ugliest things took on a new perspective with the brush of winter.

I was just beginning to take the vinyl banner down from the top of the booth when I heard a familiar voice beside me.

"Need a hand with that?"

It was my ex-husband Max, more handsome than he had any right to be, with wavy brown hair and deep brown eyes. He also had a voice that could melt my toes when he put his mind to it.

"No, thank you. I've got it," I said as I reached up for the banner and managed to grab one corner of it.

"Here, let me get that," he said as he brushed past me and took the edge from me. From his proximity, I could smell Max's subtle cologne, and despite my feelings about the man, I was ashamed to realize that I had to fight the urge to lean toward him and savor his presence.

He easily plucked the banner off its hooks, then folded it before handing it back to me. "Here you go. You must have sold out fast."

I shook my head. "No, there are dozens of donuts inside that I don't have a clue what to do with."

"Then why are we taking the banner down?" he asked.

"I don't need it now that the carnival's over."

Max looked around, and seemed to realize that most of Springs Drive was deserted. He looked at his watch as he shook his head. "What happened? It's supposed to run another two hours."

"Did you just get here?"

Max shrugged. "You know I like to sleep in whenever the opportunity affords itself," he said. "I haven't been up all that long. So, what happened?"

"Somebody was murdered under the town clock," I said.

It was pretty clear that Max was hearing this for the first time. "What happened? Who was it? Come on, Suze, give me some details."

I hated when he called me Suze, but he was too upset for me to correct him. Max, though his exterior was always cool and urbane, was a soft cookie on the inside, one of the things that had drawn me to him in the first place.

"A woman wearing Muriel Stevens's jacket was killed. I'm not sure how, nobody really said."

He frowned. "How do you know it wasn't Muriel? And why was someone else wearing her coat?"

"The murder victim had a gray-haired wig on, and Muriel never wore one in her life. Besides, Muriel told Gabby Williams she lost her jacket yesterday, so it couldn't have been her."

"If it wasn't Muriel, then who was it?"

"I don't know," I said as I handed him a set of empty trays. "Make yourself useful

27

since you're here and take these in to Emma."

"Yes, ma'am," he said, adding a grin. "I'm your man."

"You used to be, but you quit on me, remember?"

Max groaned. "Don't bring Darlene up again, would you?"

"I won't if you don't," I said. "I have no desire to ever talk about that woman again." I'd caught my ex-husband in bed with Darlene Higgins, thus the end of our marriage and the beginning of a new life for me as a single woman. I'd reacted quickly to finding them together, divorcing my husband, moving in with my mother, taking back my maiden name of Hart, and buying a rundown shop and converting it into Donut Hearts.

Max took the trays inside, then returned to help me break down the actual booth itself. It was made of plywood, two-by-fours, and enough bolts to keep it up, but still easy enough to erect and disassemble when needed. I worked a few fairs a year selling my donuts, and it was handy having a nice place to work from when I was away from my shop.

Max and I had just carried the last piece into the shop and put it all into my storage room when the front door chimed.

"Do you need to get that?" he asked, once again standing more than a little too close to me than I liked.

"No, Emma's covering the front," I said.

"Then there's no reason to rush back up there."

He was definitely pushing his luck now, and he knew it.

I said, "Tell you what. I'll buy you a donut and a fresh cup of coffee for helping me break down."

"How about two donuts, and a hot chocolate?" he countered.

I couldn't help smiling. "You never know when to quit, do you?"

"I like to think it's part of my charm."

I patted his cheek. "You would, wouldn't you?"

He followed me back to the front, and I was surprised to find Chief Martin talking to Emma there.

"I said I was sorry," I said the second I saw him. "I didn't mean to give anything away. It was just a gut reaction."

"I'm not here to see you," the chief said.

"What did I do?" Emma asked.

"You, either."

Max took a step forward. "Then you must want to see me, though I can't imagine what it could be about."

"Let's go somewhere we can talk," the chief said as he glanced over at me.

"If you have anything to say to me, you can say it in front of these ladies," Max said. "I've got nothing to hide."

"I'm not so sure about that," the chief said.

"What's this about?" Max asked, the usual playfulness in his voice now gone.

The chief glanced over at me, then said, "There's no use keeping it a secret anymore. Your ex-wife was right. It wasn't Muriel Stevens."

It was all I could do not to say, "I told you so," but I managed to contain myself. "Then who was it?" I asked.

Chief Martin ignored me. He asked Max, "Do you mind telling me where you were for the last hour?"

Max frowned. "I was sleeping — alone, unfortunately — and then I grabbed a quick shower, got dressed, and came out to see the festivities. Why do you ask? Are you just naturally curious, or do I need an alibi?"

"Why do you ask that?" the chief said.

"Because I've got the feeling you think I had something to do with whoever got killed. I can assure you, I didn't do it."

The chief frowned. "Save your assurances for someone else. Did you see anybody along the way from your place to the donut shop who can vouch for you?"

"No, I was surprised how deserted the streets were. Everyone was at the carnival, no doubt."

The chief frowned, then said, "Everyone but you."

I was amazed at Max's patience, but I knew it couldn't last much longer. I blurted out, "Get to the point, Chief."

"Stop telling me what to do, Suzanne," he snapped at me.

I took a step back from the force of his protest.

Max noticed it, too. "She's right. Why are you grilling me?"

"You have an intimate relationship with the victim," the chief said. "That automatically makes you someone I need to speak with."

"The only person I care about in all of April Springs is standing right over there," he said as he pointed to me.

"She's not the only person you've been with in your life, though, is she?"

I knew what he was going to say next before the words left his lips, but his voice still fell like muted thunder as he added, "The murder victim was an old girlfriend of yours. Somebody killed Darlene Higgins."

31

APPLE CIDER DONUT DELIGHTS

These donuts are delightful any time of year, but my family particularly enjoys them when the weather outside turns a bit chilly. In particular, the first step of thoroughly heating the apple cider fills the kitchen with more than just a delicious aroma; it also infuses a host of precious memories into the air.

Ingredients

3/4 cup apple cider
1 cup granulated sugar
1/4 cup margarine, soft
2 eggs
1/2 cup buttermilk
4 cups all-purpose flour
2 teaspoons baking powder
1 teaspoon baking soda
1 teaspoon nutmeg
1 teaspoon cinnamon
1/2 teaspoon salt

Directions

Heat the apple cider to boiling in a shallow saucepan for 10 minutes, then remove from the heat and cool. In the meantime, cream the butter and sugar together until smooth. Beat the eggs, then add them to the mixture, stirring thoroughly. Next, sift together the flour, baking powder, baking soda, cinnamon, nutmeg and salt. Add the dry ingredients to the wet, stirring just enough to blend them all together. Place the dough on a floured surface and pat out until it's between 1/2 and 1/4 inch thick. Cut out donut shapes or diamonds, or use a ravioli cutter to make round, solid shapes. Fry the donuts in canola oil at 370°F until brown, flipping halfway through the process. This will take 3–5 minutes. Drain on paper towels, then dust with powdered sugar.

Makes approximately 2 dozen donuts

CHAPTER 2

I saw Max start to wobble a little at the news, so I moved in quickly to support him before he hit the floor.

He steadied himself in my grasp, then pulled away from me, as if he were suddenly embarrassed by the close contact.

"Are you sure it was Darlene?" Max asked the chief.

"There's no doubt about it. Can you tell me why she was walking around the Winter Carnival wearing Muriel Stevens's jacket and a wig that made her look thirty years older?"

"I don't have a clue," Max said, and I knew instantly that he was lying. How odd. I was considering calling him on it, even with the chief of police standing right there, when he beat me to it.

Chief Martin asked him, "You're not putting on some kind of production right now, are you?"

Max ran our local theater group, and Darlene had joined it to be closer to him, or so I'd heard from the rumor mill around April Springs. Max had sworn their affair had been a one-time event, but Darlene's constant zeal for an encore made me doubt it.

Max ran a finger along his nose, a sure sign he was evading the truth. I just wished I'd learned to read him that well while we'd been married. He finally said, "We're doing *A New Year in Love,* and there's one part for an older woman, but she wouldn't have tried out for that. I haven't started casting it yet. Auditions aren't until tomorrow."

The chief wasn't about to let it go that easily, though. "Was Darlene's name on your list?"

Max shrugged. "To be honest with you, I haven't even studied it yet. Hang on a second. I've got it right here." He reached into his back pocket and pulled out a sheet of yellow legal pad notepaper.

"Why are you carrying that around with you?" I asked.

Chief Martin shot me a dirty look, but it was pretty clear that he wanted to know as well.

"I've got to make some hard choices, so I thought I'd walk around the carnival and think about who signed up," he said. "I purposely didn't look at it so I could save it for today. You know my process, Suzanne."

I wasn't about to respond to that.

Max scanned the list, and sure enough, Darlene's name was on it. "What do you know. She was going to try out for Penelope. What I can't figure out is why on earth she would want that part."

"What's so special about that?" I asked.

Max said, "It's an older woman, and Darlene was obsessed with her fear of getting old. She thought it was worse than dying."

"Somebody saved her the trouble of finding out," the chief said, a little too callously for my taste. Then again, he wasn't exactly vying for my approval.

"Who else was trying out for the role?" I asked.

The police chief said, "Suzanne, I'd appreciate it if you'd keep your crazy questions to yourself. No one's going to kill somebody for a role in a community theater group."

"Don't be so sure. These things get pretty heated," Max said.

He looked at the list, then shook his head. "There's no way that's right. It's got to be a coincidence."

"Whose name is on there, Max?" the chief asked.

He frowned, then admitted, "There are two other names written here. One is Trish Granger."

"Who's the other?" Emma asked. I'd nearly forgotten she was standing behind me.

Max shook his head as he said, "It's Muriel Stevens."

"I think I'd better go talk to her next," the chief said. As he started for the door, he turned back to Max and added, "In the meantime, you need to stay in town. You don't have any reason to leave, do you?"

"My calendar's wide open at the moment," he said. "I don't have any jobs outside of April Springs, or any plans to go anywhere."

"Good. Let's keep it that way."

After the chief was gone, Max slumped down onto one of our sofas. "I can't believe somebody killed Darlene."

"I didn't think you two were all that close," I said before I had a chance to realize how cold that made me sound. I was going to have to get over what Darlene had done to me, once and for all. It didn't sit right with me, holding a grudge with a dead woman.

Max stared at me a second, then said, "Suzanne, you know in your heart that's not fair. Someone was murdered today."

"You're right," I said, my voice a little softer than it had been before.

Max stood abruptly, and as he headed for the door, I said, "Max, I'm sorry."

"So am I, Suzanne."

After he was gone, I kept watching him as he walked down Springs Drive, oblivious to the falling snow. Max was in pain, and more than that, he was in trouble. I just wasn't sure what I could do about either situation.

My best friend, Grace Gauge, was waiting for me on the front porch of the house I share with my mother when I drove home around one in the afternoon.

"Don't you ever work?" I asked her with a laugh as I approached, getting my key ready for the front door.

"Why don't we save the question-and-answer session for inside? I'm freezing out here. The snow's awfully pretty though, isn't it?"

I looked back toward the park that touched our property, and took in the view of the trees and pathways covered with snow. It looked like a Christmas card, with swirling sparkles of white filling the air. It was no wonder that I cherished snowfalls so much in April Springs.

"Come on, quit stalling. I'm cold," Grace said, her teeth chattering.

"If you carried a few more pounds on you, you'd be better insulated," I said as I smiled and opened the door.

As she pushed past me inside, she grinned and said, "No, thanks. I'd rather buy a bigger jacket." Grace put her coat by the door, then settled down in front of the fireplace. Though my mother was absent, there were still a few glowing embers in the hearth.

Grace studied the fireplace a moment, then asked, "Any chance you can throw on a log or two?"

I did as she asked, then said, "Now it's your turn. Why are you here in the middle of a workday?"

She grinned at me. "They sent me home, can you believe it? My supervisor doesn't want a repeat of last year, when Anita Ricco crashed her company car in an inch of snow. The company has decided they'd rather pay us all for goofing off than take a risk with their property. I'm all for it, myself."

"I was wondering where your car was," I said as I put a pot of coffee on.

"That's why I'm so cold. I walked over here from my house. That Jeep of yours is four-wheel-drive, isn't it?"

"Why, do you want to borrow it?" I said as I put a handful of cookies on a plate and set it in front of her. They were my mother's favorite, peanut butter cookies with Hershey Kisses in the middle of each one, placed there just before they came out of the oven.

"Hardly, but if we need provisions later, I want to be sure we can get to them at the store. There are some necessities I'm not willing to live without."

I turned on the lights of our Christmas tree, then said, "I can't wait to hear what made that list."

"Why don't you leave your tree on all the time?" she asked, ignoring my question.

"Momma's afraid we'll burn the house down," I said.

Grace leaned over and touched one of the branches. "It's worth it, if you can have a live tree like this."

"I like them, too. You have a live one, don't you?"

She mumbled something, and I asked her to repeat it.

Defiantly, Grace said, "I didn't put a tree up this year, all right? It just seemed kind of pointless, since I'm the only one who'd see it."

"That's not like you," I said. "You usually love the holidays."

"I do," she admitted. "But putting a tree up this year just felt kind of pointless. Listen, I know neither one of us has to have a man in our lives to make us complete, but they can be a nice accessory, don't you think?"

"I do," I said as I got two mugs and filled them with coffee.

"Where's Jake at the moment?" Grace asked. Jake Bishop was my boyfriend, a state police investigator who traveled all over North Carolina looking for killers. He had an important job — and nobody knew how to do it better than he did — but his travel schedule didn't exactly make it conducive for a steady relationship.

"He's on the road again," I said.

"What about David Shelby?"

David was a man who'd come to April Springs earlier that year, and it had taken us quite a while to figure out that we'd gone to summer camp together as kids. I couldn't deny that there was some kind of attraction there, but with Jake in my life, I hadn't done anything to act on it.

"He's just a friend," I said as I went through a stack of cards and mail that always seemed to accumulate on our mantelpiece during the holidays. I found the card I was looking for and handed it to her. "Read this."

In a man's firm handwriting, the back of the card said,

"Suzanne, I'm off to find my last chance. David."

Grace looked at the back — a picture of the Alaska wilderness — then tapped the writing on the card with her finger. "That's cryptic enough, isn't it?"

"I'm sure the explanation was too complicated for a postcard," I said.

"Then he should have written a letter, or at least phoned before he left town." Grace shook her head, then added, "It's probably all for the best."

"You know what? He's been gone less than a week, and I already miss seeing him come into the donut shop. He was there every day, did you realize that?"

"That certainly sets him apart from Jake, doesn't it?"

I shrugged. "I care for him, honestly, I do, but sometimes I think he should find a nice lady truck driver. He'd have a better chance of seeing her than he has me."

Grace bit into a cookie, then said, "Don't worry. I'm sure he'll be here before Christmas."

"That's the plan right now, unless business calls him away," I said as I handed her a mug of coffee and then sat beside her. "Strike that. His business is probably going to bring him here by nightfall. I hate the reason he has to come to town, but at least I'll be able to see him again."

Grace put her mug down on the coffee table. "Suzanne, is there something you're not telling me? Did something happen today at your booth?"

I couldn't tell if she was teasing or not, then I realized that the entire time we'd been talking, she hadn't brought the murder up, something I should have realized was greatly out of character for her. "You haven't heard, have you? There was a murder at the Christmas Carnival today."

She didn't believe me at first — it was clear in her expression — but when I didn't back down, she finally accepted it. "What happened?"

"Darlene Higgins was killed under the town clock," I said. "The thing is, she was dressed in Muriel Stevens's jacket, and she was wearing a black-and-gray-haired wig when she was murdered, so it didn't even look like her."

After I finished bringing her up to date on what I knew, Grace put a hand on mine and asked gently, "Suzanne, are you all right?"

"Why shouldn't I be?" I asked.

"Come on, I'm your best friend, remember? I know how you feel about Darlene Higgins."

"That all happened a long time ago," I said. "I've decided to put it behind me."

Grace arched one eyebrow. "You don't really expect me to believe that, do you? Remember who you're talking to."

I let out a deep breath, and hadn't even realized that I'd been holding it in. "Maybe. I don't know. Sure, I've been angry with her for a long time. After all, she broke up my marriage." I stared at the flames in the fireplace for a few seconds longer, then added, "But it was Max's fault, too, and I've managed to just about forgive him, even if I doubt I'll ever be able to forget what happened between them." In spite of my effort to wipe the image out of my mind of finding them together, it still came back unbidden at the slightest provocation.

Grace frowned as she stared into the flames. "Has the chief asked you for an alibi yet?"

That thought hadn't even occurred to me. "No, why would he?"

"Come on, Suzanne. Think about it. You had a motive to want her dead, and you were at the carnival selling donuts. That just leaves the means. How did she die?"

It was unsettling to hear Grace's litany of reasons I might be guilty, but she had a point, one I'd been unwilling or unable to face. "You know what? I don't have a clue. I just realized that the chief didn't say how she was murdered, just that she was dead. Hang on a second, this won't take long."

I reached for the phone and dialed George's number.

When he picked up, I said, "Hey, it's me."

"Hello, Suzanne. What can I do for you?"

"I know things might be a little strained right now between you and the police force, but do you think you could find out exactly how Darlene was murdered?"

There was a pause, and then he said, "I honestly don't know, but I can try."

"Thanks, I appreciate it. Don't do it if it's going to get you in trouble."

"Now, what fun would that be? If I lived by that rule, I'd never get to do anything."

After I hung up, Grace asked, "Did you just call George?"

"Yes, I thought he might be able to find out what's really going on. I can't help wondering what Darlene was doing going around town dressed up like Muriel."

"I thought you said she was getting ready

45

for her audition."

I shrugged. "That's just one theory, but no one really knows, do they? Is it possible that whoever killed Darlene was really going after Muriel?"

"It's possible, from the way you described her wig and that coat. Somebody should warn Muriel that she might be in trouble."

As Grace reached for the phone, I stopped her. "There's no need to call her. The chief was heading for Muriel's house when he left Donut Hearts. I'm sure she knows what's going on by now."

"Where does that leave us, then?"

I looked at her for a second for some kind of clue what she was talking about. "I'm not sure what you mean."

"We're going to investigate this ourselves, aren't we?" Grace looked surprised I hadn't suggested it myself.

"No, ma'am. I'm staying out of this case, and you should, too. Let the chief find the killer this time. Darlene's death doesn't involve me."

Grace stood and began to pace as she ranted, "You aren't serious, are you? Let's list the reasons you need to get involved. First, the victim is the woman who broke up your marriage. Next in line, we have your ex-husband, a man you are still on good terms with, though why I can't imagine, as one of the lead suspects. Do you honestly need anything more than that? Suzanne, you're involved with this up to your eyeballs."

I was saved from answering when the front door opened. My mother, a petite woman who barely broke five feet in height, came into the house brushing the snow from her jacket. "It's coming down fiercely now," she said with a warm glow. I'd inherited her love of snow, and was glad it was something we shared. When Momma noticed Grace, she said, "Why, hello there. I didn't know you were here. Where's that beautiful car of yours?"

"Parked in my driveway where my boss ordered me to put it. I'm on a paid holiday until the snow stops and they can plow the streets."

"It may be longer than you've planned for, then. I just heard that our two snowplows are on their way to Charlotte. There was a problem there with some of their equipment, and our mayor offered them ours as a goodwill gesture."

"That's all well and good," I said. "But what are we supposed to do here in the meantime?"

"We endure," my mother said as she put

the bags she'd been carrying down on the table. "Fortunately, I was able to get provisions before the grocery store shelves were completely emptied. You'd think those people had never seen a snowstorm before." She looked at Grace, then added, "Dear, you're welcome to join us."

"I'd better not," Grace said as she started to get up.

My mother looked impatient about being thwarted. "Nonsense. We're having lemon chicken, and I know that's your favorite."

Grace sat down again. "Okay, you convinced me."

I touched her shoulder. "Are you all right?"

"Of course I am. Why do you ask?"

"Momma had to twist your arm so hard, I was afraid she might have broken it."

Grace grinned at me. "Mock me all you want, but I wouldn't dream of insulting your mother by turning down her most generous offer."

My mother laughed. "I appreciate that. I always enjoy it when you two girls get together over here."

Grace asked, "Mrs. Hart, is there anything I can do to help?"

"Thank you, dear, but I've got time to do everything that needs to be done, and it's something I really enjoy doing. You two sit there and enjoy the fire. I'm happiest when I'm busy."

As Momma disappeared into the kitchen, I said to Grace, "Thanks for not saying anything about the murder."

"She knows, doesn't she?"

I nodded. "She doesn't want it to ruin the day, though, and I don't blame her. Momma lives for the days when it snows, and I want her to be able to enjoy this."

Grace nodded. "I don't want to upset her either, believe me. Did you honestly think I'm going to risk losing a dinner invitation from your mother? Especially when I can't drive to the nearest restaurant to eat?"

"You wouldn't have to drive," I said. "I'm sure The Boxcar is still open. Knowing Trish, she's making a killing right now feeding the hungry folks of April Springs."

"Thanks, but I'd have to wade through the snow to get there, and these boots are designed more for style than function." She showed off her ankle-high leather boots, and I could see her point. Grace wasn't exactly dressed for the snow we were getting. I felt bad for anyone who didn't have a safe and warm place to sleep tonight.

"You're going to be here anyway. Why don't you stay over tonight?" I suggested.

Grace looked outside at the still-falling snow. "Ordinarily I'd walk home after we eat, but I think I'll take you up on your offer, if you're sure. Since we have some time to kill and your mother clearly doesn't want us anywhere near her kitchen, how about a few games of Scrabble before we eat?"

"You're on. Loser does dishes, okay?"

"Get out your rubber gloves then, because girl, you're going down," Grace said.

I got our Scrabble game and set it up by the living room window where we could watch the snow in one direction, and the fireplace in the other. With the decorated Christmas tree in one corner of the room, it made quite a lovely sight. It was too bad that as we played, I couldn't manage to completely get rid of the sight of Darlene's body lying there on the sidewalk in front of the clock. Who had killed her, and why? Was the assault meant for her, or Muriel? I was afraid that before too long, I was going to end up investigating the matter myself, regardless of my original intent to stay out of it.

Whether I liked it or not, it appeared that Darlene's death had become a part of my life.

Three hours and several games later,

Momma finally said, "Come on, ladies. Dinner is served."

"One second," I said as I played my last letter, making a paltry ME out of one of the few open squares with word possibilities. "I'm out."

"And so am I," Grace said as she played three letters, making TREE. "It's in honor of Christmas," she added.

As I totaled the score, Momma said, "If you two aren't interested in eating, I'll be glad to start without you."

Grace stood and said, "We can figure out who won later. Let's go."

I brought the sheet into the dining room with me, along with a pencil. I wasn't about to let that get out of my sight. We were tied at a game apiece, and the outcome of this one would determine who washed dishes, and who sat by the fire while the other one worked.

When I walked into the dining room, I saw that Momma had outdone herself. The good china was laid out on the table, and it positively overflowed with goodies. Besides the lemon chicken, there was her signature garlic mashed potatoes, her green beans with pearl onions, and some of her home-made cranberry sauce.

"This is almost too pretty to eat," Grace

said as she took it all in.

"Take a picture if you'd like to reminisce about it later, but I'm digging in," I said.

My mother shook her head. "Grace, I'd hoped your good manners would rub off on my daughter, but I'm afraid it's never going to happen. I should probably just give up that particular dream."

"That's probably for the best," I said with a smile as I reached for the cranberries. "It puts a lot less pressure on me."

"You know the rules. First we say grace; then we eat," my mother said.

I looked at my friend and said, "Hi, Grace. Now, could you pass the mashed potatoes?"

"Suzanne," my mother said.

"Sorry." She had worked hard putting on such a fine feast, and I knew that I was being a little too glib about it, but it was so nice having Grace with us.

As my mother gave the blessing, I found myself focusing on her prayer. She was right, we were lucky, and sometimes I took it for granted. I needed to hear her sobering words just as much as she needed to say them.

After she finished, Grace said, "I don't know which is lovelier, your presentation, or your sentiment."

"Thank you, my dear," my mother said,

obviously pleased with the praise.

"Me, too," was all I could manage, though I hoped my mother realized her words had struck a chord with me as well.

"Let's eat, shall we?" she said brightly, so we did. Dinner was full of pleasant conversation, and we all avoided the one topic that was surely on everyone's mind. If they were willing to ignore it, then I was, too.

After dinner, Momma asked, "Now, who has room for dessert?"

"I couldn't eat another bite," I said.

"I'm stuffed, too," Grace echoed.

"We've got homemade apple pie with a crumb crust topping," Momma said.

"Maybe I'll have just a sliver," I said.

Grace nodded. "I think I have room for that much myself."

Momma grinned. "Tell you what. Why don't I do the dishes and you two go enjoy the fire. After I'm finished cleaning up, we'll have dessert."

I said, "No, ma'am. We're cleaning up. Or at least one of us is. We played Scrabble for the privilege, and we won't take no for an answer."

"Are you sure?" she asked.

"Positive," Grace said.

"If you're certain," she said as she started off toward the living room. I knew her favorite part of making meals was the process and the end result, not the cleaning afterwards.

"I thought you'd put up more of a fight than that," I said, smiling.

"Then you thought wrong. Thank you both. Now if you two will excuse me, I believe I'll go enjoy that fire."

After she went into the other room, Grace asked me, "So, who lost? I know you brought the score sheet in with you."

"Let me total it up," I said as I tallied the figures. I added them twice, then laughed out loud.

"What's so funny? Did I lose?"

"Look," I said as I handed her the sheet. We'd ended in a dead tie on the last game, 234 to 234.

Grace smiled. "It looks like we're both cleaning up."

"It surely does. Let's knock these dishes out so we can have some pie."

She looked at me in disbelief. "Suzanne, are you honestly telling me that you're still hungry? I was just kidding before."

I shrugged. "I'm not saying I could eat a sandwich, but I probably have room for a little bit of pie after we finish."

Grace laughed. "Then let's get to work. I'd hate to be the one responsible for making you starve to death."

The cleanup was a breeze having Grace work with me, and we were just about to cut the pie when my cell phone rang with its signature laugh.

I thought about ignoring it, and when I didn't answer immediately, Grace said, "You'd better get it. It might be important."

"That's what I'm afraid of," I said. "I don't want to spoil this evening's light mood."

"It's fine. Besides, it'll drive us both crazy if you don't."

I shrugged, then pulled my cell phone out and said hello. It was George. "I wasn't expecting you to find anything out tonight."

He said, "I thought you should hear it as soon as possible."

"Well, you've got my attention. How did Darlene die?"

"She was stabbed straight through the coat and into the heart."

I felt a shiver go through me. "That sounds horrible," I said. "What a terrible way to die."

"I don't know. I've seen worse," George said.

"I'm sure you have, but I don't want to hear about any of your old cases. Thanks for finding out for me."

"Hang on a second," he said as Grace kept pulling out my arm, no doubt wanting to know how Darlene had died. "I'm not finished."

"Go ahead. I'm listening."

George sighed. "Don't you want to know what the murder weapon was? Come on, Suzanne, it's the next logical question, isn't it?"

"I suppose so," I said. "I just assumed it was a knife. Wait just a sec," I added as I turned to Grace. "Somebody stabbed Darlene in the heart."

"Oh," she said.

I said to George, "Sorry about that. Now, what were you saying?"

"I was talking about the murder weapon. Have you seen those candy canes around City Hall?"

"The ones hanging in the windows? Yes, I saw them. Trish was in charge of decorating, since she was running the carnival."

"No, not those. I'm talking about the ones stuck in the ground out front where the flower beds are during summer."

"Yes, I saw those, too. Kind of cute, aren't they?"

"I used to think so," George said, "until I heard that one of them was used to stab Darlene in the heart. Now I'm not so sure."

"Tell me you're joking," I said, having a hard time believing him. Who would take an ornamental display and turn it into a murder weapon?

"I don't joke about murder," he said. "It was obviously a crime of opportunity. Anyone could have taken one of those canes and used it to kill Darlene. As cold as it's been, the entire town's wearing gloves, so it's no surprise that there weren't any fingerprints on it."

"I didn't think those candy canes were sharp enough," I said.

"They've got eight-inch steel skewers on the ends so you can drive them into the ground. They're tough enough to penetrate frozen turf, so I can't imagine one having much trouble with Darlene."

"That hardly eliminates any suspects, does it?"

"Anybody at the carnival today had access to those candy canes. Anyway, I just thought you'd want to know. It's still coming down pretty hard out there, isn't it? Do you need anything?"

"No, we're settled in pretty snugly here at the house. Grace is staying with us and we're making it a party."

George asked, "You're not planning to open the donut shop tomorrow, are you?"

"Why wouldn't I?" I said. "My Jeep's got four-wheel-drive, and if I'm not comfortable driving, it's a short walk to the shop if I cut through the park."

"If you can make it through the drifts. You might want to call off work tomorrow. Even if you manage to get there, do you think many folks will be able to come buy your donuts in this weather?"

"I'll worry about tomorrow when it gets here. In the meantime, thanks again for the information."

"You're welcome," he said, and we hung up.

"You'll never believe what the murder weapon was," I said to Grace.

"I'm guessing it was something common like a knife," she answered as she looked out the window at the still falling snow.

I shook my head. "Somebody used a candy cane to kill Darlene."

Grace spun around with a look of incredulity on her face. "How is that possible? They're not that strong, are they?"

"It wasn't a real one made from sugar; it was a display piece with a spike on one end from the front of City Hall."

"So anyone could have grabbed it," Grace said. "Even Max."

"My ex-husband has many flaws — I'm

not trying to say that he doesn't — but he's not a killer. Besides, he just got to the fair as I was breaking down the display. There's no way he could have killed her."

Grace frowned, and I could tell she wanted to say something. I just wasn't sure I wanted to hear it.

After thirty seconds, I couldn't stand it any longer. "Go ahead," I said. "There's something on your mind. What is it?"

"I don't know what you're talking about."

"You want to make a comment. So make it."

She looked reluctant to speak, then finally said, "Fine, if you must know, it's pretty clear to me that Max could have killed her."

"How is that possible? I just told you, he got to the carnival half an hour after the murder."

She frowned. "No, he got to your booth then. Who knows where he was before that? He could have lied to you about just arriving, knowing that you'd give him an alibi. What better witness than someone who's not your biggest fan? He could have figured the police would be more willing to believe his innocence that way."

I started to protest when she held up one hand. "Suzanne, think about it objectively. If you alibi him, folks are going to think it's true. Nobody expects you to go out of your way to defend your ex-husband, especially when they consider who the victim was. If that's what he did, it's pretty brilliant."

"I still don't believe he could do it," I said.

"Think about it. Don't you believe it's possible that's why he came to you in the first place?"

It made more sense than I was willing to admit, but I didn't know how to rebut her. Could Max have been using me to establish an alibi? If he had, he was being more clever than I'd ever given him credit for. But one question still begged to be answered. Why would Max kill Darlene in the first place? No matter his flaws, I couldn't see him stabbing her in cold blood.

Then again, I'd proven over and over again that I didn't know everything there was to know about my ex-husband.

PEANUT BUTTER COOKIE KISSES

This one's a favorite at my house. They're especially delicious hot out of the oven, with the chocolate kiss on top still melting!

Ingredients

1 cup butter or margarine, softened
1 teaspoon vanilla extract
3/4 cup brown sugar
3/4 cup granulated sugar
2 eggs, beaten
1 cup peanut butter, chunky or smooth
3 cups flour
1/8 teaspoon salt
2 teaspoons baking soda
Enough Hershey's Kisses to top each cookie, about 1 bag

Directions

Cream together the butter, vanilla, brown sugar, and white sugar until thoroughly mixed. Next, add the beaten eggs and peanut butter, mixing well again. In a separate bowl, sift the flour, salt and baking soda together, then add to the wet mix, mixing thoroughly. Pinch the dough off into walnut-sized pieces, then bake on an ungreased cookie sheet for 10 minutes at 375°F. When the cookies are nearly done, pull the sheet out of the oven and place one kiss on top of each cookie, then return to oven to finish baking. Remove and cool on a rack, then enjoy!

Makes 3–4 dozen cookies

CHAPTER 3

At one-thirty the next morning my alarm went off, and I slapped at it before it woke everyone in the house. Grace was in our spare bedroom, and I didn't want to disturb her sleep, since we'd just gone to bed four hours earlier. I was used to working on short sleep, but that didn't make it any easier to deal with my alarm the next morning.

I peeked through my curtains and looked outside at the park. The world was covered with snow, but not the white beauty of images reflecting bright morning sunshine. This was a land bathed in shades of gray and blue, lovely in its own right, but with a hint of mystery as well.

How on earth was I ever going to get to work in this mess? I thought about staying home and going back to bed, but there was too much of the Puritan work ethic in me. What if someone needed one of my warm donuts to start their day, and trudged through the snow to get it, only to find that I hadn't opened my shop? I knew the odds were probably pretty slim, but I still couldn't disappoint anyone without at least trying to make it in.

I got dressed, and as I walked downstairs, I heard my mother's voice from her doorway. "I thought I heard you rustling around."

"Sorry, Momma," I said, keeping my voice down.

"You're not going out in that, are you?"

"I'm going to try," I said, wondering about the wisdom of it even as I spoke. I knew that if I waited around and thought about it, I'd never leave. She followed me downstairs, no doubt ready to try to talk me out of it before I got stranded in a snowbank between home and the donut shop.

Suddenly, we both heard a noise approaching from outside.

Momma frowned as she said, "That sounds like a motorcycle. I can't imagine anyone riding one at this time of night, especially in all of this snow."

The noise grew louder, and then suddenly stopped right outside our front door. As I reached for the baseball bat we kept in the hall closet, I said, "Momma, go upstairs. I'll handle this."

"Not without me," she said.

I started to insist, but from the set of her mouth, I knew there was no way she was going to listen to me. "Fine. But stay back behind me, okay?"

I flipped the porch light on and looked outside, and suddenly let the bat drop to my side.

"Who is it?" Momma asked me.

"It's George Morris, and he came on a snowmobile."

"What's he doing here?" she asked.

"Let's open the door and find out." I unlocked the door and held it open for him, but George refused to come in.

"I've got snow on my boots and pants. I don't want to drip on your floor."

Momma brushed me aside. "Nonsense. Get in here this instant and I'll get you a cup of coffee. These hardwood floors are ancient. A little snow isn't going to hurt them."

"Don't go to any trouble on my account," George said.

"It's on a timer, so it should be ready," I said. "And Momma's right. Come in here before you freeze to death."

He stomped his boots together out on the porch, then saw that snow was still firmly lodged in them. After taking them off,

George came in wearing thick woolen socks.

"I've got to admit that coffee would be nice," he said.

As we all went into the kitchen, Momma looked at me and said, "Well, if you're not going to ask him, I am. What on earth are you doing here in this kind of weather at this time of night?"

He shrugged. "Suzanne told me yesterday she was going to work no matter what, so I borrowed a snowmobile from a friend so I could give her a ride."

Momma beamed. "That's the sweetest thing I've ever heard."

He looked uncomfortable about the praise. "It was nothing. It gave me an excuse to get out in the snow and play a little."

"I know better than that, George Morris. It was a sweet gesture, but I'm still not sure Suzanne should work today."

"Suzanne wants to," I said, "So Suzanne's going in."

She looked at me oddly. "Since when did you start referring to yourself in the third person?"

"Since you started talking about me as if I wasn't even here," I said, trying to muster a laugh.

I drank my coffee, then told George, "If the offer's still open, I'd love a ride."

"That's why I'm here," he said as he stood. Before leaving though, George turned to Momma and said, "Thanks for the coffee, ma'am."

"Thank you for looking out for my daughter."

"Let's go," I said.

"Bundle up, dear," she said.

"You don't have to tell me twice, Momma," I said as I put on my heaviest coat and joined George outside.

"I've never ridden on one of these," I said as I got on the snowmobile behind George.

"They're great fun," he said. "Just remember to hold on tight."

George started the engine, and that was the last bit of conversation between us until we got to Donut Hearts. I was sure we were waking people up all along Springs Drive, but I was determined to enjoy this opportunity. While I did see some lovely scenes along the way, mostly I stared at George's back, shielding myself from the wind. At least the snow had stopped falling for now.

There wasn't another soul out, but that was typical for that time of morning on a weekday even without the snow. As George pulled up in front of the shop, I got off and felt my knees wobbling a little before I managed to right myself.

"Would you like to come in for more coffee?" I asked, the whine of the engine still whirling in my ears.

"Thanks, but I have another errand to run before I have to get this back to its owner. If you need me, call, okay?"

"I will. And George?"

He turned toward me. "Yeah?"

"Thanks for the ride."

He tipped his cap to me. "Any time."

After he was gone, I walked into the shop, glad that this snowstorm hadn't affected our power. As I turned on the lights, I hit the power switch on the fryer, checked for messages on my machine, then got to work making donuts for the day. I might end up eating them all if no one showed up, but it felt good making them, and preparing, just in case.

The phone rang as I was measuring out ingredients for the day's cake donuts.

I added a bit of pumpkin to one of the mixes, then answered. "Donut Hearts," I said, wondering about the caller.

"Suzanne? You're actually there?"

It was Emma Blake, my assistant. "Sure I am. Why do you sound so surprised?"

"Because there's like a foot of snow outside," she said.

"Don't worry. You don't have to come in

today," I said. "I can handle things here myself."

She paused, then said, "No, if you're there, I want to be there, too." Her voice muffled a little as I heard her say to someone in the room with her, "You were right, she's working. Now will you just go back to bed, Daddy? What noise? I don't hear anything. Oh yeah, I hear it now. How should I know what it is?"

"Emma," I said, then repeated louder, "Emma. Unless I miss my guess, it's George Morris. He came to get me on a snowmobile, and I'm willing to bet you are next on his list. You can send him away if you want. I don't mind, honestly, I don't."

"Are you kidding? And miss a chance to ride on one of those? No way, I'll be there soon."

She was still talking to her father as she hung up, and I wondered if Emma would make it in after all. Her dad ran our local paper, and he was one of the most overprotective men I knew. It was amazing he ever let Emma out of the house, for fear of what lay just outside the front door. I didn't blame him, though. Working with the news like he did, I knew he probably saw a lot more of the bad of the world than the good in it.

I'd just finished the first batch of old fashioned donuts when I heard George approach. Taking half a dozen from the rack and throwing them in a box, I put my boots back on and went outside to greet them.

As Emma got off the snowmobile, she said, "Suzanne, that was the coolest thing. I wanted George to take me around town, but he didn't want to wake anybody up that he didn't have to."

George smiled. "What can I say? I have to worry about my reputation. What would folks think if they saw me racing all over town with a teenage girl on the back of this thing?"

Emma kissed him on the cheek. "They'd be jealous," she said.

I gave George the box in my hands.

"What's this?"

"Half a dozen old-fashioned donuts, as fresh as you'll ever get them. Thanks for the taxi service."

"With a tip like this, you're welcome." I'd never known George to turn down an offer of donuts, and was glad I'd been able to deliver some to him now.

"I'll see you two later," he said.

After he was gone, Emma and I looked up and down Springs Drive. "You know what? He may be the only customer we have all day," I said.

As we walked inside, Emma asked, "Can you believe the mayor loaned out our plows to Charlotte?"

"I'm willing to bet he's already regretting it. If I know him, he'll have them back here working by dawn."

Emma smiled. "Then we'd better get busy."

"You didn't have to come in, but I'm really glad you're here," I said.

"There's no place I'd rather be," she said as she stifled a yawn. "Well, maybe in a warm bed. Or the Florida Keys. Or even Disney World."

"Come on, let's get busy before you wish your life away," I said as I led her back into the kitchen.

I could make donuts by myself, but it was too stressful to do it alone every day. Having Emma there always made things easier, and not just for her company. She seemed to know what I needed before I realized it myself, and we made a great team. I dreaded the day she saved enough money to go off to college, but I didn't begrudge her the opportunity. Emma saw the world as a place to explore. As for me, I'd seen my share of it, and at least for now, I was content to stay in April Springs and enjoy what I had within my grasp.

At a little before five-thirty, I looked at all of the donuts we'd made, and wondered if we'd sell any of them.

"It's time to open up," I said.

"Unless everyone in town has snowmobiles, I've got a feeling it's going to be a slow morning," Emma said, stifling another yawn.

"If it is, you can take a nap in my office."

"Where, on your chair, or your tiny little desk? No, thanks. I'm calling the sofa by the front window."

I just shook my head and laughed as I walked through the kitchen doors to the front. It was still dark out, but there was reflected light from the moon illuminating the gray blanket of snow.

Not a soul was waiting to get in, which shouldn't have surprised me. It was still a few minutes until we were due to open, so I turned on the radio to see what Lester Moorefield was ranting about this morning.

His voice came in so clearly it was if he was in the kitchen with Emma, instead of in his studio on the outskirts of town.

"All of April Springs is buzzing about two things: the snow, and the assassination of Darlene Higgins. The police admit they're stymied in their investigation, but this reporter has learned that Darlene was not the intended victim at all. In a shocking, exclusive discovery, I have learned that the intended victim all along was none other than Muriel Stevens. Tune in for my nine o'clock broadcast to learn why, and more importantly, why no one in town is safe until the Christmas Killer is caught."

I turned it back off, sick of Lester's idle speculation and wild rambling. I had to admit that part of it was because he was right. I was jumping at shadows, and would keep doing it until the murderer was safely behind bars.

It was officially time to open, so I flipped the neon OPEN sign on, unlocked the door, and was nearly back to the kitchen when I heard a truck rumbling up Springs Drive. I peeked outside and saw a snowplow veering toward the lit sign of the shop.

Leaving the plow idling in the middle of the street in front of the donut shop, two men got out in heavy overalls and came in.

"Sorry about your floor," one of them said, a big man with a ready smile. Just behind him was a small, quiet man who barely made eye contact. The big man had his name stitched on his overalls — the letters BOB written in swirling curly cues —

while the other man had a much plainer EARL stitched on his.

"That concrete has been there a hundred years. I don't think you could hurt it with a jackhammer. I thought you all were in Charlotte."

"We were," Bob said, "but the mayor pulled us off four hours ago. We had a devil of a time getting back though, didn't we, Earl?"

"Yep," his companion said.

"You got that right," Bob replied, slapping his smaller friend on the back.

Bob looked at the display cases behind me, then said, "How's about a pot of coffee and a dozen donuts, your choice."

"Is this order to go?" I asked.

"No, ma'am, I'm planning to eat them all right here." He turned to his friend and asked, "Earl, what are you having? That order was for me. You're on your own, bucko."

Earl just smiled, and Bob said, "I'm just teasing. He'll share my dozen, but you'd better bring him his own coffee. We've been up all night, and I don't figure we'll be getting to sleep anytime soon."

"Is that safe?" I asked as I poured them two coffees.

"Look at it this way. Who are we going to

hit? It's not like we've been drinking. Nothing but coffee, anyway. Nobody's parked on the road if they have any sense at all, so we should be fine."

I grabbed a good selection of donuts, and the two men sat down at the counter instead of taking one of the sofas near the window. From the looks of their overalls, I was infinitely glad of that. While the floors had been there forever and could take any mess they could throw at it, the couches and chairs were another matter altogether. At least there wasn't much damage they could do to the vinyl stools.

Earl managed to eat more donuts than Bob, something I never would have believed if I hadn't seen it for myself.

When they were finished, Bob threw a twenty-dollar bill on the counter and said, "Keep the change. We'll be back later for more."

"That's too much of a tip," I said. These men worked hard for their money, and I didn't want to take advantage of them, though I normally never protested when someone decided to leave us a tip, no matter what the size.

"Ma'am, seeing your light on was worth fifty, so in a way, we're robbing you." He slapped his coworker on the back, and for a second, I thought Earl was going down from the force of the blow, but he managed to right himself at the last second.

Bob asked him, "You ready?"

Earl nodded, and after they were gone, I realized the entire time he'd been there, he'd only said one word.

Emma came out from the kitchen with a dishtowel in her hands. "Was it my imagination, or did I hear voices out here?"

"We had our first two customers," I said. "Would you do me a favor and grab the mop?" The floor was puddled in places where they'd walked, and I wanted to get it all up before someone else came in and slipped. A lawsuit was the last thing I needed.

"We should put newspapers down on the floor," Emma said as she retrieved the mop.

I took it from her, then asked, "Do you really think they'd help?"

"Can it hurt?"

"I guess not." After the floor was dry, we laid a line of papers from the door to the display counter, before running out of newspaper.

"That's going to have to do," I said.

Outside, the plow was going up and down Springs Drive, knocking the snow cover into two walls of packed ice and snow on either side of the road. How could anyone get into my parking area with that wall blocking them? As I thought about it, the plow swung around, knocked the wall of snow down going into my parking area, and managed to plow it as well, though I don't know how they were able to do it on such a tight radius. After that, they cleared the spaces open in front of my shop as well. I smiled when I realized I was the only one on Springs Drive who got that particular service. I didn't care how much they protested, the next round of coffee and donuts was going to be on the house.

As soon as they vanished up the road, a middle-aged man bundled up in a heavy jacket came in, shaking the snow from his dress boots once he was inside. When he took his hat off, I saw that his head was shaved, and he'd tried to make up for it with the bushiest black eyebrows I'd ever seen in my life.

"Would you like some coffee?" I asked.

"Yes, thank you. That would be great."

I poured him a cup, offered a donut, which he declined, then said, "You're a brave soul, coming out on a morning like this."

"I'm in town because of the murder at the carnival yesterday. Do you know anything about it?"

I said, "Sorry, I just heard what everybody else has."

He took a sip of coffee, and then asked, "And what exactly is that, if you don't mind telling me? I really would like to know what folks around town are saying about it."

I shrugged. What could it hurt? "A woman named Darlene Higgins was dressed up like another resident, Muriel Stevens, and someone killed her, probably by mistake."

"Is that what the police think?" he asked after taking another sip of coffee.

"That I couldn't tell you. Now, do you mind me asking you a question?"

"Go right ahead," he said.

"If you're not with the police, why are you asking so many questions? Are you some kind of reporter?"

He frowned. "Sorry, I should have introduced myself first thing. I'm Taylor Higgins. I was Darlene's first cousin. Her last one too, I guess. There was just the two of us left out of the whole brood."

"I'm so sorry for your loss," I said.

He nodded, and I could see his eyes start to well up with tears, though he shook them off. "Thank you for that. We were kind of close, so this has been tough to take. It was bad enough thinking someone killed her on purpose, but to die like that by accident? That's just terrible."

"I don't know if it's true or not," I said. "It's just what some folks are saying."

"They probably know more than the police do," he said. He finished his coffee, threw a pair of dollar bills on the counter, then said, "I knew it would be hard coming here, but I'm just having a tough time believing she's gone."

"Again, I'm sorry about what happened," I said.

He waved a hand in the air, and then walked back out into the snow.

By six-thirty, we hadn't had another customer.

Emma poked her head out of the kitchen. "I just finished the dishes we've got so far. Can I grab a couch and take a nap?"

"I don't see why not," I said.

She smiled, threw her apron on the counter, and then headed for one of the couches in front of the donut shop. Emma had barely settled in when George came in, sporting heavily layered clothes and rosy cheeks.

"Have you been out in the snow all morning?" I asked as he started shedding layers.

"It's kind of habit-forming, you know?"

"I don't see how," I said.

George sniffed the air, then he asked, "Is there any chance there's fresh coffee?"

"You've got it. How about some donuts, too?"

"I might be able to handle a pumpkin one or two," he admitted.

Emma grabbed her apron. "I'll get your order," she said.

"Stay there, I've got it covered."

She nodded her thanks, and I got George a fresh mug of coffee and two pumpkin donuts, one of his favorite flavors.

As he took a great gulp, I asked, "Isn't your friend going to miss his transportation on a day made for it?"

"No, he told me I could use it as long as I wanted. I took it back to him an hour ago, but he'd never ridden it before, so he asked me to take him for a ride around town so he could get used to it. He hated it, can you imagine that?"

"It's not everyone's cup of tea," I said.

"I loved it," Emma said.

George tipped his mug to her before taking another sip.

I realized we were getting low on coffee. As I turned away from the front door to start another pot, it chimed again. I was getting more customers than I'd ever imagined.

Then I looked back and saw Chief Martin coming in. The moment I saw his face, I realized I might have been better off staying home today after all.

"Suzanne, I need to talk to you," the chief said.

Before I could answer, George asked, "What's this about?"

I cut him off before he could do any more damage to his relationship with the police chief and said, "I'd be glad to help if I can, Chief. You know me, I'm always happy to cooperate."

He looked at me skeptically as George said, "Suzanne, you're under no obligation to talk to him, you know that, don't you?"

"I know that," I said as I touched his arm lightly. "And believe me, I appreciate you looking out for me, but I really do want to help if I can."

He shrugged. "It's your call, but I'd like to hang around while you talk to him."

I nodded. "It's okay with me. How about you, Chief?"

He frowned, then agreed. "Suit yourself, Suzanne. I need to know where your ex-husband is."

The question caught me completely off guard, since I'd been expecting him to ask me about my own alibi. "How on earth should I know that?"

"He's not at his apartment, and no one's seen him after our conversation here yesterday."

"I have no idea where he went, and that's the truth. It used to be my job to know where Max was all of the time, but I quit, remember? There was no future in it. Sorry I can't help you."

He ignored me, and then looked at George and Emma. "Anyone else see him since yesterday afternoon?"

Neither one of them said anything. The chief bit his lip before he turned back to me. "There's something else I need to ask you."

"Go ahead."

"When I left here, I went to Muriel Stevens's house. She wasn't there. Then when I checked back this morning, her place was still deserted."

"Maybe they ran away together," Emma said, not taking the query seriously at all.

"I kind of doubt that," the chief said. "Have you seen her lately, Suzanne?"

"Muriel's never had a donut in her life, to my knowledge. The woman's a fanatic about what she eats." I suddenly realized what I was saying in my own shop, and added,

"Not that my donuts aren't wonderful."

I knew that my donuts weren't exactly health food, but they were good for low spirits, or for folks who wanted to indulge a little. And shouldn't they be able to? I considered what I offered the public a treat, one of those nice little things that made life worth living.

"Spare me the advertisement," he said. "I'm just concerned about Muriel."

"And not Max?" I asked.

"Him, too," the chief said. He looked frazzled, and I knew that two disappearances and a murder were stretching him beyond his usual resources.

"Are you going to call Jake?" I hated the reason for having to make the call, but it would be wonderful to see my boyfriend back in April Springs.

"I've been trying to get hold of him, but he's been too busy to return my calls."

"I'm not sure where he is," I said. Jake wasn't always at liberty to tell me where he was, or what he was doing. It was one of the things that frustrated me most about our relationship.

The chief nodded. "Well, if you talk to him before I do, have him give me a call."

He put his hat back on and started for the door when I called out, "Chief, hang on a second."

As he turned back to me, I grabbed a paper cup, filled it with coffee, then I handed it to him. "On the house. Good luck."

He looked genuinely surprised by the offer, and as he took the cup, he said softly, "Thanks, Suzanne."

"Don't mention it," I said.

After he was gone, George and Emma started talking at once about what could have happened to our two errant townsfolk.

"I really don't think they're together," George said. "It's hard to imagine that there was a love triangle going on there that nobody knew about." He looked at me and added, "Sorry, Suzanne. I didn't mean anything by it."

"Don't apologize to me," I said. "I can't see it happening, either."

"It's possible, though, right?" Emma asked from her spot on the couch.

George said grimly, "Even though I don't think it's true, for their sakes, I hope that's all it is."

The dire tone of his voice caught my attention. "What are you implying?"

He stared down into his coffee for a few seconds, then said, "Never mind. I was just thinking out loud."

"Do you honestly think I'm going to give up that easily? Come on, come clean, George."

When Emma saw that he still wasn't going to explain himself, she said, "He's wondering if they're both dead, too."

There was a shocked silence all over the room, but I noticed that George didn't deny it. Max and I had a rocky relationship — through dating, marriage, and divorce — and while I might have wished him harm at one point in our lives, I'd soon gotten over it. As long as I lived in April Springs, I knew Max would be around, a constant I could depend on to amuse and annoy me. The thought of Max being gone was more than I was ready to accept.

"I'm sure he's all right," I said. "He's probably just snuggling up with his latest girlfriend, enjoying a chance for a snow day."

Though it was clear neither one of them really believed it, they indulged me by agreeing with my statement without contradiction or embellishment, a sure sign that both of them were holding back their true thoughts on Max's status. I didn't care. Unless I saw his body, I'd never believe that Max was dead, no matter how dire the circumstances.

My black mood was interrupted by the front door chime, and I wondered if the chief had come back for something else. That's when I saw a parade of parents and children enter the shop, and I felt the gloom suddenly vanish. There was laughter and smiles as they all piled in, and I felt like giving donuts away to match their mood, though the businesswoman in me knew better. I had a chance to serve my customers and make a nice profit today. Emma stepped behind the counter with me, and George faded back to a chair by one of the windows so he'd be out of the way.

"Who's first?" I asked as one of the dads approached. It was Harry Milner, married to one of my good customers, Terri. They had eight-year-old twin girls, and Terri and her friend Sandy often came by the donut shop after their children were in school. Sometimes on Saturday mornings, Harry came by to pick up breakfast for his still-sleeping family.

He slapped two brand-new, crisp one-hundred-dollar bills on the counter and said, "Breakfast is on me, for everybody and anybody who walks through that door. If you run out, let me know and I'll settle up when I leave."

There were protests from the crowd of

parents, though I noticed none of the kids were complaining.

Harry smiled at them all and said, "I just had a bit of luck in the stock market, and I want to share it with my friends. Surely no one's going to begrudge me that, are they?"

He was good. No one could protest, so Harry turned back to me. "As for me, I'll take a cup of coffee and a bearclaw." He hesitated, then said, "Cancel that. Make it hot chocolate."

"Do you still want the bearclaw?" I asked.

He grinned. "What do you think?" He started to rejoin his friends when he stopped and asked, "Is there any chance we can get some Christmas music in here? All this snow has me in the holiday spirit."

"Sure thing," I said, tuning the radio to a station in Charlotte that started their holiday tunes around Labor Day. It wasn't my usual background music for the donut shop, but then again, I didn't normally get two hundred dollars in orders either, so it was a day for surprises.

I got Harry a hot chocolate in my biggest mug, then heard shouts from the children, and told Emma, "We need another gallon of hot chocolate. And fast."

"I'm on it," she said. Emma was what passed for barista at my place. I let her choose the daily coffee specials, order the products, and make the hot chocolate, though we never had a tremendous demand for it. I loved it myself, and was constantly asking Emma how she made hers so tasty, but so far, it was a secret she hadn't been willing to share with me.

"It'll be a few minutes for the hot chocolate," I said.

There were disappointed groans all around, then I added, "but in the meantime, you can all pick our your donuts, and by then we should be ready to serve you drinks. Let's see how many want hot chocolate? Raise your hands so I can get a count."

Every hand in the place went up, except George's. I asked, "Are you the lone holdout sticking with coffee?"

He nodded, and some of the kids gave him a look like he was crazy, which George chose to ignore. It was all I could do not to laugh, so I ducked back into the kitchen to give Emma the count.

She had an array of spices out on the counter, and it was pretty clear that I wasn't welcome in my own kitchen.

"Was there something you needed?" Emma asked as she tried to hide the selection from my gaze.

"I just wanted to tell you that we need

sixteen hot chocolates," I said. "I had to be sure you made enough."

"There will be plenty," she said. "Don't worry about that."

"You know what? You'd better make it seventeen. I haven't had your hot chocolate in a while, either."

"I've got a feeling we'll need more than that, so I'm making a triple batch. Now shoo."

I hid my smile from her as I went back to the front.

"It's on its way," I said, and there were more whoops of delight, and not just from the children.

I loved the sounds and sights of people filling the shop. I had to find a special way to thank George for coming to get me. I wouldn't have missed a day like today for the world.

By eleven-thirty, we were out of hot chocolate, despite Emma's constant battle to keep up with the demand. I thought about closing early, but people kept streaming in, clamoring for a treat to celebrate the snow day. I was sure there were people holed up all over April Springs grumbling about the snow accumulation, but none of them came into Donut Hearts. I decided to leave the

89

station tuned to Christmas music, at least until the day after the holiday. Carols were interspersed with orchestral music, and to my relief, everyone was safe from reindeer hit-and-runs, especially Grandma.

At noon, we locked our doors, with two donuts left in inventory, barely a cup of coffee left in the pot, and a bank deposit that needed an armed guard escort. I stuck it in our safe. It would easily keep there for another day.

All in all, it was a good day, one that I'd savor if it weren't for the fact that my ex-husband was missing, along with a woman I liked, but didn't really know all that well. I wondered if the chief had any luck tracking either one of them down yet. If he had, he wasn't sharing the information with me.

And of course, that left me wondering about Jake Bishop, and whether Chief Martin was going to ever get hold of him, or if he was going to try to handle things himself.

Honestly, I realized that it wasn't my job to worry about it. I was tired, and it was time to go home. I bagged up the last two donuts, grabbed my purse, and then left the shop, turning my back to lock the door.

As I did, I heard a disguised voice behind me say, "Give me the bag, and no one will get hurt."

SIMPLY MY BEST APPLE PIE

These pies are great year round, but the best time to make them is when the apples are in season in the autumn. It's a quick and easy dessert that is always a hit. The crumb crust topping is wonderful. Enjoy a slice of pie with the coldest milk you can find!

Ingredients
8 or 9 inch pie crust, premade

Filling
1/2 cup granulated sugar
3 tablespoons flour
1/2 teaspoon nutmeg
1/2 teaspoon cinnamon
Dash of salt
5–6 cups thinly sliced firm, tart apples (Granny Smiths work well, so do Staymen)

Topping
1 cup flour
1/2 cup brown sugar
1/2 cup butter, room temperature

Directions
Peel and core the apples, then cut into thin slices. In a bowl, sift together the sugar, flour, nutmeg, cinnamon, and salt, then stir

this mixture into the apples until they are thoroughly coated. Add to shell, then in another bowl, combine the flour and brown sugar, then cut in the butter. The mix should be crumbly, and the butter still in small chunks. Add these to the top, then bake uncovered in a 425°F oven for 30–45 minutes, until the crust is golden brown and a butter knife slips into the top easily.

CHAPTER 4

I started to hand my purse backward when I heard a laugh. "Not that bag. Who cares about money? I want the donuts."

I turned around and saw Grace grinning at me. "Those *are* for me, aren't they? I can't believe you bought it."

"You were very convincing," I said as I handed the bag of donuts over to her. "You're welcome to them. But surely you've had breakfast already."

She smiled and shrugged at the same time.

"Grace, are you telling me you just got up?"

"Of course not," she said as she peeked inside the bag. "I was just teasing. I've been up for hours. Your mother insisted I eat a full breakfast, and then she wouldn't let me leave until the snowplow came and dug you all out. I just now made a break for it."

"Sorry, I know how she can be sometimes."

"Are you kidding me? I love the way she pampers me."

I looked around Springs Drive and saw that I wasn't the only business open, though I had to believe mine was doing better than the rest of them. I was glad to see that Two Cows and a Moose — our local newsstand — was doing brisk business. I'd been in the other day getting a magazine, and saw that the proprietress — pretty and young Emily Hargraves — had adorned her beloved stuffed animals in Santa suits, from their shiny black boots to their red and white caps perched precariously on their heads, though Moose had presented a particular challenge for her because of his antlers. I thought she'd been crazy naming her business after her favorite three stuffed animals, but I had to admit, they were a crowd pleaser, perched on a shelf in a place of honor above the cash register. I couldn't wait to see the outfits Emily had planned for St. Patrick's Day.

"Let's get something to eat," I said. "It looks like The Boxcar is open."

"Sure, that sounds good."

"I know what my mother considers a balanced breakfast. The sausage pile has to match the stack of bacon on your plate, and the eggs outweigh them both. You've got to be stuffed, and I just gave you donuts."

She smiled. "Okay, so I'm not hungry. That doesn't mean I can't join you. I'll have coffee and keep you company while you eat. Come on, let's go."

We walked down the abandoned tracks, now covered with a layer of snow, toward The Boxcar grill.

Trish smiled at us as we ascended the stairs, then pointed at the Donut Hearts bag in Grace's hands. "You're not really going to bring food into a diner, are you?"

"No, ma'am," Grace said. "This is inventory that Suzanne had to liquidate, so I agreed to take it off her hands. Believe me, I'd never break your rules."

Trish's faked grimace broke into a smile. "Fine, but you'd better make sure that inventory stays in the bag while you're here."

"I can check it with you, if you'd like," Grace said. "I'm really too full to eat them anyway."

Trish laughed. "Then you came to the right place. I can see why a diner might appeal to you," she said.

"I'm here to keep Suzanne company," Grace said. As she handed Trish the donuts, she said, "Honestly, you're welcome to them."

She peeked inside the bag, then looked at

me. "Do you mind, Suzanne?"

"Help yourself," I said. "But I thought no one could bring food to your diner?"

"I make the rules, I can break them," she said as she tucked the bag behind the counter.

As she led us to a free booth in back, Trish asked us in a lowered voice, "Have you heard the news?"

"About Max and Muriel being missing?" I said.

Grace grabbed my arm. "What? What happened now?"

Trish said, "Don't look at me. That's all I know. Suzanne, have you heard anything new?"

I shook my head as I slid onto the bench seat of the booth. "Just rumor and idle speculation."

Trish's eyes lit up. "That's what I like the best. What have you got?"

"Feed me first, and then I'll tell you," I said.

Trish shook her head in mock disgust. "I can't believe you're withholding information on me."

"Believe it," I said. "I'll have a turkey club with no tomato, fries, and a Diet Coke."

"Diet?" Trish asked.

"I'm trying to cut back," I said.

"Diet it is." She turned to Grace. "Do you want anything?"

"Make it two diet Cokes," she said.

"You two are a couple of wild gals out on the town, aren't you? Hang on, I'll be right back."

As soon as she left, Grace whispered, "Before she gets back, tell me everything you know, and don't you dare leave anything out."

"There's really nothing to tell. Chief Martin came by the donut shop early this morning wanting to know if I'd seen Max, and when I told him no, he informed me that Muriel Stevens was missing as well. Emma said she thought they were off somewhere together."

Grace shook her head. "She had to be joking. Honestly, I don't see them as a couple, do you?"

"It's hard to see Max with anyone but me," I admitted, "unless we're talking about Darlene Higgins. I saw that plainly enough."

"Have they made any progress in that investigation?" Grace asked as Trish slid the diet Cokes in front of us and nudged Grace to scoot over.

Once she was sitting with us, Trish said, "I told you two to wait for me. Now what did I miss?"

"I just said Emma thought that Max and Muriel were holing up somewhere together," I explained.

Trish appeared to think about that for a few seconds, then shook her head. "No, I can't see it."

"Me, either. Is that the investigation you were talking about?"

"No," Grace said. "I was wondering if the police have found out anything about Darlene's murder yet."

Trish looked at me. "And what did you say?"

"I didn't have a chance to say anything. But no, if the chief knows anything, he's not sharing the information with me."

"Curious, isn't it?" Trish said. "What was Darlene doing in Muriel's coat, why was she wearing a wig, and why would someone stab her with a candy cane?" She shivered a little as she added, "It's a pretty odd way to die."

I nodded. "Isn't it strange that someone grabbed a candy cane, of all things, for a murder weapon?"

"They have some pretty deadly points on the spike that goes into the ground," Grace said.

"How do you know that?" I asked.

"Before I came by the donut shop today, I

walked over to City Hall and pulled one out of the ground to check for myself."

"Did anyone see you do it?" I asked.

"Not that I know of, but I wasn't exactly furtive about it. Why?"

I shook my head. "You shouldn't have done that. What if someone saw you, and another person gets stabbed with one?"

Grace looked at me critically. "Seriously? Do you really think that's a concern? What can I say? I was curious."

Trish said, "I would have looked too, if I'd thought about it."

Grace asked, "Why did they leave them out on display, anyway? I find that kind of disturbing in its own right."

"Who knows?" Trish said.

"Traditions around here are pretty tough to break," I said, "and decorations at the courthouse are near the top of the list."

Trish glanced over her shoulder and said, "It looks like your club is ready. I'll be right back."

After she delivered my food, Trish was so busy with other customers that she didn't invite herself to sit back down with us.

I offered Grace a French fry.

"I couldn't. I'm stuffed," she said.

I grinned at her. "Why do you think I offered you one?"

She stared at my plate, then after hesitating, reached over and grabbed a fry after all.

"What?" she asked as she saw me smiling at her. "Can't a girl change her mind?"

"Absolutely," I said. "Have some more."

She nodded, took another fry, then asked, "Did you invite somebody else to lunch with you?"

"No, why do you ask?"

She pointed over my shoulder and said, "There's a cop coming this way, and he's looking right at you."

I felt my heart jump, hoping it was Jake, but instead, it was Officer Steven Grant, a policeman in April Springs who was also a good customer at my donut shop.

"Would you like to join us?" I asked as he neared us.

"Sure," he said as he slid onto the bench seat beside me. "I've already had lunch, though."

Trish came over. "Need anything, Steven?"

"Pie and coffee," he said as I looked at him with one raised eyebrow. He added, "I didn't say I had dessert, did I?"

Trish asked, "What kind of pie would you like?"

"You know me, Trish. Surprise me."

She shook her head as she walked away, and Grace said, "Excuse me, I need to powder my nose."

"You don't have to leave on my account," Officer Grant said.

"Don't worry, I'll be back," she said.

After Grace was gone, I said, "Did you come in here to have some pie, or was there something you wanted."

He lowered his voice, then said, "I thought there was something you should know before it gets out on the grapevine. It's only fair, you know?"

"Since I don't know what you're talking about, I really can't say."

He frowned, then said, "Here goes. I could get fired if you repeat this, but the chief seems to think you might have had something to do with Darlene Higgins's murder."

I felt a cold, sweeping dread come over me. "What did he say?"

"Yesterday before the snowstorm hit, he had me check your alibi during the time of the murder."

"He never asked me for one," I said, trying to keep the outrage out of my voice.

"Don't worry, I found three folks who agreed you were in your booth selling donuts the entire time, including Gabby Williams next door. You're fine."

"That's good, because I didn't do it." I looked hard at him, then asked, "But why tell me? You don't owe me anything."

He shook his head. "Maybe not, but you've gotten a bad shake in the past from the department, and I thought you should know about this. I just reported to the chief, and he seemed to accept it, so you're off the hook."

"Has he got any other suspects?" I asked. It was bad finding out I was on the list, but the fact that my name had already been crossed off helped a little.

"That I can't say."

Trish brought him a slice of lemon meringue pie and a cup of coffee. He smiled when he saw it, then asked, "Can I get that to go?"

"Why not? I enjoy putting things in boxes."

He laughed. "Then you should love me."

Officer Grant started to go as Grace came back. "You're not leaving because of me, are you? I can always come back later."

"No, ma'am, I need to get back to work." He smiled at Grace, then turned to me. "What I told you was confidential, okay?"

"I won't tell a soul," I said.

"Good."

The second Officer Grant was out of The

Boxcar grill, Grace said, "He's gone. So tell me, what did he say?"

"Grace, you just heard me promise not to tell anyone."

She looked shocked by the suggestion that I'd keep my word. "You didn't mean me, though, did you? Come on, Suzanne, you have to tell me."

"Sorry," I said, "I promised."

Grace chewed that over for a second, then said, "I understand, you gave him your word. Now, if you don't mind, I'm going to have another fry."

"Like I said, help yourself."

She grabbed a handful, then didn't know what to do with them. After a moment's hesitation, Grace grabbed a wad of napkins from the dispenser and plopped them down there.

I laughed. "Wow, you took me at my word, didn't you?"

"What can I say? You offered, I accepted."

Trish walked by with a coffee pot topping everyone off when she saw Grace's pile of my fries.

She looked at me and said, "What's wrong, Suzanne, don't you like my French fries anymore?"

"I do, but someone else appears to like them even more than I do."

Grace just smiled, and Trish shook her head as she walked away.

Two minutes later, she came back with a huge plate mounded with French fries. "There you go. That ought to satisfy you both."

"It's too much," I said. "I'll never be able to eat all of these."

"I've got a feeling you'll put a dent in them," she said. "Do your best."

I looked at the fries, then at Grace. "This is all your fault. If we don't finish them, it will hurt Trish's feelings."

Grace reached for another handful of fries as she said, "Then we'd better finish them, hadn't we?"

By the time we'd eaten most of the plate, Trish came by and swept it away. "You two look miserable. I've punished you enough," she said as she took the remnants away. "Is there anything else you'd like?"

I was stuffed beyond belief, but I couldn't help myself from teasing her. "Any more of that lemon meringue pie left?"

"You're kidding, right?"

"I'm kidding, right," I said with a smile. "Just the bill, Trish."

She had it ready for me, and I was surprised to see that the extra plate of fries wasn't included.

"You forgot something," I said.

Trish shook her head as she leaned forward. "I'll swap you donuts for fries, how does that sound?"

"Like you're getting robbed," I said.

She shrugged. "Then let's just call it an early Christmas present, okay?"

"Okay, but now I have to get you something."

"I'm partial to your pastry pine cones," she said with a smile. "I'm just saying."

I paid our bill, and Grace and I walked back outside. Since we'd been inside the diner, the sky had darkened, and fresh snow was falling again.

"It's really coming down, isn't it?" I said as I pulled my coat closer.

"I'd better go by the grocery store before I go home," she said.

"You're welcome to come home with me again," I said.

"I don't want to be a bother."

"Are you kidding me? You're not a bother, you're a buffer. Momma and I will drive each other crazy if just the two of us are snowbound in that house."

Grace bit her lip, then said, "Well, if you're sure. Normally I like living alone, but I'm not too fond of storms of any kind."

"At least there's no lightning," I said. As I

spoke, there was a diffused flash in the sky, and a few seconds later, thunder rumbled in the distance.

I looked at Grace. Without cracking a smile, she said, "I'm just glad you didn't say there wasn't a hurricane."

"We'd better get home before this gets any worse," I said. "The last time I saw lightning in a snowstorm, we got a foot overnight."

Grace shivered at the prospect. "Can we swing by my house first? I want to pick up a few things."

"Sure, but we have to do it on foot. My Jeep's still at the house."

"Then we'd better get going," she said. "It looks like this isn't going to let up anytime soon."

At least Grace's house was on the way to my place. The sidewalks were all a mess, but there was barely any traffic on the road, so we decided to walk there. It made the going a lot easier, especially since the new snow added a little traction. The daytime temperature hadn't gotten above freezing, but at least our plows had been followed by salt trucks, so for now, it wasn't bad.

"Should we get some groceries, too?" Grace asked. "I don't have enough in my pantry to feed a mouse."

"If I know my mother — and if not me, who — she'll have enough for a monthlong siege. That woman believes in being prepared for just about anything."

Grace nodded. "Not a bad trait at the moment, wouldn't you say?"

"Hey, I'm a big fan of the lady myself." I had to admit that sometimes it took Grace's presence for me to remember some of my mother's good qualities. Both of Grace's folks had passed away years ago, and Momma had kind of adopted her.

We climbed the steps up to Grace's porch, and before I could approach the door, she put her hand out and stopped me.

"What's wrong?" I asked.

"Look," she said. "There are footprints on my porch, and I haven't been home since yesterday."

"Maybe it was the mailman."

"My box is on the street," she said.

"A neighbor worried about you?" I asked.

"I doubt it. Suzanne, something's wrong here."

"Let's not jump to conclusions," I said as I walked to the door.

Grace nodded. "You're right; I guess I'm a little jumpy."

"Or not," I said as I noticed that door was slightly ajar. "You locked up yesterday, didn't you?"

"I always do, you know how paranoid I am about that," she said. "Why? What's going on?"

I pointed to the door and said softly, "Let's go back to the diner and call the police."

She backed up without saying a word, but from the expression on her face, I knew she wanted to scream.

We hurried back a dozen paces, then she said, "I've got my cell phone. I'm going to call from here."

"I just realized that I have mine, too," I said. "But don't you think this is a call we should make with other people around? We're kind of vulnerable out here in the street all by ourselves."

"I don't like this, Suzanne," she said, her voice starting to crack.

"It's going to be okay," I said.

She reached into a deep pocket for her phone when I said, "Hang on a second."

Driving up the road was one of our April Springs police cruisers, and I'd never been so happy to see one in my life. I threw out my arms and started waving frantically, so the officer would make no mistake that I was trying to flag him down and not offering an enthusiastic greeting instead.

It was Officer Grant, my one real friend on the force.

He pulled up to the lip of snow bracketing the road and rolled down his window. "What's wrong, Suzanne?"

"It looks like somebody broke into Grace's house," I said as I pointed toward it.

He nodded. "Stay right there. I'll check it out."

Officer Grant somehow managed to pull the cruiser up over the piled snow, and I saw that the car had chains on its tires. As he got out, I started toward him, but he held one hand up for me to stay where I was as he unbuckled his gun and pulled it out.

Okay, I know when to take a hint, even if a direct order is lost on me at times.

Grace stood beside me in the cold, falling snow, but neither one of us said a word. I didn't know about her, but I was bracing myself for the sound of a gunshot. After what felt like a lifetime later, the front door opened again, and Officer Grant came out, his revolver back in its holster.

He waved for us to approach, and we hurried toward him.

"Whoever was in there is long gone," he said.

"Are you sure?" Grace asked.

He nodded. "Oh yes. I checked under

every bed, and in all the closets. Trust me, he's gone."

"Could you tell if anything is missing?" I asked.

"No, the television's still there, and I found some jewelry in the bedroom that looked valuable, along with four one-hundred-dollar-bills in the bottom of the case. You really should find a better hiding place for your money."

"I keep meaning to, but I never seem to get around to it," she said.

Officer Grant frowned as he added, "There are a few dirty dishes in the sink, and there's a pillow and blanket on the couch. I'm guessing that whoever broke in just wanted a place to ride out the storm last night."

"What if he comes back?" she asked, the edge of hysteria clear in her voice.

"When he sees that your lights are on, he'll move on to someplace else. In the meantime, I'll keep an eye on your house."

"Thanks, but I won't be staying here tonight," Grace said.

I put my arm around her. "That's not even an option. You're coming home with me, remember?"

She nodded, then Grace asked Officer Grant, "Would you mind staying here a few minutes, just long enough for me to pack a few things?"

He nodded. "Sure thing. Just don't take too long."

"No problem there."

She started inside, then said, "I know I'm being silly, but would you two mind coming into the living room while I pack?"

"We'll be glad to," I said, trying to be as reassuring as I could. "Now, let's get you packed so we can head back to my place."

Officer Grant and I did as Grace asked, and as we stood in the living room, I realized both of us were intently listening to her move around in the other rooms.

After a minute, I pointed to the front door and asked, "Is there something we should do about that in the meantime?" It was pretty clear from the inside that someone had forced the door open. The jamb was split, and a few shards of wood were on the floor.

He nodded. "We'll barricade it for now, and use the side door when we leave. Give me a hand with this couch, okay?"

I nodded, and we shoved it into place, blocking the door as firmly as we could. Grace had a side entrance, and though we were going to have to muck through some snow to get out that way, it was better than leaving the front door wide open for another intruder to just walk on in.

"Do you really think that will discourage him?" I asked.

"I'm guessing he won't come back. If he was interested in robbing her, he would have done it already."

"And what if he was planning to sleep here again tonight?" I asked softly enough so that Grace couldn't hear.

"Then he would have done a better job disguising his break-in. You didn't exactly have to examine the lock to know someone had been there, did you?"

"No, it was pretty clear the front door was kicked in."

"That's my point. This guy isn't a finesse criminal. He took advantage of your friend's absence, and he's long gone by now."

"I hope you're right."

He nodded, and then the radio on his belt beeped, and he took it out in the kitchen so he could answer in private.

Grace came back in with an overnight bag and looked wildly around the room. "Where did he go? He left us?"

"Take it easy. He's in the kitchen," I said.

"I know I'm jumpy, but I can't help it. I admit it. I'm rattled." She looked at the couch in front of the front door, then added,

"You're kidding, right?"

"It was the best we could do on the spur of the moment."

She shook her head. "Thanks for trying, but we're going to have to do better than that."

She reached for her phone book, and I asked, "Who are you calling?"

"Tim Leander. He does all of my handyman chores."

I put a hand on the phone. "Don't you think he's probably busy right now handling emergencies?" I knew Tim was a mainstay in April Springs, keeping the town repaired and together with apparent ease. Tim was a master at fixing just about anything, and he was on speed-dial at our house, along with just about everyone else in April Springs.

"You don't call this an emergency?" she said shrilly as she dialed his number.

"Tim? This is Grace. I need you." She listened to his response, no doubt learning that he wasn't about to drop everything.

Grace smiled at me a few seconds later as she said, "That's great. I'll see you in five minutes. And Tim? Thanks."

After she hung up, I said, "Okay, now I'm impressed. I don't know what you've got on him, and I'm not sure I want to."

She shook her head. "Suzanne, he owes

me a favor, and I decided there wasn't going to be a better time to call it in than now."

"What kind of favor did you do for him? Or do I even want to know?"

Grace laughed for the first time since we'd seen her busted front door, something I took as a good sign. "I should let you supply the reason yourself with that overactive imagination of yours, but I'm not going to. Tim needed some advice once, and I supplied it. It's as simple as that."

I shook my head. "I don't think so. Details, girl; come on, I'm listening."

Grace wouldn't tell me, though. "I can't, Suzanne. I promised, so don't ask."

"Okay, I can respect that," I said. "But I've got to admit, you've got my curiosity roused."

"Some mysteries in life aren't meant to be explained," she said as Officer Grant rejoined us.

"Ladies, we need to go. I've got an emergency call on Oakhurst."

"You go on," Grace said. "We'll be fine now."

"I'm not leaving you alone here," he said in a voice that left no room for debate.

"We won't be. Tim Leander is on his way," Grace said. "Will you help me move the couch back before you go?"

114

He nodded and added a grin to the mix. "Absolutely, if it keeps me from trudging through the snow."

We pushed the couch back to its original position, and Tim knocked on the door as Officer Grant reached for the handle.

"Come on in," he said. "I was just on my way out."

Tim, a heavyset older man with a head full of gray hair, nodded as he said, "I imagine you're a little busy today."

"Right back at you," Officer Grant said.

"A little snow is always good for business," Tim agreed, and then Officer Grant was gone.

Tim said, "Good afternoon, ladies. Let me see what we've got going on here." He studied the splintered door frame like it was a Picasso, then said, "I can make it hold for now, and then replace the jamb after things settle down. Does that suit you?"

Grace asked, "Will it keep whoever broke in out?"

He nodded. "I guarantee it. I can't say it will work throughout the house, but he won't get back in through this door."

"That's all I ask," Grace said.

"Let me get a few tools from my truck," he said. "I'll be right back."

As he walked out to his pickup, I said,

"You'd never know the town was in turmoil all around him, would you?"

"That's what I like about him. He's so calm all of the time."

Tim came back with a large canvas tool bag filled with a cordless screwdriver, a well-worn handsaw, a hammer and chisel, and a piece of wood a little bigger than the one someone had shattered. As he removed the remnants of the old wood with his handsaw, I swear I heard him whistling.

"You don't mind if we watch, do you?" I asked.

"No, ma'am, I never said 'no' to an audience." Then he looked at me and grinned. "But if you start giving me advice on how to fix this, the bill starts to double by the minute. I like to call it my irritation tax."

"I won't say a word," I said. "I promise."

In no time at all, he had the new jamb piece in place — drilled to accept the locking mechanism as well — and I wondered if it was really just a patch. "Do you really have to replace that later?" I asked as he started putting his tools away.

"It's solid enough for now," he said as he thumped the new wood with his hand. "But it's not a very elegant fix, is it? Don't worry, when I get finished with it, you'll never know it was broken."

Grace reached for her wallet. "How much do I owe you, Tim? I'll pay whatever you ask. I'm so grateful you came over here so quickly."

He said, "It was my pleasure. As to the bill, you know better than to ask."

"I have to pay you something," Grace protested.

"The debt I owe you is beyond payment," he said.

"You don't have to do this," Grace said.

I swear, he winked at her. "Don't have to. Want to."

After Tim was gone and Grace tested the lock a few times, I said, "You really aren't going to tell me what's going on, are you?"

"I'm sorry, I can't."

"I just ask one thing, then."

Grace looked at me expectantly. "What's that?"

"If I'm ever in a jam, will you use your pull for me?"

She laughed as she grabbed her overnight bag. "I'm not making any promises. Let's go."

"Hey, it was worth a shot," I said.

By the time we got to my house, it was clear that Grace was feeling better about the break-in, but I couldn't blame her for being upset. I hadn't lived alone for more years than I cared to remember, and though I doubted my mother could defend me in a break-in at our place, it was good to know that someone else was there all of the time.

Grace didn't have that, and though she was a strong, independent woman, I had to believe that a roommate would be better for her, even if it was just a pet.

No one should live alone, in my opinion. But it was her life, and I wasn't going to butt into it.

Well, no more than I already did.

HOT CHOCOLATE SUPREME

Some folks might think it's silly to bother with a personalized hot cocoa mix when there are so many good products readily available, but I worked on this recipe for months until I got the perfect explosion of flavor. It's an easy recipe to make, so during the next cool evening, give it a try!

Ingredients

2 cups non-fat dry powdered milk
3/4 cup granulated sugar
1/2 cup Hershey's Cocoa, natural unsweetened powder
1/2 cup Special Dark Hershey's Cocoa, Dutch Processed powder
1/2 cup powdered non-dairy creamer
A dash of salt

Directions

In a large mixing bowl, combine all of the dry ingredients and mix well until thoroughly blended. Store in an airtight container until you're ready to use it.

When you are, put 1/4 cup of the mix into a mug, then add 3/4 cup of hot milk and stir until the powder is dissolved. Marshmallows are optional.

CHAPTER 5

"Come on, you two. You'll catch pneumonia if you stay out there too long." As expected, Momma was thrilled to see that Grace was with me. Oddly enough, as Grace and I had walked down the road toward my house, the snow stopped suddenly, and I swore I could feel the temperature drop with every step. We'd taken a short cut through the park — not the most prudent decision — sinking into the drifting snow, but avoiding the longer walk around to the front of the house.

"Can you believe it stopped snowing?" I asked my mother as Grace and I took our jackets off by the back door.

"I have a feeling it's only a temporary lull," she said as she looked outside at the gray clouds.

"You could be right. Would it be okay if Grace stays with us again tonight?"

"I just assumed she would," my mother

said with her gracious southern charm.

Grace asked, "Are you sure it's okay, ma'am?"

"Child, I've been cooking all day with every intention of having you with us. If you didn't show up, I was going to send Suzanne after you."

"Thanks. I appreciate it."

We'd decided not to tell Momma about the break-in at Grace's house on the walk over. There was no need to worry her unnecessarily.

Momma stared hard at me for a few seconds, then asked, "Suzanne, is there something you want to tell me?"

"You look nice today," I said, wondering if she'd heard anything I didn't want her to know, which could be just about anything.

She scolded me, "You didn't say a word about what happened at Grace's house. Are you trying to shield me from the world again? Young lady, need I remind you that I was handling things before you were a glimmer in my eye? I'll continue to do so for the rest of my life. You should know better than hold anything back from me."

I smiled. "You know, I really should. I don't know why I'm so surprised that you already knew about what happened. This town has one big mouth." I wanted to know who had said anything to her, but the time for subtle interrogation was long gone. "Who told you, anyway?"

Jake Bishop stepped out of the dining room and smiled at me. "I did. I heard it on my radio while I was having coffee with your mother."

Jake was tall and thin, with sandy blond hair that made me want to run my fingers through it, but I wasn't about to do that at the moment. He'd been distant lately, not making nearly enough effort to spend time with me. I knew he was busy, but so was I, and I was willing to make changes in my schedule for him. Well, as long as it didn't interfere with my donuts. And that pretty much took a big chunk out of every day, seven days a week. Okay, so maybe it hadn't been as one-sided as I liked to think.

I gave him my best hug, but he didn't reciprocate nearly enough to satisfy me.

Then I looked into his eyes, and I knew there was something going on.

In a somber voice, he asked, "Suzanne, do you have a minute? I need to talk to you about something."

"Uh oh," Grace said softly beside me, a sentiment I wholeheartedly agreed with.

Momma said, "Grace, come help me with the mashed potatoes. I've got too much to do in that kitchen by myself."

"Glad to," Grace said.

Before she and Momma disappeared into the kitchen, my mother asked, "Will you be staying as well, Jacob?"

"No, ma'am, I have to be in Asheville tonight, so I need to get going soon. Thanks for the offer, though." There was a drawn look in his eyes that told me he wasn't there to deliver any good news.

"You know that you're always welcome here," she said, and then it was just the two of us.

"What's wrong, Jake?" I asked, wondering what made him look so solemnly at me.

"We need to talk," he said flatly, and I felt the bottom suddenly drop out of the day. "I can't do this anymore. I'm so sorry. It's not you, it's me."

"Which means it's really me," I said. "Go ahead, I'm tough. Tell me the truth. You owe me at least that much." I felt my tears start to come, but I forced them to at least wait until he was gone.

I could swear that he was going to cry, but that didn't make sense. After all, he was the one ending it.

After a moment, he composed himself and said, "I guess what it all boils down to is that I'm still in love with my wife. Before you say a word, I know how crazy it sounds. Don't think I don't realize she's not coming back. When she died, my heart couldn't let her go. I thought I could make a fresh start of it with you, that I could get my life back, but her memory is just too strong. I'm so sorry. I never meant to hurt you."

And then he did start to cry, something that was hard to imagine from this tough state police inspector. I moved toward him and hugged Jake, stroking the back of his head as he cried softly, and to my surprise, I found my tears suddenly joining his.

After what seemed like forever, I stroked his hair for the last time and said, "Jake, don't feel bad about this. You can't help what's in your heart. I'm just sorry it didn't work out between us."

"So am I, Suzanne. More than you'll ever know."

He wiped the tears away from his cheeks with the back of his hand, started to touch mine, but then pulled away at the last second. After a moment, he said, "I really do need to be going. I'm sorry I can't stay."

"What's so important in Asheville? I figured you might be called on to investigate the murder here in town."

"I was, originally. But as I drove here from Raleigh, a town councilman was murdered in his office in Asheville, and April Springs got bumped."

I walked him to the door with a heaviness overtaking my heart with every step.

We said a nearly silent good-bye, and then he was gone.

As his cruiser pulled out of the driveway, I let out another stream of tears before I finally got my emotions back together. I was really crying more for what might have been than because Jake had just broken up with me. We'd dated enough so that we were comfortable with each other, but I'd never been sure that he'd end up being the great love of my life. I'd tried and failed to make a marriage work with Max, and for a long time, I'd told myself that I was through with that particular institution, but lately, I wasn't so sure. It wasn't that I needed a man in my life — I managed just fine on my own — but I seemed to be happier when there was someone I could look forward to seeing, even on the unpredictable basis my relationship with Jake had been founded on.

I dried my tears, then went into the powder room to dash cold water on my face before I walked into the kitchen. I was nearly at the door, but paused to take a deep breath before allowing myself to face the gauntlet of Grace and my mother. I knew

Jake's reason for coming would be the elephant in the room that nobody wanted to talk about, so I decided to come clean and get it all out at once.

"Jake just broke up with me," I said.

"Suzanne, I'm so sorry," Grace said as she started toward me. "Are you all right?"

"Not so much right now, but I will be."

I looked at my mother, who was shockingly silent, given the bombshell I'd just dropped. "Do you have anything to add, Momma?"

She frowned, then asked softly, "No, but I have a question. Did he give you a reason?"

I nodded. "He said he was still in love with his late wife. How do you compete with that?"

My mother put down the hot pad in her hands and hugged me, with Grace half a step behind her. Momma said, "You can't fight a ghost, Suzanne, and the sooner you found out his true feelings, the better off you are. I'm sorry, I know it's hard, but there's somebody out there who is just right for you. You're a smart, strong, beautiful woman. No matter what happens, you'll be fine."

Now I really wanted to cry. That kind of praise from my mother, though always implied, was barely ever spoken aloud. I hugged her, squeezing a little tighter than necessary, then I whispered, "Thank you," into her ear.

Momma pulled away, dabbed at a few fresh tears on my cheeks, then said, "You're most welcome. Now, if you don't mind, I need you to set the table. Go on, Grace, you can help her, I've got things under control in here now. Thanks again for your help."

"Glad to pitch in," she said as we walked out into the dining room.

"She barely let me hold a spatula in there," Grace said softly. "That woman reigns in her domain, doesn't she?"

"She always has," I said.

Grace looked into my eyes. "Are you sure you're all right?"

"I'm a little beat up, sure," I said. "But I'll be okay. Jake was right, and I think I knew it all along myself. I feel bad for him, if you want to know the truth."

"I guess it's tough being haunted by someone you loved," Grace said.

"I didn't say she came back as a ghost or anything."

"Suzanne, there are more ways of being haunted by your past than being visited by specters." She looked at the bare table, then added, "We'd better get busy. Unless I miss my guess, dinner will soon be served."

"What are we having? Did you manage to get that out of her?"

"Pork tenderloin with more of her famous garlic mashed potatoes and baby carrots. There's some kind of banana pudding concoction for dessert. I peeked into the fridge when she had her head in the oven." Grace smiled. "Okay, that didn't come out right."

"I know there are a great many people in this world who might commit suicide, but my mother's not one of them. Should we use the good china again?"

"I think that's an excellent idea," Grace said. "After all, in a way, this is your independence day, isn't it?"

"I suppose so," I said. "I'm just not sure I'm ready to be independent again."

"Come on," Grace said as she nudged me. "It'll be fun."

"If you say so," I said.

As we set the table with three settings, we avoided any more talk about Jake, or men in general. This was going to be a strictly estrogen evening, from the meal all the way to bedtime, which, given my early morning wake-up call, wouldn't be all that long after we ate. I normally didn't mind my hours. Well, at least I'd gotten used to them since

I'd opened Donut Hearts, but it was a lot harder for me to get to bed at a decent hour while Grace was staying with us.

I found myself nodding off after dinner as we played Scrabble, and finally, Momma said, "Suzanne, you're putting me to sleep with all that yawning. Go to bed before you collapse from exhaustion."

"But what are you two going to do?" I asked, not willing to give in yet.

"We'll manage somehow to carry on without you," she said with a smile.

I looked at Grace. "I *am* beat. Are you really okay if I desert you?"

"I don't know how you've managed to stay up this long," she said. "Go on, we'll be fine. Really."

I wanted to argue with them, but in all honesty, I was too tired to put up much of a fight. I'd been weary before, but the break-up with Jake had taken the last ounce of energy out of me.

I went upstairs, changed into my flannel pajamas, then went straight to sleep. I'd been concerned that worries over what had happened with Jake might keep me awake, but in a way, it was good to have closure, and I admired Jake for telling me some rather difficult news so well.

As I drifted off, I thought more about

what tomorrow might bring, and tried to focus on the possibilities for the future, instead of the realities of the past. It must have worked, and why not? I was getting good at it, since I'd given myself the speech countless times before.

Instead of my alarm clock waking up the next morning, I heard a voice calling me from the bedroom door. "Suzanne, are you awake?"

I sat up and looked at my clock. I still had three minutes before it went off, and I tried to keep the irritation out of my voice when I spoke.

"Grace, is something wrong?"

"No. I just wanted to know if I could come to work with you this morning. My boss still wants us off the roads, so I'm free to do what I please. I've been threatening to tag along with you forever, so why not today? Would you mind?"

I rubbed the sleep from my eyes. "Come on in."

When she did, I saw that she was fully dressed. "I know why you're doing this, and don't think I don't appreciate it, but you should change and go back to bed. I don't need a babysitter. I'm all right."

"I know you are, you nit. I want to come

to work with you today and see how donuts are really made. What's the matter? Don't you want me to come?"

"Sure, if you're serious," I said as I stifled a yawn.

I could see her grin from the light coming in from the hallway.

She said, "I'm up, aren't I? Speaking of which, why aren't you?"

Just then, my alarm started beeping at us. "I'm awake. Go grab two coffee mugs and I'll be right down."

"Sounds great," she said as she disappeared. Grace had been teasing me since I'd first taken command of the donut shop that she was going to join me someday, and I wondered if Jake hadn't visited the night before if she'd be making the offer now, but I wasn't about to turn her down. I knew Emma wouldn't mind, or at least I didn't think she would. Her mother came by about once a month to work with us, just to keep up to date on what we were doing, in case I took one of my rare days off from Donut Hearts. Grace shouldn't be any problem at all.

I pulled on jeans, a T-shirt, and a heavy sweater, then went downstairs to find Grace waiting for me with a travel mug full of coffee.

I took a deep drink, then said, "Are you really sure you want to do this?"

"I'm beginning to think you don't want me," she said.

"No, I just think anybody who gets up in the middle of the night and doesn't have to is insane. Let me warm up the Jeep, and we'll be ready to go."

"I took care of it while you were downstairs. We didn't get much snow last night. Maybe it's over."

"It's hard to tell around here, isn't it?" I threw a heavy coat on over my sweater, then added, "If you're coming, let's go."

She grabbed her jacket, and we got in the Jeep and drove slowly toward the shop. A trip that usually took three minutes took us fifteen because of the slippery roads. I was glad again that I'd bought a vehicle with four-wheel drive. While it wouldn't help on ice — nothing I knew would — it managed the snow-crusted roads fine, as long as I didn't push my luck.

I parked in front, smiling when I saw that Bob and Earl had yet again made sure my parking was scraped down to the asphalt.

Grace noticed, too. "How do you rate that kind of treatment?"

"I take care of the two men driving the snowplows," I said. "As long as I keep them

in coffee and donuts, I've got a clean parking lot."

"That's kind of like offering them a bribe,
isn't it?" she asked as we got out of the Jeep.

"No, it's exactly like one," I said. "Why,
do you have a problem with that?"

Grace laughed. "Are you kidding? We
hand out bribes all the time in my business
to buyers. We just call them premiums."

As I unlocked the front door, Grace said,
"Go ahead and do your work. Act like I'm
not even here, and I'll do my best to stay
out of your way. Unless you want me to help
you."

"Thanks, but Emma and I have it covered."

I dragged the barstool from my office and
put it in a place where she'd be out of the
line of fire while Emma and I went through
our morning routine.

I flipped the fryer on, checked for messages, and wasn't surprised to find that we
didn't have any. Not a legitimate one,
anyway. There was one on the machine, but
it consisted of thirty seconds of breathing,
and then a hang-up. That happened more
than I cared to think about.

I heard voices in the kitchen, so I poked
my head out of my office and saw that
Emma had arrived.

She looked at me steadily as she said, "I didn't realize we'd have someone with us today."

"I came to watch you two work," Grace said. "I think it's fascinating."

"Okay," Emma said, "if you say so."

As we started to prepare our cake donut mixes, Grace kept up a constant chatter. I didn't mind it, but it was pretty clear that Emma wasn't all that happy about us having company. That was just tough. Donut Hearts was still mine, and as long as it was, my friends would be welcome. I fried the old-fashioned donuts, Emma added the glaze, and Grace kept up a running commentary, bombarding us with questions as we worked. I added plain cake batter to the donut dropper, a metal contraption that resembled a large steel funnel. A spring-operated piece dropped a perfect ring of batter into the oil every time, but it was a dangerous tool to use around other people.

"You need to go out into the front area for a few minutes," I instructed Grace.

"I'm sorry. Am I being too chatty?"

I thought I saw Emma nod, but I didn't think Grace caught it. "No, I have to swing this around to get the batter to drop, and I don't want to take any chances that it might slip out of my hand."

She looked surprised by my confession. "Does that happen often?"

Before I could answer, Emma pointed to a spot on the wall just on the other side of Grace's head. "That's where she threw it the last time it slipped, so I'd take her advice and leave."

Seeing the gash in the drywall was all that Grace needed. "I'll be in front if you need me."

After she was gone, I put the donut dropper on the counter and looked hard at Emma. "Do you want to tell me what that was all about?"

"What?" she asked. "It's true, isn't it?"

"It happened the third day the shop was open," I said. "And that's not what I mean, and you know it."

Emma pretended to wipe down the counter beside the glazing area, though I'd seen her clean it twice already. "I don't have a clue what you're talking about."

"Your attitude. Why are you being so distant with Grace?"

Emma frowned, then said, "What should I do, welcome her with open arms?"

"That would be nice," I said.

"No, thanks. If you want to train somebody to take my place, fine. But don't expect me to be happy about it."

I couldn't help myself, I laughed out loud.

Emma misinterpreted it, though. "You think it's funny?"

"Emma, dear, sweet Emma, Grace has no interest in taking your job, and even if she did, I wouldn't hire her. Your place here is yours as long as you want it."

She looked at me carefully, then asked softly, "Is that the truth, or are you just trying to save my feelings?"

"Believe me, it's the complete and utter truth."

Emma frowned at me, then looked toward the front. "Then why is she here?"

"She stayed all night with me, and she's been threatening to come in since I opened this place. Trust me, Grace has no interest in replacing either one of us." I didn't mention that my best friend made more in a few days than I cleared in a month, and she didn't work a tenth as much as I did.

She'd be insane to quit her job to come work for me.

"I guess I owe her an apology, then," Emma said.

"It wouldn't be out of order," I said. She really hadn't been openly rude to Grace, but I didn't want there to be bad blood between them.

"I'll take care of it right now."

She disappeared into the front room, and I dropped in a batch of old fashioned donuts. I hadn't even turned them when Emma came back into the kitchen. That had to be the briefest apology in the history of mankind, but I was busy with donuts frying in scalding oil at the moment, and I didn't want to get into it until they were out of their sizzling bath.

As I pulled the finished donuts out of the fryer with my beefed up chopsticks, Emma was ready with the glaze.

Before I added another dollop of batter to the dropper, I said, "That didn't take long, did it?"

"I didn't apologize," Emma said.

"Hang on a second. I thought we agreed that would be the right thing to do. Why did you change your mind between here and there?"

"Go out and see for yourself," Emma said with a smile.

I walked through the kitchen door, and for a second, it looked like Grace was gone. Then I noticed her feet sticking out beyond the edge of one of my couches, and as soon as I spotted her, I heard a gentle snore.

She'd fallen asleep in less time than it took to fry a donut, a feat that would have been a record in my book.

I came back in and saw that Emma was grinning. "I didn't have the heart to wake her up."

"That's fine," I said. "But you're still going to apologize to her, right?"

"I'm glad to," Emma said. "Why is it so important to you?"

I hugged her shoulder. "Because I don't want to see two of my best friends fighting, especially when it's not necessary."

Emma looked at me oddly. "Is that true?"

"Of course it's true. You know how much I hate confrontation."

"I'm not talking about that part," she said, her gaze never leaving mine. "I mean the part about us being friends."

"Absolutely. I like to think we're more than just two people who work together. Why, am I being presumptuous?"

"No, I think of you as a friend, too. I just never said it out loud."

I smiled at her. "Well then, it's high time you did, wouldn't you say?" I picked the donut dropper back up, then said, "Let's get back to work, shall we?"

"I'm ready," she said, and as she ducked into my office, I slung the dropper back and forth a few times, driving the batter into the bottom.

"Clear," I called out as I started dropping

fresh rings of batter into the oil, and Emma came out to get to work on the next phase of our operation. As I finished the cake donuts, she got the ingredients out for the glazed dough. We slid into our routine without a misstep, and I was sorry Grace couldn't see us. It was like a choreographed dance, one that had grown out of practice six days a week for the past few years.

Finally, it was time for our break.

Emma asked, "Should we just stay back here so we don't wake Grace?"

"I don't know about you, but I need some fresh air," I said. "I don't see any reason to break with tradition now, do you?"

"I don't want to wake Grace."

I laughed. "Did you hear her snoring? I doubt you'd be able to rouse her with a cannon until daybreak. Come on, let's go outside and see if it's started snowing again."

We walked through the front, and I saw that Grace hadn't moved an inch from her spot on the couch. Her breathing was deep and rich, and a part of me envied her the rest. Outside, it was clear that the snow had come again briefly, then it had tapered off to nothing. From the look of the sidewalk and the road, we hadn't accumulated much more than a dusting since we'd been inside.

Emma studied the scene, then said, "So, I guess the majority of the snow's over, isn't it?"

"It looks like it. Have you seen a weather report lately?"

"No, but when's the last time we got two or three snows so close together?" she asked as she kicked at an errant chunk of frozen ice and slush.

I thought about it. "Not for years, anyway. I'll just be glad to finally see it go."

"But maybe it could stay until Christmas," Emma said.

"I thought you were the one who worshipped the sun and the heat?" I asked.

"Come on, Suzanne. Everybody likes a white Christmas," she said. "Even me."

As we took in the early morning, we were each left to our thoughts. The break we took between making cake donuts and the yeast ones was an important one for us. It allowed Emma and me to clear our heads of what we'd done, and focus on what we had ahead of us. Inside the proofing box, the yeast donut rounds were safe and warm, but I was happy to be outside despite the cold weather. It made me feel alive in a way that a warm day in August never seemed to manage.

I glanced at my watch, and saw that we'd

gone over our break-time by a full four minutes.

"Let's go," I said.

Emma nodded, and as we walked back in, the timer was beeping, and I worried that it had roused my friend. I glanced over at Grace, who looked so peaceful in her sleep, and saw that she hadn't moved an inch.

Two minutes before opening, it was time to wake Grace so we could unlock the front door and welcome our customers. I couldn't believe that loading the display cases with donuts hadn't awakened her, or the freshly brewed coffee, either.

I poured a mug of it, walked over to her, then gently shook her shoulder. "Hey, sleepyhead, it's time to wake up."

"What? Where am I?" Grace said as she slowly awakened. "Suzanne?" It took her a second, then she spotted the coffee in my hand. "Must. Have. Coffee."

I handed her the mug, then as she took her first sip, I said, "I hate to wake you, but I'm opening the shop in one minute."

"I fell asleep?" she said as she rubbed her face with her free hand. The one holding the coffee wasn't going anywhere.

"Yes, before we even took our break."

"Why didn't you wake me?" she asked.

141

"Seriously? You looked so peaceful, I didn't have the heart to do it."

Emma surprised me by getting a fresh yeast donut and handing it to Grace. "I owe you an apology. I'm sorry I was a little snippy this morning."

Grace took the donut gladly, then said, "Girl, if I had to get up every morning when you did, I'd be biting people's heads off like they were made of chocolate."

Emma said, "That's no excuse. I was afraid you wanted my job."

"Not if it paid a million dollars a month," she said, then paused before adding, "Well, maybe then." She smelled the fresh donut, then took a healthy bite. "This is wonderful, but it's not worth it. Suzanne, I don't know whether I have a whole new level of respect for you, or if I think you're completely insane."

"Why can't it be both?" I said. "Why don't you move to a booth, unless you want to go back to the house. You can take the Jeep, if you'd like."

"I don't think I'm ready to go back to my place yet." For the first time that morning, a look of fear crept into her expression, and I hated myself for bringing it up.

"I meant you could go back to my house. I'm sure Momma would be thrilled to fix you a big breakfast again this morning."

"Donuts and coffee, that's what I need," she said. "Unless you don't want me hanging around."

"Are you kidding? We'd love to have you. Right, Emma?"

To my assistant's credit, she didn't even hesitate. "That's right. Would you like another donut? We've got all kinds."

Grace shook her head. "This is great, for now. You two have work to do. Don't let me stop you."

"We didn't, and we won't," I said with a smile.

I unlocked the front door, but since nobody was waiting to get in, it was more a formality than anything else.

Five minutes later, customers started streaming in, and it felt good to have something to offer them. A day without donuts was a day without joy for a lot of my regulars, and I didn't ever want to be responsible for taking that away from them.

An hour later, I was pleased with the morning's sales so far when Chief Martin came in, with Officer Grant in tow. From the expressions on their faces, I had a feeling that my joy quotient for the day had just run out.

CHAPTER 6

"Why do I get the feeling that you're not here for donuts," I said as the chief approached the front counter.

"Suzanne, we need to talk."

"Is that why there's two of you?" I asked. "Are you actually ganging up on me now? What's going on, Chief?"

"It's about Max," he said, and I felt the blood drain from my face.

"He's dead, isn't he?" All of a sudden, I found myself regretting every harsh word I'd ever hurled at him, every door I'd slammed in his face. Now I'd never get the chance to say I was sorry, to wipe the slate clean between us.

The chief looked surprised by my question. "What makes you say something like that?"

"Then it's not true?" I asked.

He shook his head. "Not as far as I know. Kind of an odd question coming from you, wouldn't you admit?"

"I don't know, what's the proper response in situations like this? I know my ex-husband is missing, and I also know that you think he might have had something to do with Darlene's death. Is it that crazy to think that something might have happened to him?"

Chief Martin shrugged. "I don't know, I'll have to think about that."

"If he's not dead, then why are you here?"

Officer Grant started to say something, but one look from his boss was enough to shut him up.

Instead, the chief said, "We have reason to believe that you're harboring your ex-husband, and I came here personally to tell you that if you are, it's going to mean big trouble for you."

"Harboring him? What is he, a boat? I don't have any idea where he might be, and that's the truth."

The chief didn't look like he believed me, but I didn't really care.

He said, "If that's true, then who broke into Grace's house yesterday? And why was she with you all night instead of at her own place?"

At the sound of her name, Grace came on the run. It was pretty clear she'd been listening to the entire conversation, so there was no need to bring her up to speed on what had been said.

She stared hard at him and said, "I've got a question for you, Chief. If we were hiding Max, why wouldn't we give him a key to my house, instead of making him break the door down?"

"I already thought of that," the chief said. "You wanted some deniability if he was caught hiding out there."

"Maybe, but if that's true, why did I flag Officer Grant down when I did? More of a smoke screen, Chief? You've been watching too many episodes of *Columbo*."

He decided to ignore that. "If you're hiding him, or you know where he is, I'm coming after both of you. This is your last chance to come clean. Where is he?"

"I don't have a clue," I said.

"Don't look at me," Grace said. "I wouldn't protect that man from a pack of dogs if he was wearing a suit made out of bacon."

The chief shook his head. "Suzanne, are you still claiming that you don't have any idea what happened to Darlene?"

"Which one of us are you accusing, Chief, me or my ex-husband? What about Muriel? Is she still missing? Did you drop her from your list, or she still on it?"

"Suzanne, you don't get to ask the questions. I do."

"If you give me some information about what's really going on, maybe I'll be able to help you," I said.

He looked like he wanted to bite my head off, then obviously changed his mind before he stormed off toward the exit. Officer Grant wanted to say something — it was pretty clear by the way he was looking at me — but he never got the chance.

His boss hesitated at the door, then barked at him, "Let's go. Now."

Once they were gone, Grace said, "Imagine the nerve of that man, coming in here accusing us of hiding your ex-husband. The man's way out of line."

I frowned. "You know what? He's not. If Max had come to me, I might have done what the chief was accusing me of, and I would have roped you in to help, too. I don't think there's a chance on earth that he killed Darlene Higgins, no matter what Chief Martin thinks, and if it meant keeping him out of jail, I'm not sure I wouldn't do everything the chief just accused me of doing."

Grace said, "He kind of implied that you might have had something to do with Dar-

147

lene's murder yourself, didn't he?"

I bit my lower lip, then said, "You caught that too, did you? It doesn't sound like he believed my alibi."

I'd nearly let the information I'd gotten from Officer Grant slip out, something that would have killed me to do. Maybe Grace hadn't noticed.

"I didn't know you had to provide him with your alibi," she said.

"It just makes sense, doesn't it? I can see how he'd think I had a reason to want Darlene dead. You know what? I've been doing my best to stay out of this case, but it looks like I don't have much choice. If the chief's going to focus on me and Max, it's time I started looking for the real killer myself."

"That's the spirit," Grace said. "Where should we start?"

"I'm calling George, and you're welcome to sit in. This has gone on long enough."

Grace nodded. "You know me, I'm ready for anything. Just give me a job, and I'm all over it."

"Let's wait until George gets here, shall we?"

"Okay," Grace said. "I'm going back to my booth, but if you need me, just give me a shout and I'm there."

I was just about to call George Morris when the man himself walked into the shop.

"I need to talk to you," I said.

He nodded, then asked, "Can I eat first, or is it an emergency?"

"I think we've got enough time for a donut or two," I said as I grabbed him a cup of coffee and a pair of fresh cinnamon apple cake donuts. "I'd hate the idea that I was starving you."

"Not as much as I would," he said.

After he took a bite and followed it up with a sip of coffee, he said, "That's better. Now, what's so important?"

"Hang on a second." There was a good crowd of customers in the shop, and I didn't want to broadcast what we were about to do. I took care of everyone at the counter, then knew I had to talk to George before another surge came in. There was something about snowy weather that made April Springs crave donuts.

I turned back to George just as I saw Darlene's cousin, Taylor Higgins, walk in.

I had a cup of coffee ready for him as he approached the counter.

"Good morning," I said, offering him my cheeriest greeting. I thought I had problems, but he'd just lost someone he'd been close to, and that trumped anything I'd experienced lately, including getting dumped. "How are you today?"

"Not good," he said. "I'm here about my cousin. I'm worried the police aren't doing all they should to find her killer."

"I don't know what to tell you," I said.

"I know. It's not your problem. I'm going to the station to talk to Chief Martin in a little while, but I wanted to come here first to get my nerve up."

"I wish I had more than coffee for you, if that's the case," I said.

"Thanks. I appreciate the thought, but I'm on the wagon anyway." He grabbed his coffee after declining a donut and took a seat by the window.

I turned back to George. I was pretty sure the chief wouldn't approve of our conversation, and I'd done enough to get on his bad side in the past few years that I had no desire to add to it.

Lowering my voice, I said, "Why don't you go over and sit with Grace? She's involved in this, too."

"Imagine my surprise," he said with a soft smile.

After a minute I joined them.

"Don't you have to wait on customers?" Grace asked.

"No, I spoke to Emma, and she's going to

take care of the front for me. She hates working with the customers, but this is too important to wait until closing."

George nodded. "Okay, you've got us here. Now what?"

"This is going to be a lot more complex than what we've done in the past," I said. "We need to look into the lives of three people, and there are just three of us. Are you sure you're both willing to help me again? I'm afraid I've found my way into another jam."

Grace said, "Suzanne, you don't even have to ask. We're here for you, you know that."

George nodded his head in agreement. "Just tell us what you have in mind."

I looked carefully at him, and knew that he was overly sensitive to my meddling in active police investigations, since he was a retired cop himself. "Do you have a problem with any of this? Because if you do, we'll all understand if you want to bow out of this one."

George moved his mug around on the table in front of him for a few seconds before speaking. "Suzanne, I'm loyal to you, but I have to admit that sometimes I feel kind of cheap spying on the department for you. Is there any chance Chief Martin is going to call Jake? That could be your pipeline into the investigation instead of me."

Before I could warn her not to say anything, Grace blurted out, "She could, but Jake came by the house last night and broke up with her. Don't worry about it, George, we'll find someone else. You can go, if you're uncomfortable."

"Hang on a second," I said. "I'd appreciate it if you'd ease up on George. He's being pulled in a lot of different directions lately, and if he doesn't feel right about helping us, that's going to be perfectly fine, okay?"

"I'm just saying," Grace said, "you're either with us, or against us."

George scowled at her, then said, "I don't remember asking you one way or the other what you thought about me."

She shrugged. "Suzanne needs my help. I don't care what you think; I'm going to help her."

"So am I," George said as he slammed his hand down on the table. It was loud enough to attract attention all around the shop, but after everyone saw that the fireworks were over, they went back to their own conversations.

I said, "That's it. You two, follow me."

I didn't even look back to see if George

and Grace were behind me as I walked into the kitchen. If they hadn't followed, I was going to look like a first-class idiot, but to my relief, they did just as I'd asked.

"Okay, let's clear the air here and now."

Grace said, "I'm just watching your back."

I took her hands in mine, mainly so I wouldn't be tempted to strangle her. "Grace, George is my friend, too. Don't question his loyalty to me ever again. Am I making myself clear?"

She looked properly chastened. "Yes, ma'am."

When I didn't say another word, she got the message and dropped her hands from mine. As she faced George, I wasn't sure what kind of scene we were about to get, but to my delight, she said softly, "George, I'm sorry I acted like a brat. Someone broke into my house last night, and I think it's related to what's going on in town. When it sounded like you weren't willing to help, I took it personally, and I shouldn't have. Please forgive me."

That was one of the things I loved about Grace. When she laid it on the line, there was no doubt about her sincerity. It was probably one of the traits that made her such a great salesperson.

George nodded, then said gruffly, "Sorry

about the break-in. It must have been tough, knowing that someone was in your place without your permission. It's kind of a violation, isn't it?"

Grace said, "That's exactly what it's like. How did you know?"

"I was a cop once, remember? You can't do the job without some empathy, no matter what some people believe."

"I believe it," Grace said.

"So what am I supposed to confess?" George asked me.

"Nothing that I know of. Why, do you have a guilty conscience?"

"Me? No, I sleep like a baby at night. I just figured you brought me back here for something."

I hesitated saying anything, but then realized that with friends, sometimes the easiest choice isn't always the best one. "I'm worried about you. Slamming your hand down on that table is not something I'd expect you to do. What's wrong?"

"Nothing," he said, but there was a hitch in his voice, and I wasn't about to let it go at that.

"George, tell me," I said.

Grace said, "If you two will excuse me, my coffee's getting cold."

After she was gone, it was just the two of

us. I decided to press him one more time. "George, you know you can talk to me about anything. We're friends."

"Yeah, that's the problem sometimes, isn't it?" he said as he started pacing around the small workspace.

"I'm not sure what you mean by that," I said, thoroughly confused by the odd declaration.

He stopped pacing, then stood and looked at me. "Do you think that fact has escaped the chief's attention? No matter what you might believe, deep down he's a good cop. He sees a lot more than you give him credit for."

I'd never considered that possibility. "What are you saying? Is our friendship hurting your connections with the police?"

"Suzanne, they aren't connections. They are my friends. And lately, I've been hearing some grumbling about where my loyalties really rest. You know what? I wonder sometimes myself. There's a brotherhood among law enforcement officers, and sometimes I play kind of fast and loose with it."

It was the longest speech I'd ever heard him give. I touched his shoulder lightly. "George, I'd never ask you to betray a friendship, you know that, don't you?"

He nodded, then pulled away from my

touch. "I know that, but sometimes I think maybe they don't." He took a deep breath, then said, "You know what? If you need me, I'm here for you. I'll find out whatever I can."

"I don't want you to burn any bridges on my account," I said.

"I didn't say I would. But if I can help you without crossing any lines, I will."

I started to protest when he added, "Suzanne, you're not my mother, or my boss, or my shrink. You're my friend, and if I choose to help you, there's not much you can do about it. Now can I go back and eat my breakfast? I feel like a kid having to stay after school for something he didn't do."

"Go on. Eat your donuts," I said, laughing as I followed him back out front. George headed back for the table, but I stopped at Emma's position behind the cash register.

"Good, you're relieving me," she said.

"Not quite. We have a few more things to discuss. You can handle things here, can't you?"

She gave me an exaggerated thumbs-up signal, then said, "If customer service is going to be part of my job description, then I want a raise."

"As for me, I'd like a pony," I said, "but I've got a feeling neither one of us is going to get our wish."

The table was quiet as I approached, and they both looked expectantly at me. I took a deep breath, then said, "First things first. Are we all good right now?"

I got two nods of assent, which is what I'd been hoping for. We were a team.

"Okay, here are my thoughts. We need to look into Max's disappearance, as well as Muriel's sudden absence. While we're doing that, we need to dig into Darlene's life and see who might have reason to want her dead. We also need to look into Muriel's life, because whoever killed Darlene could have just as easily been going after her."

Grace asked, "Can you honestly think anyone could make that mistake? The two women were as different as night and day."

"You didn't see her lying on the ground," I said. "I didn't know until I saw that the wig Darlene had been wearing had slipped and some of her blonde hair poked out from underneath it. Remember, she was trying out for the lead in Max's play, so she was emulating Muriel pretty closely."

"Okay," George said. "Who gets what assignment?"

"Here's what I had in mind. Grace, I need you to ask around as delicately as you can about Darlene's and Muriel's finances. See

157

if either one of them owed anyone any money, if they had large life insurance policies, or big savings accounts waiting to be inherited. Any angle that could involve money as a motive would be helpful."

"I can't imagine Darlene Higgins leaving much of a financial legacy," she said.

"Honestly, I can't either, but we shouldn't guess. We need to know."

"I'll do my best," she said. Grace glanced at her watch, then she added, "Most of the people I need to talk with probably aren't even up yet. I'll have to wait a few hours before I make any calls."

George looked at me steadily for a few seconds, then asked, "So, what did you have in mind for me?"

"Are you sure you want to do this?"

He nodded. "Tell me what you need."

I took a deep breath, then said, "You have the hardest job of all. I need you to find Max and Muriel."

"Martin's got his men working on it pretty hard," George said.

"I know that, but none of them have your experience and expertise."

"You don't have to flatter me, Suzanne, I already said I'd help." Though he was protesting the compliments, it was pretty clear he enjoyed them.

"I'm just telling the truth," I said.

"Sure, whatever," he said as he got up and headed for the door.

He stopped halfway there. "What do I owe you for breakfast?"

"It's on the house," I said.

He nodded, and then he walked out the door. George had no problem taking free donuts, something that always made me laugh, given his past job experience, and the reputation cops had for loving donuts.

That left me. I decided I needed to ask around town to find out any dish I could on Muriel and Darlene from the gossip mill, and there was only one place I could go for that, next door to Gabby Williams.

It was too bad her shop wasn't open yet.

Grace must have had the same thought as I had. "We have to talk to Gabby, don't we?"

"Yes, but that comes later. The first thing we need to do is get our hair done," I said.

"Suzanne, do you really think that's fair, since George is out looking for clues about what really happened?"

I grinned at her. "I didn't say where we were going, did I? I'm going to call and get us the next two appointments at Wilma Jackson's Cutnip."

"That's asking too much," she said as her hands went protectively toward her elegantly styled coif.

"Tell you what. I'll take a hit for the team, and you can just come along for the ride. How's that sound?"

"Better for me than it does for you," she said.

"Why do you say that?"

"Have you seen the women around town who all have the exact same hairstyle? They have one thing in common; they go to Cutnip to get their hair done."

"It can't be that bad, can it?" I asked, as my own hands went to my beloved ponytail.

"Maybe I'm just exaggerating," she said.

After a long pause, she added, "Then again, maybe I'm not."

My fingers trembled a little as I called Cutnip, and a part of me hoped they were booked solid through July.

Unfortunately, they'd just had a cancellation, and could take me in the next fifteen minutes.

When I told Emma I needed her to watch the front a little longer, she asked, "Where are you going? Why can't I run your errand for you?"

"I'm going to Cutnip to get my hair done so I can snoop around," I said as I lowered my voice.

"That's okay, you go on ahead. Take your

time, I'll even close up at noon, if you want me to."

I shook my head, and I would have laughed if I wasn't so worried about what was going to happen to my hair, all in the name of the murder investigation. I'd have to keep telling myself it was something I had to do. Maybe that would keep me in the beautician's chair. Otherwise, Wilma was going to need a hefty set of straps to confine me as she tortured my hair.

I hesitated at the door of the salon as another woman came out. Her hair sported Wilma's signature teasing, a big hairdo that looked more at home in the sixties than it did now.

"You want to know something? I'm not so sure about this anymore," I said. "Is it really worth it?"

"Come on, don't be such a baby," Grace said as she started to give me a little nudge toward the door.

"If I'm being a baby, why don't you get your hair done instead of me?"

She laughed low enough so only I could hear it. "Suzanne, do I honestly look that crazy to you?"

Before I could come up with an answer that had just the right bite to it, it was too late; we were inside.

There were five chairs in Wilma's salon, and four of them were full, with one woman waiting. The place was certainly hopping. The one empty chair was covered with a black smock that had DARLENE embroidered in red on it.

Wilma nodded in our direction as we walked in. A woman holding onto her forties with both hands, she was dressed in tight black stretch pants, and I could see hints of a leopard-print blouse under her smock. Her hair had been teased into a giant ball of henna, and I could see she didn't have to look far for her inspiration.

"As I live and breathe, it's the donut lady herself," she said. "Are you finally ready to get rid of that ponytail and grow up?"

My hand went to my hair as I said, "I thought I'd come by and look at some options today," I lied. "But I'm not ready for a drastic change yet. I need some time to come to terms with it. Could I still get a shampoo and a trim in the meantime?"

Wilma waved her scissors in the air, barely missing removing a chunk of her current customer's left earlobe. "Honey, we do everything here but change your oil."

As Grace and I took our seats, Wilma said, "What about you, darlin'? You need a touch-up, too?"

"No, I'm good. I just came along to give my opinion on her new hairstyle. Suzanne needs my advice on just about everything."

I kicked her foot, but nobody else noticed it.

Wilma looked carefully at Grace, then said, "That's fine, then. You're a little too trendy for my taste, if you don't mind my saying so."

I tried to bite back the laughter, and instead found myself choking. After a few seconds, I managed to get it back under control, but not before garnering some odd looks from everyone else in the beauty salon.

Grace said, "Do you want to know the truth? We can't all pull off your style, Wilma."

The salon owner nodded. "It's wise of you to realize it, dear. Don't sell yourself short, though. You do pretty good, with what you have and all, I mean."

I expected Grace to say something biting, but she managed to smile, then said, "Coming from you, that's a real compliment."

I had to look at her to check, but she didn't even roll her eyes as she said it.

Wilma took a few more snips with her scissors, then she removed the smock from the woman in her chair. After collecting her fee, she turned to me and patted her chair and said with a smile, "You're next."

"How about her?" I asked as I pointed to the woman who'd arrived before we had.

"Sally? She's waiting on Mary Fran. Nobody else touches her. Come on, don't be shy, I won't bite."

No, but I was willing to bet her scissors did. I reluctantly climbed into the chair, and she draped the smock around me like it was some kind of cape.

She instructed me, "Now, you just lean back into the sink and we'll give you a good wash first."

"I washed my hair last night," I said in protest, suddenly wondering if this was that good an idea after all.

She sniffed it, then said, "If you don't mind my saying so, you smell like donuts, Suzanne."

"There are a lot worse things I could smell like," I said. In my head, I added, "like a Parisian nightwalker like you," but I kept that comment to myself.

She patted my shoulder, and as she did so, Wilma tilted me back until my neck touched the sink basin. "Just relax. You won't feel a thing."

That was kind of what I was afraid of.

As she doused my hair with warm water, I

said, "It's a terrible thing about Darlene, isn't it?"

Was that sharp tug in my hair a comment on my question?

Wilma said, "Sorry about that, my fingers got caught in a knot. Yes, I thought long and hard about closing the shop all week in her honor, but Darlene would have wanted the show to go on."

"That's right," one of the other hairdressers said as she accentuated her point by stabbing her scissors in the air. "She was a real trooper."

Wilma said, "Excuse me for saying so, but I never thought I'd hear a word of sympathy from you towards her, Suzanne Hart."

I started to protest when she added, "I'm not saying I'd blame you. Darlene lost her head over that Max, and even you have to admit, that man could charm water from a dry well."

"He's got a way about him, I won't deny it," I said, trying to keep my temper in check. I was there for information, not to defend what little there was of my ex-husband's honor.

"Just between us girls, I knew that man was trouble from the first day he got his driver's license," Wilma said. "I tried to warn Darlene about him, but she just wouldn't listen to me."

I got a sudden whiff of the shampoo before she put it in my hair, and I smelled bananas and apricots, a powerful and pungent aroma. If I had my druthers, I would have kept the deep fried scent.

As she rubbed it into my scalp, she said, "There now, isn't that better?"

"Hmm," I said, not trusting myself to speak.

As she rinsed the shampoo out of my hair, I decided to dig a little deeper.

"Wilma, do you know anybody who had a grudge against Darlene?"

"Do you mean besides you, sugar?" she asked.

I fought the urge to protest my innocence again. "Yes, besides me."

"Funny you should ask. The chief asked me the same thing."

"What did you tell him?" I asked as I wiped a bit of the errant shampoo away from my eyes.

Wilma seemed to think about it, then said, "Nobody's ever had a problem with her, and that's the truth. Besides her one little slip with Max, she was a good girl." Wilma hoisted me back upright, wrapped a towel around my wet hair, then studied my face for a few moments. "Let's see, I think the most attractive cut for you would be my specialty. I call it the Cascade. Isn't that lucky for you? Dear, it will do wonders for you, and you'll finally look your real age, instead of like one of the kids."

There was no way I was going to put up with that. I'd seen too many of Wilma's cascades walking around April Springs to ever want one myself. I glanced over at her clock. "Oh my gosh. Is that the time? Wilma, I hate to do this, but I've got to run. I've got a dentist appointment I forgot about completely. I'll come back another time, I promise," I said as I ran the towel through my hair a few times, then shoved that and the smock into her arms. "How's ten sound for the wash?"

"I charge twenty," she said coldly.

"Seriously?" I asked as I pulled another ten from my thin wallet. "Okay. Gotta run now."

Grace met me at the door, and once we were outside the shop, I used my fingers to scrub my still-wet hair back and forth in the cold. It was freezing, and I quickly regretted abandoning the towel.

Grace grinned at me and said, "You're go-ing to get pneumonia, you know that, don't you?"

"That's still better than getting one of her

167

specialty hairdos. She's got a lot of nerve calling it a cascade. It's more like an avalanche, if you ask me."

The salon door opened and one of the stylists, Cynthia Trent, came out with a towel in her hand. I'd gone through school with her brother, Tom, a nice guy who'd ended up going to Duke and was now a doctor in Charlotte. Most of the girls had been more interested in the bad boys at our school, and most of us regretted the choices we'd made back then. If I'd known then what I knew now, I would have dated more math majors and fewer aspiring actors and wannabe rock stars.

"I was hoping you'd still be here," she said as she handed me the towel.

"Thanks, Cynthia. You're a lifesaver," I said, then ran the fresh towel through my hair until it was dry enough to hold me until I could get home and finish the job.

As I handed the towel back to her, I said, "That was sweet of you."

"Wilma just lied to you," the stylist said, her voice barely above a whisper, though there was no one near but Grace.

"The shampoos are really just ten, aren't they? I knew it."

Cynthia shook her head. "They're twenty, all right. That's not what she lied to you about. Darlene had one enemy in April Springs, at least one that I knew about, and you deserve to know who it was."

BREAKFAST PUFFIN MUFFINS

These treats are a nice change of pace from deep frying everything, and bake in the oven. They're perfect for a quick snack or a bite on the run. Light in texture and flavor, these are a real hit at my house!

Ingredients

1/3 cup margarine or butter, soft
1/2 cup sugar
1 egg, beaten
2 cups flour
2 teaspoons baking powder
1/4 teaspoon salt
2 teaspoons pumpkin pie spices
3/4 cup milk, whole or 2%
1 teaspoon cinnamon
1 teaspoon nutmeg
2 ounces raisins (optional)

Directions

Blend margarine, sugar, and beaten egg together until the mixture is smooth. In a separate bowl, sift the flour, baking powder, salt, pumpkin pie spice, cinnamon, and nutmeg together. Add the dry ingredients and the wet to the milk, alternating and mixing as you go. If you'd like, now is the time to add the raisins to the batter.

Fill the muffin cups halfway (I always use liners), then dust the top of each muffin with cinnamon sugar (1 tablespoon granulated sugar for 1 teaspoon of cinnamon) before you put it into the oven, which should be preheated to 350°F. Bake for 18–22 minutes, or until a toothpick comes out of the center of each muffin clean. Cool the muffins on a rack for five minutes before removing them from the pan.

CHAPTER 7

"Who are you talking about?" Grace asked.

Cynthia glanced back toward the door, then admitted, "Wilma herself. She thought Darlene was stealing from her here at the salon, and they had a horrible fight just before Darlene was stabbed. If you ask me, it's a little too much of a coincidence that she turns up dead just a little later, don't you think?"

"I do," I said. "Why tell me, though? Did you talk to the police?"

She looked at me like she thought I was crazy. "Are you kidding? The chief's not a big fan of mine, and I doubt he'd believe me. He still thinks I painted the town clock pink the night we graduated, and he's never let up on me since."

I shrugged. "Join the club. He doesn't really care for me all that much either, but that hasn't kept me from telling him what I know when it's important, and believe me,

172

this matters."

The door of the salon opened, and Wilma stepped out. "Suzanne, I thought you had an appointment you had to rush off to make."

"I do, but my hair was still wet, and Cynthia was nice enough to offer me a towel. She's really sweet."

Wilma looked at her employee. "Yes, she's an angel in disguise. One who has someone sitting in her chair at the moment, I might add."

"Sorry, I'll get right on it," Cynthia said as she ducked back inside.

"We've got to go, too," I said.

"How convenient that Grace has the same appointment you do," Wilma said, the sarcasm dripping from her words like honey off a spoon.

"My boss asked us all to stay home until the roads are completely clear, so I'm shadowing Suzanne today. I even helped her make donuts this morning."

That was an outright lie, but I wasn't going to say anything about it. I just smiled and nodded. "Come on, Grace. After my dentist appointment, I'm getting a manicure."

"Finally, something I can do, too."

We headed off toward Dr. Frye's office,

and as we neared his door, I looked back to see Wilma still standing there watching us. We had no choice; we had to go inside.

At the front desk, Vicki looked surprised to see us. "Ladies, I don't have either one of you on my books for today."

"We just thought we'd check to see if you had any open cleaning appointments."

She scanned the appointment book in front of her. "I have a few slots after July," she said.

"Seven months away? Really?"

"Really," Vicki said. "We're working four days a week, so it takes some time to get to everyone."

"I didn't know you worked a four-day week. Are you hiring?" I asked. "I work seven myself."

Vicki laughed. "No, we're good, but thanks for asking. Should I put you two down for August?"

Grace said, "I'll have to check my planner. I'm not sure I'll even be in town next August."

"Just let me know," she said, "but don't wait too long. Appointments have a tendency to fill up quickly around here."

I peeked out the door to see if Wilma was still watching us, but the coast was clear, at least for now. I pulled Grace outside with me, and we started back toward the donut shop.

"We're not done investigating, are we?" Grace asked.

"No, but I need to dry my hair, and I just remembered that Emma keeps a blowdryer in the bathroom."

"Why on earth does she do that?"

"Are you kidding? Sometimes in the summer she comes in with her hair still wet and she doesn't dry it until she gets to the shop."

"And you don't mind that?"

I shrugged. "Good help is hard to get. I let her do a few things I probably shouldn't, but all in all, she's a good worker, and she doesn't complain about the killer hours or the less-than-stellar pay."

"If you say so," Grace said. "It's kind of casual, isn't it?"

I laughed. "You've been working in corporate America too long. The real world's a little tougher, trust me."

"I'm not disputing it," she said. "I've long said you're insane trying to run your own business. It's nice to let someone else worry about the big decisions, like how they're going to pay me, and how much vacation I get every year."

"Vacation? What's that? I haven't had one since I opened the donut shop."

Grace said, "Then wouldn't you say it was high time you did? Let's just chuck all this, close the shop, and head for Aruba. I can be ready in an hour."

"Sorry, I'm not as flexible as you are, even if I could afford the trip, which we both know I can't. I've got commitments here, and a big one is to Max. I'm not about to leave him hanging out in the wind."

"I don't see why not," she said. "What's he done for you, besides break your heart in so many pieces I thought it would never heal."

"That's not the point, Grace, and you know it. We were married at one time, and not all those days were bad ones. I owe it to him to help if I can, but if you want to go to a warm beach somewhere with cold cocktails and hot nights, don't let me stop you."

"It wouldn't be any fun going by myself," she admitted.

"Cheer up. Maybe some time we'll do it," I said. "But not right now."

"Agreed, but I'm holding you to that." Grace hesitated as we neared the shop, then she asked, "What are we going to do after you dry your hair? Have you thought about that yet?"

"I've got to put in some time at the

counter, but I have a plan after that."

"What is it?"

"I'm not going to tell you just yet."

"Why not?" she asked.

"Because I want you to be surprised," I said as we walked into Donut Hearts. There wasn't a single soul inside, including Emma, my assistant.

After a few seconds, she came up front.

At least she had the decency to look embarrassed when she saw us. "Sorry, I had to go to the bathroom. Nobody came in, though."

"How do you know?" I asked as I looked around the shop. "You were in the other room."

"I would have heard them," she said. Emma did a quick look around the place, then looked relieved as she said, "See? Nothing's changed."

"Have you checked the cash register?" I asked.

With an obvious sense of panic, she hit the NO SALE button, and I didn't even have to see inside the drawer to know that while Emma had been in back, someone had come into the shop and robbed us.

"Suzanne, I'm so sorry. I don't know what to say." Emma looked close to crying, and I wasn't far behind her. I couldn't let her see that, though.

"Don't worry. It wasn't your fault."

"Whose fault was it, then?" Grace asked, and I could have strangled her at that moment for voicing what all three of us were thinking.

Grace immediately realized she'd made a mistake. "I didn't mean that the way it sounded, Emma. I'm sorry."

My assistant looked as though she couldn't feel any worse than she already did. "No, you're right. If I hadn't left the cash register unattended, we wouldn't have been robbed. I should have at least put a sign in the door and locked up. Sometimes I forget our small town can still have its share of crime."

I patted her shoulder. "Don't be too hard on yourself. If I hadn't gone to Cutnip digging into something that didn't concern me, I would have been here to watch the front myself. We both share the blame on this one," I said.

Grace asked, "Suzanne, hadn't you better call the police and report this?"

"I suppose I have to," I said. "Chief Martin's going to have a field day with this." I reached for the telephone. "I might as well get it over with."

I was hoping for Officer Grant, but just my luck, the chief answered the telephone himself.

"I need to report a robbery at my donut shop," I said.

For some reason, I'd been expecting him to laugh at my misfortune, but he asked solemnly, "Was anybody hurt?"

"No, as a matter of fact, no one was up front. Emma was in back, and I'd stepped out of the shop for a minute. While we were gone, somebody cleaned out our cash register."

"That's pretty careless, Suzanne, even for you."

I felt bad enough about losing a day's receipts without his added, unsolicited commentary. "Would you send someone over here?"

I was hoping he wouldn't come himself, but that quickly turned out to be in vain. "I'll be right there. Don't touch anything until I get there, okay?"

"I wouldn't dream of it," I said.

After I hung up, I said, "The chief's coming himself."

I turned to Emma and added, "He's already scolded me about leaving the register unattended, so prepare yourself for a lecture."

"He can't say anything worse than I'm thinking myself," she said. "Suzanne, I'm going to pay you back every dime that was taken."

I patted her shoulder. "Emma, I appreciate the gesture, I honestly do, but I won't take your money."

That didn't do anything to cheer her up. "You're going to fire me then, aren't you? Not that I blame you."

I held her shoulders with my hands. "Nobody's getting fired, either. Now, don't you have some dishes to do?"

She asked, "Doesn't the chief want to dust for fingerprints?"

"I doubt it. Besides, whoever came in never made it in back, so we'll be fine cleaning up there. Go ahead, take care of it."

She nodded. "I'll do it right now. I'm so sorry. I don't know what else to say."

After she was gone, Grace looked at me solemnly, then said, "You're firing her, aren't you?"

"No," I said, not managing to conceal my surprise. "You heard what I told her. I meant it. She made a mistake, she's sorry about it, and I'm willing to bet it won't happen again. People deserve a second chance, Grace."

She shrugged. "You're a better person

than I am. I'm not sure I could keep my temper in check."

I frowned a few seconds, then explained, "Don't get me wrong, I'm not happy about what happened, but I meant it when I said it was as much my fault as it was hers. I should have waited until noon to talk to Wilma, but my curiosity got the better of me. Emma's not the only one who needs to learn a lesson from this."

"You're not going to quit investigating the murder, are you? It's not like you to just give up when things get tough."

I looked out the window as I said, "No, but I'm going to try to keep my priorities a little straighter. I've got a business to run — first and foremost — and if I don't take care of that, I won't have any way to support myself, and I'd rather die than ask anyone for help."

Grace nodded. "Don't think we all don't realize that," she said. "In the meantime though, if you need a little extra to tide you over, you know I'm always willing and able to help. All you have to do is ask."

I hugged her. "Thanks, but we'll be fine. It was a slow morning, so we should be able to bounce back. I *am* going to tell Emma that if it ever happens again and she's here by herself, she needs to do as she suggested and lock the front door before she goes to the bathroom."

"That's all I'm saying," Grace said.

Chief Martin drove up, parked in front of the shop, and came in with a clipboard in his hand. "Okay, let's hear it again."

"I told you everything over the phone," I said. "We don't know anything else. You're not going to shut the shop down, are you?"

"Why on earth would I do that?" he asked.

"I don't know, that's what they do on TV. I don't want fingerprint dust all over my donuts."

He shook his head. "Suzanne, there are going to be a million prints in this place, and I'm willing to bet that the only ones that matter were smudged when you opened the register to see that you'd been robbed."

"So you're not even going to look for prints?" Grace asked, not even trying to keep the aggravation from her voice.

"Of course we'll check it out," he said. "I've got an officer coming to dust the register for prints, and the front door handle. Other than that, I don't think we have much of a chance to find anything, but we'll try. How much did you lose?"

"I'm not sure yet, but it wasn't a whole lot. It was a slow morning. I'll run a report on the register, but I have to hit a few buttons to do that, and I don't want to obscure the prints anymore than we already have."

Chief Martin nodded, and we all watched as Officer Grant came in, carrying a gray case in one hand.

"Where should I dust?" he asked.

"The register, and the front doorknob," the chief said.

Officer Grant did as he was told without saying a word.

The chief looked at me and asked, "Where were you when this happened?"

"Grace and I stepped out for a few minutes," I said.

"Would you mind telling me where you were?"

I ran a hand through my unkempt hair and admitted, "I was at the beauty shop, if you must know."

"Why am I not surprised you were at Cutnip. Suzanne, are you digging into Darlene Higgins's murder?"

"I was getting my hair done," I repeated.

He studied my unkempt hair, then the chief frowned. "Then why didn't you let her finish?"

This was getting complicated. Lies usually were. That's why I stuck to the truth whenever I could. "I felt bad about leaving Emma here all by herself, okay?"

"At least that instinct was on the money," he said. "Where is she?"

I pointed to the back. "I've got her doing dishes. I thought it might help steady her nerves."

Before he could go back into the kitchen, I said, "She already feels bad enough about this. Don't scold her too, okay?"

He merely shrugged as he disappeared in back, and as I started after him, he shook his head. "Thanks, but I don't need you at the moment. Don't wander off, though. I'll be right back."

I started to protest, but it was pretty clear he wasn't about to back down.

As soon as the chief was in the other room, Officer Grant frowned at me. "Sorry this had to happen to you. Petty crime's been way up in town lately." He must have realized how that sounded, because he quickly added, "Not that your robbery's petty. You know what I mean."

"It's fine; I understand. Are you getting any good prints?"

He shook his head. "No, they're all smudged on the register. I'm guessing the oil from handling the donuts makes it tough to get a decent print on the best day."

"What about the door?" Grace asked.

"I'll dust there too, but I'm pretty sure it's

not going to help. I'm afraid this is a dead end."

He was just starting on the front door when the chief walked back out. "You'd better go talk to her. I can't get her to stop crying."

"What did you say to her?" I asked as I rushed past him to Emma.

"Nothing that didn't need to be asked," he said.

Grace started to follow me when the chief said, "Hang on a second. I want to talk to you."

Grace wanted to argue, but I shook my head. I needed to see Emma alone, and the chief was doing me a favor by restraining her, whether he meant to or not.

Emma was indeed crying when I went into the kitchen. "What's wrong? What did he say?"

"He wanted to go through my purse. He said if I wasn't guilty, I wouldn't mind."

"Guilty of what?" I asked, though I was starting to suspect just what the chief had in mind.

"Suzanne, he thinks I stole the money myself. I didn't, I swear I didn't. You've got to believe me."

I hugged her, and the sobbing intensified.

After a minute, she managed to get control

of it again, and as I pulled away, I said, "I trust you with my life. I know you'd never steal from me."

"Thank you for believing me," she said through her sniffles.

"There's nothing to thank me for," I said.

"Should I let him search my stuff? I don't have anything to hide."

"You don't have anything to prove to me."

"But I do to him." Before I could stop her, she walked to the door and said, "Chief, I changed my mind. You can look wherever you want. I don't have anything I'm afraid for you to see."

"Good," he said.

He took her purse, riffled through it, then said, "You've got eleven dollars and change here."

"Surely we made more than that," I said, trying to treat it lighter than it really was. It had shaken me, having Chief Martin suspect Emma of the theft. I knew in my heart she hadn't done it, but had Wilma shared the same confidence in Darlene? It was more than a theft, if it was true. It was a betrayal of trust, and I could suddenly realize how Wilma could have taken it so personally.

"Do you want to search me, too?" As she spoke, Emma took off her apron, revealing an outfit underneath of tight blue jeans and a t-shirt that wouldn't have hidden a quarter, let alone a handful of bills.

"No, you're fine. But I need you two to wait out front for me."

We did as we were ordered, and after about ten minutes, the chief came back up front. "The money wasn't there, or in the alley, either."

"I told you it wouldn't be," Emma said.

"I have to look, Emma. It's part of my job," he said, almost sad about the truth of it.

"Then I feel sorry for you," Emma said as she went back into the kitchen.

He turned and asked Officer Grant, "Did you find anything?"

"Lots of partials, nothing we can really use. Half the town's been in here over the past two days. Sorry I couldn't do more."

"That's fine. Go on back to the station and wait for me there."

After he left, Grace asked, "So, what happens now?"

"I fill out this report, and Suzanne calls her insurance company. That's really all we can do at this point."

I said, "I'm not filing this. My premiums will jump more than I lost. This is one I'm just going to have to eat."

The chief finished the form, then tore off

the bottom copy and handed it to me. "Again, I'm sorry about this."

"It'll be fine," I said. "Thanks for coming so quickly."

After he was gone, I asked Grace, "What did he say to you when you were alone?"

"He wanted to know why my hair wasn't wet, too."

"What did you tell him?"

Grace smiled. "The truth. I said that I was too smart to let Wilma within half a mile of my hair."

"What did he say to that?"

"I thought I saw a grin, but it was just there for a second, so I can't be sure. Where do we go from here?"

I glanced at the clock. "It's almost eleven, so I have to stay around until closing." I looked at the display case, which was still loaded down with donuts. When I ran the report, I'd know exactly how much we'd lost, but I had a pretty good idea just seeing the inventory we still had on hand.

"I've got some calls to make, remember?" she asked.

"You can use my phone in the office," I said.

"Thanks, but I'd rather do it somewhere else. I'll be back around noon."

"Okay."

After she left, Emma and I tried to do anything we could think of to dispel the pallor in the air, but nothing seemed to work. Several customers drifted in, but none of the sales were all that large, and the till was practically bare when Grace came back ten minutes before noon. Emma had withdrawn into the back, and I had grown tired of trying to make her feel better, especially since I was the one who'd lost the money.

Grace said, "You look like death."

"Thanks. You're particularly lovely yourself. What did you find out?"

She looked toward the back. "Is Emma still here?"

"She is. Why?"

"I'd rather not talk about this until she's gone," Grace admitted.

I didn't care one way or the other, but Grace had long had a mind of her own. "Help me box these up, and we can all get out of here," I said.

I called out to Emma, "We're closing early. Can you come out here?"

"Sure, what do you need?" she asked as she came out, wiping her hands on a clean towel.

"Would you mind taking these by the church?" I asked as I pointed to the donuts we'd readied for transport.

She patted her hands dry on her apron. "I'd be happy to do it. If there's anything you need, all you have to do is ask."

She grabbed her jacket, then said, "Save the rest of the dishes. I'll take care of them when I get back."

"I'll do them," I said. "You can go home after you drop these off."

"Suzanne, let me do them. That's my job. Please."

I couldn't bear the hurt look in her eyes. "Fine. I won't touch a thing."

After we loaded up the car and my assistant drove off, I asked Grace back inside the donut shop.

"Were you able to find anything out?" I asked as I started sweeping the floor. I'd leave the dishes for Emma, but that didn't mean I had to put the entire burden of cleaning up on her shoulders. She'd made a mistake, a costly one, true, but I'd forgiven her, and it wasn't in my nature to keep punishing her for it.

Grace grinned at me. "You're not going to believe this."

"Try me," I said.

Grace nodded. "Here's what I was able to come up with so far. I started with Muriel, and I was frankly surprised by what I found. She looks like she's been doing well to the outside world, doesn't she? It's all a lie. Her house is mortgaged to the hilt, she's taken cash advances out on three credit cards, and her combined savings and checking accounts have less then forty dollars between them."

I had a hard time believing it. "Are you sure?"

"My sources are pretty accurate," Grace said. "I didn't see the numbers myself, but I believe it's true."

"So she's in some kind of dire financial trouble," I said.

"That much is pretty clear," Grace said. "What I don't know yet is what happened to all of her money. At one time she was supposed to be loaded. I've got a few people looking into it, and I should know something more pretty soon."

"I'd say that's a lot you found out," I said. "What about Darlene?"

"Hey, I only had an hour. I've got some calls out, but I haven't heard anything yet."

"You did great," I said as I patted her shoulder.

Grace asked, "So, where does that leave us?"

"Before we do anything else, I'm going to run a report to see how much I lost today, and I want to finish it before Emma gets back. You can wait here with me if you want, or I can catch up with you later."

Grace grabbed the broom from my hands and started sweeping. "If you don't mind, I'll hang around."

I knew she'd have to go back to her home sometime, but it was clear she wasn't ready to do it just yet.

"Thanks. I appreciate all the help I can get."

As Grace swept up, I ran the report. In the end, we lost a little over two hundred dollars. Not a fortune by anyone's standards, but more than I'd hoped it would be. Still, things could have been a lot worse, and if it taught Emma to be on her guard when she was at the shop alone, it might have even been worth the price it was going to cost me.

I finished the report, bagged the change and the checks left behind, then turned to Grace, who'd completed her task.

"What now?" she asked.

"We forget about the robbery and keep digging into the murder," I said. "There's somebody else I'd like to talk to, and I'm hoping we get more out of her than we did with Wilma."

"Who did you have in mind?"

"Darlene's roommate," I said.

"What do you think she can tell us?" Grace asked.

"There's only one way to find out, isn't there? Let's go."

"Aren't we going to wait for Emma?" she asked.

"No, I think this is something we need to take care of right now." I left Emma a note telling her that we were gone for the day, and urging her to go home as well. There was no use crying over the money we'd lost. We'd just have to get over it, and make amends to try harder keeping our money safe in the future.

Grace and I locked up the shop, and I looked over toward Gabby's used clothing store. Oddly, it was dark inside, and I wondered if she'd closed for some reason. I'd been meaning to go talk to her just before I found out about the robbery, and it had completely slipped my mind in the turmoil.

"My car's this way," Grace said as I started toward ReNewed Clothing.

"I know, but I need to check on something first."

Grace touched my arm lightly. "Suzanne, if we go in there, we're never going to get out, and you know it."

She followed me anyway, and we both

stopped by the front door and read the sign posted there.

To our loyal customers,

We're closed until further notice. If you have something on consignment with us, try back next month. We appreciate your business. If you want to buy something, I'm afraid you'll just have to try again later as well.

We appreciate your understanding.

Sincerely,

The management.

"What's going on?" Grace asked. "I didn't think Gabby ever closed her shop."

"Not without telling me," I said. "Something must have happened to her. Come on, let's go back to the donut shop."

"What good is that going to do?"

"I've got her home number written down someplace there, and there's an emergency contact if something happens at her shop and she's not there. We traded numbers the day I opened, but I've never had to use hers."

We walked back in, and Grace followed

me to my office. I had to flip through my numbers notebook twice before I found Gabby's entries. I tried her home number, but there was no answer, and strangely enough, she didn't have her answering machine on, either.

There was an emergency contact, but no name was listed. When I dialed it, it too rang for ten times without anyone picking up, but then the oddest thing happened. Suddenly Muriel Stevens's voice greeted me. "I'm not able to come to the telephone right now, but if you leave your name and number, I'll get back to you as soon as I can."

"That's bizarre," I said as I hung up without leaving a message.

"What is?"

"I dialed Gabby's backup number, but I got Muriel's phone instead."

"No way."

I nodded as I hit the "redial" button, then I handed her the telephone so she could hear the message for herself.

Grace listened for a few seconds, and after the message ended, she said, "Muriel, I need you or Gabby to call me as soon as you get this. It's important. Oh, this is Grace Gauge. I'm in the book."

"Why'd you do that?" I asked as she handed the phone back to me.

"We want to know what's going on, don't we? I thought it made sense to leave a message. I didn't realize Gabby and Muriel were that good friends."

"Neither did I," I said. "What I don't get is why Gabby didn't mention they were close when we first saw Darlene's body."

"I don't know," Grace said, "but we're not going to figure anything out until we talk to her again. Now let's go find Darlene's roommate, Kimmi Erickson. That's the one thing I was able to find out about Darlene when I started asking around."

"Let me guess," I said. "I bet she spells her name with an 'i' on the end, doesn't she?"

"I don't have the faintest clue," Grace said as I looked her name up in the thin April Springs telephone book.

I found the listing, then said, "It just says K. Erickson here, but we can ask her how she spells her name when we see her. Come on, are you driving, or should I?"

"Ordinarily I'd volunteer, but where exactly do they live? I'd hate for anything to happen to my company car, and if the two of them live out in the country, the roads might not be plowed yet."

"So if something happens to one of our cars, it should be to my Jeep and not your

Mercedes, right?" I asked with a slight smile.

"Suzanne, not to be mean about it, but what's one more ding on your car going to matter?"

"I'd love to argue with you, but I can't," I said as I laughed. "Let's go."

"In your Jeep, right?"

"Right," I said. Apparently Kimmi and Darlene lived on the outskirts of April Springs, and from the address, I was guessing it was in a trailer somewhere out in the sticks. I was pleasantly surprised when I discovered a quaint old cabin at the address I'd found in the telephone book. It wasn't run down at all. As snow layered on the roof, it made the place look like it belonged on a calendar page, and I wondered how these two women could afford the rent for a place as nice as this looked.

We walked up the steps and rang the door bell twice, but no one answered.

"Nobody's home," Grace said.

"Give it a second," I said. This time I used the brass knocker, giving it a hard set of raps.

The door opened almost immediately, and inside, we found a girl in her mid-twenties dressed in a tight white t-shirt and a pair of red short shorts that looked like they'd been painted on. If I had a body like that, I'd probably go around wearing the same thing myself. She said a little breathlessly, "I'm Kimmi. Sorry, I was just doing my yoga. Come on in, I'm almost finished."

This girl had no idea who we were, or why we were visiting her, but she opened her home to us like we were long-lost friends.

Kimmi got back on a bright blue mat in front of the wide-screen television, and hit a button on her remote control. As she dropped into a pose that would have sent me straight to a chiropractor, I looked around the room. It was wonderful and homey, with a fire burning in the stone fireplace. Darkened hardwood floors glistened with shellac, and heavy wooden furniture matched the structure of the house itself.

As Kimmi contorted her body, she said, "We can talk right now. I know this part by heart."

"We were just driving by, and I have to tell you, I love this house," Grace said. "Do you own it, or are you renting it?"

"Neither," she said. "My dad's letting us stay here until he can sell it. Well, it's just me now, and he's not crazy about me living by myself." She looked over at us, then asked, "Do either of you need a place to stay? I'm looking for a roommate so I don't have to leave."

"I might be interested," Grace said.

I looked at her and tried to keep my mouth closed. Grace winked at me, and said to Kimmi, "Could I see your extra bedroom?"

"Sure, but there's still stuff in there, and it's a real mess. My roommate . . . moved on," she added lamely.

I suppose you could call dying moving on, but Kimmi didn't strike me as the metaphorical type.

Grace nodded. "Where is it?"

Kimmi pointed with a free foot. "Down the hallway and on the left. It's the only door that's closed. I'll be with you in three minutes."

As we hurried down the hallway, I said, "You have a perfectly good house of your own. Why would you want to live here?"

"To be honest with you, my place has lost some of its charm since somebody broke in and went through my stuff. Having a roommate might not be a bad thing."

"Are you telling me you're actually considering living with Bambi?"

"Her name's Kimmi," she said as she opened the door. "We came to snoop, so I got us through the door. What more can you ask for? Now let's start digging before she finishes that howling dog pose she's doing."

"I don't think that's what it's called," I said.

"I don't care if it's called dog and hydrant," she said. "Hurry up. We don't have much time."

I looked around the room, and saw Darlene's sad little attempt to decorate for the holidays. There was a small artificial tree on top of the dresser — complete with twinkling white fiber optic lights — and tiny little boxes were wrapped as presents and arranged under it. All of that sat on a blanket of cotton that had been spun to resemble fallen snow. On her nightstand, she had a familiar wooden tree six inches tall covered in gumdrops. For a second I thought I was seeing things. I had the exact same tree myself, and up until that moment, I thought I had the only one in town, but apparently I'd been mistaken. On the other nightstand, there was a folk art Santa, a thin woodcarving that was nearly two feet tall. Ragged and worn at the edges, this Santa didn't look jolly at all. Instead, the woodcarver had chosen an intricate, sad face, with eyes that showed how tiring it must be to deliver presents all around the world in just one night.

I was suddenly aware of Grace standing by my elbow. "Suzanne, we don't have all day. I'll go through her closet, and you check out her purse."

It made sense, so as she began rooting around inside Darlene's closet, I emptied her purse on the bed. There was a collection of business cards there that I found odd, until I looked on the backs of them and saw several different telephone numbers scrawled on them. I shoved them all into my pocket so I could look at them later. There was nothing else inside that really helped — just a mishmash of car keys, makeup, lip balm, and other flotsam and jetsam a purse tends to accumulate over the years — so I shoved it all back into her bag and put it back on the bed. It felt like I was violating Darlene somehow as I went through her things, but in a way, I was trying to help her. I was sure she'd thank me if she could for trying to find out who had really killed her. I found a bookcase bulging with paperback novels, and I leaned over to read a few of the titles. They were all romances, and from the looks of the spines, they'd been read and reread many times. I felt a twinge of sadness for her when I realized that she had just been looking for someone to love, but when I remembered that the someone she'd set her sights on had still been my husband at the time, some of my sympathy started to wane. Still, I knew as well as anybody else that it wasn't easy being alone. I just wished she's stuck to men who were free to return her affection.

"Look at these," Grace said. I joined her at the closet and looked inside. It was evident that Darlene had an odd fondness for spiked pumps with seven-inch heels, especially for a woman who stayed on her feet all day.

"These are nice," Grace said. "I'd borrow a pair, if I could. Have you found anything yet?"

"Not really," I said, and then I spotted it. Tucked inside on of the shoe boxes in back of Darlene's closet was the edge of a hundred-dollar bill.

"What's that doing in there?" I asked as I retrieved the box.

As I opened the lid, I'd expected to find more money — maybe even stacks of it — but what I found there rocked me back on my heels, and I nearly dropped the box as I looked inside.

Before I could show Grace what I'd found, the door burst open, and I knew that we'd been caught.

How on earth was I going to explain this?

CHAPTER 8

Kimmi asked heatedly, "What are you two doing in her closet? I didn't mean you could snoop around."

"We didn't know her things were still here," I said as I covered up the box lid and hid it from her view. "Why did she leave everything behind?"

Kimmi wasn't budging, though. "You still haven't told me why you were snooping around in there."

"We weren't snooping," Grace said indignantly. "I had to see how big the closets were, didn't I? Wouldn't that be the first thing you looked at if you were thinking about moving into a new place?"

"I guess that makes sense," she said as she rubbed her ear. "I just can't get used to the fact that she's gone." Kimmi took a deep breath, then said, "I should probably tell you, my roommate didn't move away. Somebody killed her."

I had to make sure she thought we didn't already know that. "That's terrible. Did it happen in here?" I pretended to look around for bloodstains, and Kimmi caught my implication.

"No, it happened in town." She frowned a second, then looked at me and said, "I know you. You run that place, Donut Darts."

"It's called Donut Hearts," I corrected her. "I heard someone died, but I never found out who everybody was talking about."

"You're Max's wife," Kimmi said guardedly, and I was beginning to realize that I may have underestimated the girl's intelligence, or at the very least, her knack for local lore.

"I'm his ex-wife. Why should that matter?"

I looked at the dresser where I'd seen a photo of Darlene and Kimmi together earlier. "It wasn't Darlene Higgins who was killed, was it?"

"She was my best friend," Kimmi said as she nodded.

I glanced at Grace, took a step closer to the bed so I'd be certain I'd hit it, then I let myself collapse.

"She's fainted," Grace said as she hovered over me. "Go get me some water. Quickly."

As soon as Kimmi went after my water, Grace whispered, "What was in that box, anyway? We just have a few seconds."

"Go look," I said, refusing to move.

Grace grabbed the box, flipped it open, and then must have seen what I'd seen.

"It's a picture of you," Grace said. "What's it doing in here?"

"You're asking me? I almost fainted for real when I saw it. There's five tattered old hundred-dollar bills in there too, and something that looks suspiciously like a lock of Max's hair. What was she up to?"

"I don't know," Grace said, "but I'm taking this with us." She emptied the box and slid the contents into her purse just as Kimmi arrived.

She handed Grace the water, then asked, "You're not going to pour it on her, are you? I don't want the bed to get soaked."

Knowing Grace, that was exactly what she had in mind. It was time to end my part of the charade.

Letting my eyelids flutter, I pretended to come to. "What happened?"

"You fainted, Suzanne," Grace said as she got close to my face.

"It was the shock of it all," I said. "Suddenly I'm not comfortable staying here anymore. Can we leave?"

"I think that's for the best," Grace said as she helped me up.

"Are you going to be all right?" Kimmi asked me. There was genuine concern in her voice, and I felt bad about duping her, even if it was for a good cause.

"I'll be fine. It was just the shock of it all, you know?"

"I guess so." Kimmi turned to Grace. "What do you think? Would you like to move in here with me? I can have her things out of here by tomorrow."

"I'm going to have to think about it," Grace said. "I'm afraid there's some kind of bad karma in here."

"The car's out in the garage," Kimmi said, obviously misunderstanding. "I don't know who to call about it, since it belonged to Darlene."

"I wonder if it will be for sale," Grace asked. "I'm looking for new transportation so I won't have to continue relying on the kindness of strangers."

Kimmi said, "It's never been a problem for me. If I need a ride, I just call one of the guys I work with, and they come right over and pick me up."

"What do you do?" I asked, not able to resist the question.

"I work for my dad. He's a contractor,

and he has lots of nice men working for him. I'm his secretary, and they all seem to like me."

"I don't doubt that for one second," I said, knowing they would come running at her slightest whim, especially if they saw her dressed as she was at the moment.

"You're sweeter than I thought you'd be," Kimmi said to me. She must have realized how I might take that, because she quickly added, "Not that I didn't think you'd be nice before. Sometimes hearing things from Darlene, I think she was really jealous of you."

"Why on earth would she be jealous of me?" I asked, startled by the admission.

"Max loved you, and Darlene believed he always would. That's something a lot of women would give anything to have."

"I guess so," I said. "I never really thought about it that way."

"Well then, maybe you should," she said. "Let's see, her keys are around here somewhere. There's her purse, I bet they're in there."

I felt my back stiffen as she reached for Darlene's purse. Would she notice the missing business cards, or that the purse was more disheveled than normal from my impromptu search? Fortunately, she didn't even bat an eye as she reached in and pulled out a heavy key ring that I'd examined and discarded earlier. As we walked outside, I saw that Darlene favored a black Trans Am, a particular favorite of some of the younger women in town.

Grace plucked the keys out of Kimmi's hands, then said, "Why don't you two chat while I have a quick look."

As she ducked in through the driver's side door, I asked Kimmi, "How long have you and Darlene known each other?"

"She used to babysit me, can you believe that? I never thought we'd get to be friends, but we did. When Dad finished redoing this house, he offered it to me rent-free for six months, and Darlene was thrilled to move in with me. She was living back home with her mother. Can you believe that? It's too pathetic to think about. I mean come on, grow up and leave home already, you know?"

I felt my cheeks redden, and wondered if Kimmi was taking a shot at me, but there wasn't an ounce of guile in the girl's expression.

"I'm sure she had her reasons," I said.

"I can't imagine what they'd be," Kimmi said.

We were both stranded at a loss for words

when Grace handed Kimmi the keys. "Thanks for letting me look."

"Aren't you even going to start it? It runs great."

"I'll bet it does, but I need something with a little more room," Grace said.

"I can see that. Maybe Daddy will buy it for me," she said as she frowned at the car. To my credit, I withheld the sarcastic comments swirling around in my head, as she added, "I guess I could always learn to drive. How hard could it be?"

As we got back into the Jeep, I pulled away. "That was a great idea. Too bad it didn't pan out, but it was worth checking, anyway," I said.

"What are you talking about?"

"The Trans Am. I'm just saying, not every lead can have a clue."

"This one did," Grace said as she smiled at me. "Yours wasn't the only photo Darlene had in her possession. What do you think of this?"

She handed me a snapshot from her jacket pocket, and I saw that it was of Muriel Stevens, dressed in her signature multicolored jacket.

I frowned as I studied the photograph. "What does it mean, though?"

Grace shrugged. "I just find the clues. It's

your job to interpret them."

"Well, okay, as long as I get the easy part," I said.

As we drove back toward town, I asked, "Should I drop you off at your house?"

"If you don't mind, I'd rather come with you," she said.

"Grace, you've got to go home sometime."

She bit her lip, then said, "I don't know. I'm not so crazy about it anymore." She tried to laugh, but it had a hollow ring to it as she added, "I guess if things get desperate, I could always live with Kimmi."

"If it comes to that, you can stay with Momma and me, no matter how pathetic some people might find it."

"I never said anything like that," Grace protested.

"I'm not talking about you, you nit. Kimmi kept telling me how lame it was that I was living with my mother."

"How'd she know that?"

"She didn't. She was making fun of Darlene when she lived at home, but the barbs worked just as well on me. Funny thing is, I thought my hide was thicker than that, but if you hadn't come out of that car when you did, Kimmi and I were about to have words, and there wasn't going to be anything pleasant about them."

"Suzanne, I'd take everything that girl said to you with a grain of salt. She doesn't get it, and she may never understand, but I do. I think you're doing the right thing living back at home."

"I'm not planning to stay there forever," I said, "but for the moment, it's where I want to be."

"In spite of the fact that your mother drives you crazy sometimes?"

I smiled as I drove toward home. "As long as I get to return the favor every now and then."

I drove another few minutes, then I asked, "Should we at least drop by your place to get some clean clothes?"

"No thanks, I'm good. I packed enough yesterday for a week." She added quickly, "Not that I'm planning to stay with you that long."

"Grace, as long as I'm welcome there, you are too. Okay? I'm not trying to push you out."

"I appreciate that," she said. "When I think I need a nudge, I'll be sure to ask you for one."

"That's all I'm saying. Now let's got home. I could use a nap before dinner."

"Really? I'm as fresh as ever."

"That's because you already had your nap

212

this morning," I said. "Remember?"

"I just nodded off for a few minutes," she protested.

I couldn't let that go without a jab of my own. "Should we go by Emma's place and ask her how long you were asleep?"

Grace laughed. "No, let's spare me the embarrassment, shall we? Okay, you've earned your nap, and I'll keep your mother company while you're sleeping."

"That's a bargain I'll never pass up," I said as I pulled into our snow-crusted driveway. The precipitation had finally ended, apparently once and for all, but that didn't mean the remnants from the storm were gone as well. Part of our driveway never saw the sun during winter, and the snow and ice were persistent visitors that often refused to leave until the very last second. I felt the Jeep slide a little sideways as I rounded the corner, and saw Grace's hands bite onto her seatbelt.

"Relax, I haven't hit anything in days, weeks even."

"I just don't want to be your passenger when the streak ends," she said.

I pulled in behind Momma's car and turned off the engine.

Grace asked, "Should you go in first and make sure it's all right that I stay a little longer?"

"Can you honestly believe my mother would say no to you?"

She shook her head. "I guess not, but I still think we should check with her first. It's the right thing to do."

"Then wait right here," I said as I turned the engine on again. "I'll be back in a few minutes, but there's no reason you have to freeze to death in the meantime."

I walked in, and Momma instantly looked back at the door. "Where's Grace? Why isn't she with you? Suzanne, have you no manners at all? You shouldn't let her stay in that house all by herself in the middle of a snowstorm."

I raised one hand and started ticking off fingers as I made my points. "One, I didn't leave her alone, she's out in the Jeep. Two, I have plenty of manners. I just don't always choose to use them when you'd like me to. And three, there hasn't been a snowflake falling in all of April Springs today, so you can hardly call it a storm."

"Are you quite finished?"

I nodded. "I think so."

"Then go invite her in. She'll catch her death of cold out there."

"I don't see how with the motor running."

Momma asked, "Why didn't she come in

with you in the first place?"

"She wanted to make sure it was okay with you if she stayed with us for a few more days," I explained.

Momma frowned, then reached for her jacket. "Stay here. I'll be right back."

"Where are you going?"

"I want to talk to Grace," she said.

"Should I come with you?"

"Let me handle this," she said. "Why don't you take off that jacket and warm yourself by the fire."

I thought about arguing with her, but her suggestion sounded so good, I decided to capitulate instead. At least I was sure to get some shock value out of my surrender.

If she was surprised by my sudden acquiescence, she didn't show it.

I took off my boots and jacket, stretched out on the couch as I pulled a light afghan off the back, and lay down so I could watch the flames.

The next thing I knew, a hand was shaking me. "Suzanne? Wake up. Dinner's ready."

I sat up and rubbed my eyes, then looked at Grace. "I must have fallen asleep."

"That's good to know, because if you were awake and snoring like that, we'd have to call the paramedics."

"Did you and Momma have a nice talk?" I asked as I stretched me arms high over my head.

"We did," she said simply.

"Sorry to leave you hanging like that," I said softly. "But she insisted she talk to you alone."

"Don't worry about it. Everything's settled," Grace said.

My mother called out from the dining room, "Girls, are you going to stay in there chatting while our dinner gets cold?"

"No, ma'am," we said in perfect unison, something that made us both laugh.

Grace offered me a hand, which I took, and she helped pull me off the couch.

"That nap felt great," I said as we walked in.

"I'm glad, dear," Momma said. "Now let's eat, shall we?"

"It smells wonderful," Grace said. "What are we having?"

"It's nothing special. I made stuffed peppers, cooked some peas I froze from the farmer's market last spring, and threw a salad together."

"That all sounds great to me," Grace said, and I nodded my agreement.

As we ate, I kept avoiding telling Momma about our robbery, and I nearly made it through the meal when the phone rang.

As she got up to answer it, I asked, "What happened about our rule of no telephone calls at meals?"

"This is important, Suzanne. I'm expecting to hear from your aunt Patty."

She answered the phone, frowned, then said, "I'm sure you're mistaken."

Another long pause, then an abrupt "Thank you" and she hung up.

"You didn't talk very long. What's going on with Aunt Patty?"

"That was Shelly Rice. She said something about a robbery at your place today. Surely she was mistaken."

"It was more a theft than a robbery," I said. "We made the mistake of leaving the front unattended for a few seconds, and someone took advantage of the situation and cleaned out our cash register."

Momma started to say something, but I cut her off before she could. "I know we should have been more careful, but we weren't, and we're paying the price for it. No lectures tonight, okay, Momma?"

"I was just going to say that I was glad no one was hurt," she said.

"And no more?" I asked.

"No more."

"Good," I said as I pushed my empty plate

away. "Because I'd just as soon forget about it, if it's all right with you."

There was a knock on the front door, and I stood quickly to get it. "Maybe this is what I need, some kind of distraction."

It wasn't. When I answered the door, I found Emma standing there, but she wasn't alone. Her father was behind her, and from the scowl on his face, I knew this wasn't going to be pleasant for any of us.

Ray Blake said, "Suzanne, we need to talk."

"It's been a long day, Ray, and Emma and I are both worn out. Can't it wait until another time?"

"It can't," he said as he nudged his daughter toward me. I had no choice but to step aside or she would have run me over.

As we all walked into the living room, Ray nodded toward Momma and Grace, and then told Emma, "Go on. Say what you need to say."

"Suzanne, I'm sorry about what happened today, and I've come to make things right with you." She held out a wad of bills that I knew would add up to exactly what we'd lost that morning.

I steadfastly refused to take it as I said, "Put that away, Emma. We've already resolved this."

"That's what I told him, but he wouldn't listen," Emma said, her glance going furtively back to her father.

I said, "Ray, you want your daughter to be a grownup, don't you?"

"That's why we're here," he said stubbornly.

"No, you're here to impose your sense of how this should be handled, not Emma's or mine. I won't take her money. It was just as much my fault as it was hers. She's a levelheaded, responsible, hard-working young woman. What more do you expect from her, Ray?"

He frowned. "I want her to do what's right."

"She already has," I said, my voice getting louder than it should have. I couldn't help it.

"Suzanne, watch your tone of voice," my mother said.

"Momma, I love you with all my heart, and you know it, but this doesn't concern you. Let me handle it."

She looked taken aback, then nodded. "Grace, I believe we have a table of dishes to clear. If you all will excuse us, we'll get to them."

Grace followed her back into the dining room, and as soon as they were gone, Ray

219

said, "I have to say that I'm not surprised you talk to your own mother that way."

I had to do something shocking to get his attention, or he wouldn't hear anything else I had to say. "I was hoping you'd get the point. You're trying to dictate Emma's actions just like my mother's been trying to do to me for years. And if I were Emma, I'd treat you the same way. That's exactly what you deserve at the moment."

I saw his jaw jut out, so I eased the harshness of my tone as I added, "Ray, you two didn't need to come here. Do you honestly think Emma hasn't already apologized for what happened? She feels bad enough about it without you rubbing her nose in it. She's not nine years old anymore."

Ray started to say something, then bit it back. He tugged at his daughter's arm and said, "Come on, Emma. We're leaving."

"In a second," she said as she lunged forward and hugged me. "Thank you," she whispered in my ear. "Nobody's ever stood up to him for me before."

"Then it's high time somebody did," I said softly. "I'll see you tomorrow."

"If he lets me come to work," Emma said before she caught up with him at their car.

I closed the door and found Grace standing in the doorway. She said, "What was that about? Or do I even need to ask?"

"Ray still thinks Emma's a little girl, and I had to spank him pretty hard to get him to see that she's not."

"He's not the only one you spanked," Grace said softly.

"I know, but she shouldn't have said anything, especially while I was trying to make a point."

"I agree with you a hundred percent," Grace said.

"But you still think I need to apologize."

"I never said that," Grace said as her gaze stayed steadily on me.

"No, but you're thinking it."

She smiled. "Suzanne, how on earth could you know what I'm thinking?"

"We've been friends for a long time, remember? Okay, I guess it's time for me to go eat a little crow."

"Sometimes it's the only meal we can get," she said. "I'll give you some privacy, so at least you won't have to do it in front of an audience."

"Thanks. This won't take long. I've grown pretty adept at saying I'm sorry."

I walked into the kitchen, but before I could say a word, Momma said, "Suzanne, I owe you an apology. I barked out at you as a reaction, not as a consciously formed thought. You're a grown woman, and I trust your judgment to use harsh words if they are required to get someone's attention. Do you forgive me?"

I couldn't help myself; I hugged her as I said, "Only if you promise to forgive me, too. I shouldn't have snapped at you."

"Well, it certainly got *my* attention," she said as she pulled away. "How did Ray take it?"

"He wasn't too pleased with me, but at least it might have deflected a little heat away from Emma. I understand the way he feels, but he needs to let her lead her own life. Emma's everything I said she was, only he seems to have trouble seeing it."

"It's not easy for a parent to let go," she said.

"I know. Do you think I owe him an apology?"

"I doubt it would do much good at this point," Momma said. "You gave him some things to think about, and I've got a feeling Ray Blake is going to have a pretty sleepless night ahead of him."

"How do you know what I said to him?"

She smiled. "I eavesdropped, of course. Suzanne, this is still my house, no matter who else is living here. Now, why don't we serve dessert by the fire? I know the snow's stopped, but it would be nice to eat in the glow from the Christmas tree and the flickering flames of the fireplace. I so love this time of year."

"It must be hereditary, because so do I," I said. "What are we having?"

"I made a trifle," she said.

"Yum. Should we divvy it up, or should we just grab three spoons and attack it all at once?"

"I think plates and spoons are in order," she said.

"Spoilsport," I said with a laugh as I helped her grab three plates, some spoons, and a handful of napkins. Momma got the trifle, and after plating up three portions, we carried them into the living room, where Grace was sitting staring at the fire.

When she looked up at us, I could swear that she'd been crying, and I wondered what had triggered it in her. I wouldn't ask, though. I'd learned long ago that if Grace wanted to share something with me, she'd do it on her own schedule, and not mine. It had been a hard lesson to learn not to comfort my friend when she was in such obvious need of it, but learn it I had.

"Who wants trifle?" I said, trying to pump a little joy into my voice.

"That looks wonderful," she said, the tears

now wiped away as she took a plate from me.

"I've always loved a good trifle," my mother said.

"Me, I'll eat whatever dessert you decide to make that day," I said. "Just no donuts. I sample enough of those as I'm working to last me the rest of the day."

"You probably shouldn't sample your wares so much, Suzanne," my mother said with a smile.

"There are a great many things I shouldn't do, but I can't seem to help myself," I replied.

Momma laughed, and it filled the room with the warmth of its glow more than the fireplace could. "That does seem to be a family curse, doesn't it?"

We finished our desserts as we watched the fire, then Momma collected the dishes and said, "If you ladies will excuse me, I got a new book today that I'm dying to read, so I'm going to call it an early night."

After she excused herself, Grace looked over at me and said, "She did that on purpose. She wants us to have time to talk."

"She saw you crying, too," I said gently. I was walking a fine line here, and I knew it, but I wanted Grace to know that we both cared about her, and we wanted to help her if we could.

"That was nothing," she said.

I shook my head. "I know nothing when I see it." She grinned at me, and I suddenly realized how ridiculous it must have sounded. "You know what I mean."

"If it's all the same to you, what I'd really like to talk about is what we found at Darlene's apartment, and what Cynthia told us. The fact that Muriel is broke should come up, too."

"It's a lot to process for one day, isn't it?" I said. "Where should we start?"

"Definitely with Cynthia," Grace said. "First off, was she telling the truth about the fight between Wilma and Darlene?"

"Why would she lie?" I asked. I hadn't even considered the possibility that she hadn't been telling us the truth.

"Who knows? Maybe she's hiding a fight she had with Darlene herself. Or maybe Wilma's done something to her, and this is her way of getting her back."

I thought about that, but it just didn't add up in my mind. "I don't know, I had the feeling Cynthia was telling us the truth."

"I did, too," Grace said, "but we can't accept everything we hear at face value. We have to question everything people tell us."

"So how do we prove if it's true or not?"

225

Grace frowned. "There's only one way I can think of. We have to ask one of the other beauticians."

"If you think I'm getting back into one of those chairs, you've lost your mind. It's your turn this time, Grace."

She shook her head. "I was thinking of something a little more subtle. Why don't we take a dozen donuts by the salon in the morning, and we can question one of them then."

"Do you think I should really leave Emma by herself so soon after what happened?" I wasn't sure how she'd react, and I didn't know if I wanted to know, either.

"What better way to show her that you trust her? I'm sure she needs a little ego boost after being marched over here this evening like a child."

"You know what? You're absolutely right," I said. "That sounds like a good plan."

"Now, how about the things we found at Darlene's?"

As we put our collected piles on the coffee table in front of the fireplace, I said, "I'm beginning to have second thoughts about taking all of this. We could have really mucked up a police investigation this time."

Grace said, "I don't see how. Chief Martin should have searched Darlene's room the day she died, and if he hasn't gone by there yet to look around, do you honestly think he ever will? Somebody's got to dig into this, Suzanne. Why not us?"

"Why not?" I echoed. I wasn't sure the chief would agree with our line of reasoning — and I knew Jake would have protested — but then again, he wasn't in the picture anymore, was he? It was up to me and my friends to figure out if that deadly candy cane had been meant for Darlene or Muriel, and more importantly, why someone had decided to kill either one of them.

I picked up the photograph of me, then felt my fingers shake as I stared at it. "This was taken in front of the donut shop," I said. "And it was right around Easter."

Grace glanced at the photo. "How can you be so sure?"

"Look through the window. I have poster-sized Easter eggs hanging up behind the counter."

She looked a little closer, then nodded. "I see them now. What does that mean?"

"Well, it's pretty clear that she took this picture nine months ago."

"I know that, I can count as well as you can. I just don't understand why."

"Join the club," I said as I pushed the photo away. I refused to touch the lock of hair, though it did look like it could have easily belonged to Max. The five tattered bills lay there, and they had a story to tell, I was sure of it, if only I was smart enough to figure out what it was. I examined each bill in turn, and had just about given up finding a clue when I saw a three-digit number carefully hand-lettered on the edge of the back of one of the bills. It looked familiar, and in a second, I realized why. Searching through the business cards I'd found in Darlene's purse, I found the perfect match to the number on the bill.

As I turned the card over to see who it belonged to, Grace asked me, "Suzanne, did you find something that I missed?"

"I think I may have found another clue," I said, as I stared at the name embossed on the other side.

BLUEBERRY SURPRISES

These blueberry treats are perfect on cold days. They promise to warm you up, especially if you snack on them with some coffee or hot chocolate.

Ingredients

1 package blueberry muffin mix (7 ounces)
3/4 cup flour
3/4 cup buttermilk
1 egg, beaten
Fresh blueberries (optional, and certainly not required, but they make a nice addition to the treats)

Directions

Add the flour to the powdered muffin mix, then add the beaten egg and buttermilk. Stir everything together until the dry ingredients are all absorbed into the liquid, but don't overstir the mix.

In canola oil heated to 360°F, drop in half-teaspoon-sized bits of batter. Turn them once as they brown, then drain on paper towels and add powdered sugar if desired.

CHAPTER 9

"Don't keep me in suspense," she said. "Who does the card belong to? And how does it tie into the murder?"

I studied it another second, then said, "I'm not positive it's connected to Darlene's death, but it is kind of fishy, wouldn't you say?"

"If you're not going to tell me whose name is on it, give me the card so I can see for myself, Suzanne."

I held it up long enough for her to read the name on it.

She whistled. "Why would Darlene have a card from Lester Moorefield? I didn't even realize Lester had business cards."

Lester was the morning news voice on our radio, local station WAPS. I doubt they had more than a thousand listeners, and yet Lester prided himself on breaking big scoops over our newspaper. He and Ray had a heated rivalry, and each one loved to beat the other to a story.

But that didn't explain why Darlene had a hundred-dollar-bill in her possession that matched an odd, three-digit number written on the back of Lester's business card.

"I know there's got to be a reason for this," Grace said. "But I can't imagine for the life of me what it is."

"There's only one way we're going to find out," I said as I tapped the card on the table. "We're going to have to ask him."

"That's not going to be fun, is it?" Grace said.

"I completely understand if you want to take a pass on it."

"Are you kidding? I signed on for the whole investigation. Maybe between the two of us we'll be able to come up with a way to question him tomorrow morning after his shift on the radio is over."

"Does that mean you're coming to work with me again tomorrow?" I asked as I glanced at the clock. It was just after nine, and technically past my bedtime, but with Grace staying with us until the further notice, I'd found that I kept pushing the hour back, and that meant less and less sleep for me.

"No, I don't think so," she said. "Suzanne, I don't know how you and Emma do it

231

every morning. Your schedule is already kill-ing me."

"You get used to it after a while," I said, fighting back another yawn.

Grace matched mine, then said, "Okay, if you keep that up, you're going to put me to sleep, too. You don't have to stay up and baby-sit me, Suzanne. I'm perfectly capable of entertaining myself."

"I know you are," I said. "I just hate to leave you alone."

"With you and your mother upstairs, I feel safe here."

I grinned at her. "Really? I doubt either one of us would be much help if there was trouble."

"Just having two other people around is enough to ease my mind." As I stood, she did, too, and Grace retrieved my softball bat from the corner by the door. "Besides, if somebody tries anything, I'm ready for them."

"If you're sure, then."

"Go to bed, Suzanne."

I did as she asked, and found myself fall-ing asleep even as I tumbled into my bed.

The next morning, I crept downstairs and found Grace asleep on the couch. A blanket was falling off her shoulders and the softball bat was tucked firmly in her arms. I covered her back up, stoked the fire, and added another log, then grabbed a quick bowl of cereal and headed off to the donut shop.

To my surprise, the lights were all on when I got there, and I could see Emma working inside on her hands and knees, cleaning the painted concrete floor.

"Morning," I said as I walked in, locking the door behind me. "Did we agree to come in early today?"

"No," she said as she continued to scrub the floors of the dining area. "I just thought with all this snow we've been having, it might not be a bad idea to spruce the place up a little. Don't worry, this isn't on the clock."

"If you're here and you're working, it's on the clock," I said, and then it hit me. "Emma, I don't care what your father said, you don't owe me anything, not restitution, and not extra hours of work."

"He doesn't even know I'm here," she said, "but Suzanne, please don't make me stop. I feel so bad about what happened, I have to do something, or I'm afraid I won't be able to work here anymore."

"You'd quit before you'd let me make you stop?" I asked.

"I don't want to. I love working here, but

233

if you don't give me any choice, then yeah, I guess I'd have to leave."

"Then work on," I said as I stepped around her. "You missed a spot," I added as I pointed to a place in the corner.

She started to get up when I said, "I'm kidding."

"No, you're right. I can see it from here."

I hung my coat up in back, then grabbed a pair of rubber gloves and joined her.

She looked startled by my presence on the floor beside her. "You don't have to do this. It's my job."

I took a sponge from the bucket and started wiping down a section of the floor she hadn't hit yet. "Let's just say you're not the only one who should do penance for making a mistake." As I wiped away some mud and a little grime, I said, "Besides, this kind of work can be really cleansing, you know?"

I watched her get my pun, and saw a smile break out of the tense gloom she'd been expressing a few minutes before. "Yeah, it's really nice to be able to wipe away a problem, isn't it?"

"A clean sweep, that's what we need here. Now enough with the puns. Let's finish this so we can start making donuts."

"It's tough being clever this early in the

morning, isn't it?"

"I don't know," I said as I wiped the last section we hadn't hit yet. "Sometimes I feel like I wake up brilliant and get dumber by the minute as the day goes on."

"I'm just the opposite," she said. "I'm a night person, myself."

"Then you really aren't suited temperamentally for this job, are you?"

She grinned at me as we both stood. "That depends on how you look at it. I like to think of it as the night before, not the morning after."

"Hey, as long as it gets you in here on time, I'm all for it." As I took off the gloves and handed them to her, I said, "You finish cleaning up, and I'll get started on the cake donut batters."

"I won't be a minute," she said.

She was as good as her word, and as I mixed the batters for our morning supply of cake donuts, Emma said, "Suzanne, in all seriousness, I love it here. I really do."

"Me, too," I agreed. "There's really nothing else quite like it."

"So," she said as she looked down at my batter stations, each ready for their special ingredients. "Do you think I could try a new cake donut recipe today? I've been dying to try it, and this is the perfect chance."

"Be my guest," I said. "As soon as I'm done with these, the kitchen's all yours." As I mixed the ingredients for the old fashioneds, the plain cakes, the blueberry, pumpkin and whole wheat donuts, Emma began amassing an odd assortment of things for her own mix. I liked to experiment myself, and I was glad to see she was taking an interest in trying her own hand at coming up with new recipes. Sometimes it was tough offering enough things that were different to keep my customers out of a rut. I figured if I kept adding new items to the menu, they'd keep coming back to try them.

"Candy canes? Really?" I asked as I saw her crushing some of the candies in our mortar and pestle.

"You mind your donuts, and I'll mind mine," she said with a smile.

"Okay, but you're cleaning the mess up."

"Don't I always?"

As I added different batters to the donut dropper and fried them, Emma left her batter for a few minutes and started helping me glaze mine after they'd been turned and pulled out of the fryer.

"I think I'm ready," she said as she returned to her blend and put the finishing touches on her batter. I could see chunks of candy canes in the mix, and wondered how they'd turn out.

At least she'd made a small batch.

"Would you like to fry them yourself?" I asked as I handed her the stainless steel dropper. I'd rinsed it out in the sink, and it was now ready for her mix.

"No, I'd rather you do it, if you don't mind."

"I'd be glad to." I spooned the batter into the dropper, and as I did, I caught the overwhelming scent of peppermint.

"That's not all from the candy, is it?"

She admitted, "No, I used some peppermint essence to give it a little boost. Why, did I use too much?"

"We won't know until they're fried," I said. I had my doubts, but I was going to keep them to myself.

I dropped half a dozen donut rounds into the fryer, waited for them to finish on one side, then flipped them with my wooden skewers so they'd cook on the other side.

"They're certainly colorful," I said as I pulled them out and put them on the glazing rack. I didn't know how many candy canes she'd used, but I would have cut that portion in half myself. As for the peppermint flavoring, I had no idea how strong or weak it might be, but from the aroma, I had a feeling they were going to be awfully sweet.

Emma glazed them, then said, "I can't taste it, I'm too nervous. You try one."

I wouldn't let her chicken out, though. "Come on, you made the recipe; it's your privilege to try the first one."

"Privilege, or obligation?" she asked, but she still took one, broke it in half, and tried a bite of it.

"Wow, too much peppermint flavoring," she said as she waved a hand in front of her mouth.

"Let me see," I said as I broke off my own bite. I took a smaller piece than Emma had, but I could still feel my nasal passages opening up from the strong flavoring.

"They're horrible, aren't they?" she asked.

"It's not bad for a first try. Next time, I'd cut the candy cane portion and the peppermint in half."

"Or more," she said.

I pointed to the prep counter. "Go ahead and mix up another batch; we have time before we have to start the yeast donuts."

"If you don't mind, I think I'll wait until another day to try it out again. I'm not sure I could face tasting another one right now."

"Coward," I said as I started to clean the donut dropper out in the sink. The batter washed down easily enough, but there were bits of peppermint blocking the strainer.

Emma watched me for a few seconds, then she nudged me to one side. "I'll do that. It's my job, and besides, I'm the one who made the mess."

"What do you want to do with these?" I asked as I pointed to the five donuts remaining on the glazing grid.

"Toss them out," she said.

I started to do as she asked, then on an impulse, I set a few aside. If Max had been around, I would have been tempted to serve him one out of pure meanness. Thinking of him made me wonder what my ex-husband was up to, and where he was at the moment. Was he still in April Springs, or had he taken off as soon as he'd realized that Chief Martin was after him? And what about Muriel? Was she holed up in someone else's house, or was she in more trouble than that? If she was someone's target, I wouldn't have blamed her for leaving town, and might have done the same thing myself if I didn't have a donut shop to run. I discounted the theory that they were together, since I still couldn't wrap my head around that particular idea.

But I still wished I knew where they were, and if they were safe.

Maybe today would offer some answers.

It would be a nice change of pace.

So far, all I'd been able to generate was more questions, and I had more of those than I could handle at the moment.

George was waiting at the front door at 5:30 when I walked out to open the shop. The snow looked to be finally gone for good, but the temperatures had plummeted, and I couldn't imagine why he was outside braving the cold just to get into my shop.

I held the door open for him, and as I stepped aside to let him in, I said, "Come on in. It's freezing out there. Why didn't you knock on the door? I didn't know you were out here."

"I could wait," George said as he took off his coat.

"That's just silly," I said. "Come on in and warm up."

George shrugged as he looked at me. "Is that what I get for being considerate? It's like I always say, no good deed goes unpunished."

"Have some coffee," I said as I filled a mug and shoved it into his hand.

He took a healthy sip, then said, "That hits the spot."

I nodded. "I think so, too. Let me get you

a couple of donuts, and then we can talk."

George sniffed the air. "Is that peppermint? I love peppermint. I'll take three of whatever that is I smell."

"They aren't ready for sale yet," I said. "We got the flavor too intense in the first batch, but we might have some ready in a few days."

"That's not fair," George said. "You know I've never had a problem with being a guinea pig. At least bring me one to try."

He'd insisted, and I could see from the look on his face that he was serious. "Hang on." I walked back into the kitchen to get one for him.

"Customers already?" Emma asked as she looked up from the sink where she was doing another round of dishes.

"George is out there," I said.

I tried to sneak one of her peppermint donuts from the place where I'd stashed them, but she caught me at it. "I thought I smelled those. You were supposed to throw them away."

"I was going to, but George really wants one."

Emma stepped in front of me, blocking my way. "You're not giving him one, are you? Suzanne, those things are lethal."

"I figure he's a big boy, he can make up

his own mind. Besides, he's not going to give up until he gets a bite."

She reluctantly stepped aside, then followed me out of the kitchen. Before I could give the donut to George, Emma said, "I just want you to know that she's doing this against my will. They're too strong."

"I don't mind. I like things strong," George said.

We were both watching him as he raised the donut to his lips.

He hesitated at the attention, then George said, "I'm not in the circus, you don't have to watch me."

"We're not about to miss this," I said, "So you might as well go ahead and take a bite. Hang on a second." I grabbed a bottled water from the mini fridge and put it down in front of him.

"What's that for?"

"I've got a feeling you're going to need it," I said.

He shook his head. "This is nonsense." George took a bite, chewed it, and beyond my expectations, somehow managed to swallow. He kept his expression even as he said, "I got a bit of candy cane in that bite. I don't know what you two are talking about. I think they're good."

Emma said, "Trust me; I don't think this

242

recipe is ready for prime time yet."

George shook his head. "I really liked it. In fact, if you have any more, I'll take another one."

Emma said with disbelief, "I'll be right back." In a second, she returned with the last two. "There you go."

As George took another healthy bite, she shook her head. "If you don't need me, I'm going back to the dishes."

After she was gone, I said, "Now, would you like more donuts, or did you get up at this abysmal hour to discuss something more important?"

"I wanted to catch up with you before things got busy," he said. "I've had some luck in my investigation."

"I found something out that was pretty interesting myself," I replied. "Do you want to go first?"

"You go ahead," George said. "I'm waiting for one more call before I can tell you what I might have found out."

"Okay," I said. "Hang on one second." I grabbed a cup of coffee, then rejoined him. After taking a sip, I said, "First of all, going to Cutnip wasn't as productive at first as I thought it might be. Wilma stonewalled us the entire time we were there, and from the way she spoke about Darlene, she was a saint to work with, and a dear friend to everyone who met her."

"That's a natural reaction, isn't it?" George said. "No one likes to speak ill of the dead."

"Just wait; there's more. One of the other beauticians caught up with us outside, and before Wilma could lasso her back in, she told Grace and me that Wilma had a blow-out fight with Darlene just before she was murdered."

"What were they fighting about?" George asked.

"From the sound of it, Wilma accused Darlene of stealing from her, and it got pretty ugly. That's when Grace and I decided to go by Darlene's and see what we could find at her place."

George frowned. "Tell me you didn't go in."

I'd heard that scolding tone of voice from him before. "George, the chief has had plenty of time to search Darlene's place. I don't know what assumptions he's working under, but if he ignores the murder victim, how good could he really be?"

He didn't say anything, but I could tell George wasn't happy about it. Just then, his cell phone rang. He looked at who was calling him, then said, "I need to take this."

George grabbed his coat and walked out into the bitter cold.

A minute later I heard the front door chime, and I expected to see George walk back in, but it was Taylor Higgins instead.

"One coffee to go, please," Taylor said.

"Will you eat a donut if I give you one on the house?" I asked, trying to joke him into taking one.

"Just coffee," he said. "Any news on what's been happening?"

"Nobody tells me anything," I said as I got him his coffee, sliding a fresh glazed donut into a bag and pushing it toward him.

He managed to resist the bait. "Sorry, no sale."

"It's on the house," I said.

"You keep it," he said, trying to avoid looking at the bag.

"You honestly don't like donuts, do you?" I said, staring at him in open wonder.

He frowned, bit his lower lip, then said, "No, I'm sorry. I never acquired a taste for them."

"And yet you keep showing up here," I said, retrieving the spurned donut.

"I like the coffee, and the company," he said, and then left, disappearing back out into the early morning darkness.

George came back in, stomping his feet at

the door. "It's going to be a few more minutes."

"Until what?" I asked.

He shook his head. "Not yet. So tell me, what did you find at Darlene's place?"

"What makes you think I found something?" I asked.

"Come on, I was a cop too long not to be able to see the signs. You might as well go ahead and tell me."

"Don't get mad," I said.

"No promises."

I shrugged. If I wanted George's help, I was going to have to trust him with everything I knew. If that meant another chewing out, then so be it.

I reached into my jeans pocket and pulled out Lester's business card — complete with the odd number written on back — and the matching hundred-dollar-bill.

George looked at both items, then got a clean napkin and took them from me. After a full minute, he asked, "Suzanne, where did you find these?"

"The hundred dollar bill was in a box in her closet, and the card was in her purse."

I could tell he was uneasy with what I'd done, but at least he kept it to himself. I asked, "Do you have any idea what this might mean?"

246

He shook his head, so I said, "After I lock up today, Grace and I are going to talk to Lester about it at the radio station."

"That's probably not the smartest thing you've ever done in your life," George said. "You should let me handle it."

"If you go, it will seem like the police are investigating. I want him off-guard."

"I'm not a cop anymore, remember?"

"George, you might not have a badge, but every single mannerism you have screams police."

He shrugged. "I still think you're taking a risk."

"Grace and I are going together, and honestly, what's Lester going to do in broad daylight? Can you truly see him trying to hurt us?"

"If he's covering up for another murder, absolutely," George said.

"Don't worry, we'll be careful."

George waved the bill in the air. "You said you found this in Darlene's closet. Was there much money there?"

"All I found was five individual hundred-dollar bills," I said.

"And did any of the rest of them have numbers on them?" he asked.

"No, just this one. Several of the cards had numbers written on the backs of them, though. Why?"

George took a sip of coffee, then frowned. "I'm not sure."

"Don't hold out on me," I said.

He thought about that, then said, "That five hundred dollars could be money she stole from Wilma."

"I suppose it's possible," I said. "But would she take hundreds? Those are easy to miss, whereas tens or even twenties might be simpler to take without Wilma realizing she was even being robbed."

"Don't worry, we'll figure it out," George said. "In the meantime, I see why you want to talk to Lester, but be careful, okay?"

"We will." I looked at his empty mug. "Would you like more coffee?"

George nodded, but just then, his telephone rang. He ducked back outside before I could top his mug off, and I waited patiently until he came back in. From what I could see, he was doing most of the talking, never a good sign with George. I was about to go outside to see what was going on myself when the front door opened, and George rushed in.

He said, "Okay, it's time for a field trip. Grab your coat and let's go."

"Where are we going?" I asked.

"I just found out where Muriel's been hiding, but if we don't hurry, we're going to miss her."

I shouted out, "Emma, I'll be back in a little bit. You've got the front until I get back," as I grabbed my jacket and rushed out the front door with George.

It probably wasn't fair to keep sticking her with a job she hated, but I couldn't let that stop me.

Maybe it was time I was finally going to get some of the answers I'd been searching for.

CHAPTER 10

"I'll drive," George said.

I didn't have any problem with that, so I got into his Cadillac. "Be careful. The roads are still a little tricky."

I had a sudden insight into where we were going. "We're heading over to Gabby Williams's place, aren't we?"

George took his eyes off the road for a second and looked at me intently. "Which is it, Suzanne? Are you a lipreader, or a mind-reader?"

"Neither one," I said. "Why do you ask that?"

"Because unless you saw me mouth the name or read my mind, how else would you know where Muriel's been hiding out? You haven't been holding out on me, have you, Suzanne?"

"Of course not," I said. "It just makes sense, doesn't it?"

"Not to me," George said. "Go ahead and

explain, I'm listening."

"You probably didn't realize it because you don't know Gabby the way I do. She suddenly closed her shop sometime in the last couple of days and disappeared, which is odd enough to mark her behavior, but then she didn't come by my place first to tell me what was going on. Gabby feels it's her personal obligation to tell everyone whatever she's doing, and she seems to take particular pleasure in keeping me in the loop of what's happening in her life. If there was something big enough to get her to shut her shop down until further notice, trust me, she'd take an ad out in the paper."

I looked back at George to see if he believed me. "I swear, I'm not holding out on you."

"I believe you," he said. We were nearing Gabby's place, and there was one question I had to ask before we got there. "I told you how I reasoned it out, but you didn't mention how you knew."

He pointed ahead, and there was a car parked on the street with its lights on, and from the plume of smoke, it was idling, ready to take off at a moment's notice. We were just a hundred yards from Gabby's house, but George pulled in behind the idling car instead of driving up to Gabby's.

I couldn't have been more surprised if the Easter Bunny had stepped out of the car when I saw Officer Grant get out.

He and George shook hands, and he nodded to me before addressing George. He said, "You have five minutes, and then I'm calling the chief."

"Got it," George said. "Let's go," he said to me.

I looked quizzically at the police officer, but he didn't meet my gaze.

I quickly caught up with George, then asked, "What's going on? Why is he helping us?"

"He owes me a favor, and it's a big one," George said. "I called in the marker to get his help, but he wasn't all that happy about me being here before his boss. That's what took me so long on the phone. He's a good cop, and this goes against his grain."

"That must have been some favor he owed you," I said.

George just shrugged. "Come on. We don't have much time."

He walked up the front steps, then pounded on the door. "Gabby, open up. I see your light's on in the hallway and I noticed your shadow a second ago, so don't try to pretend you're not awake yet."

There was no response, then George said,

"Everyone knows Muriel's there. You've got four minutes until the police get here, so you might as well talk to me first."

There was no response.

I said, "Let me try."

George shrugged, so I said, "Gabby, it's Suzanne Hart. Let us in. We're here to help Muriel, but if the police get her first, we might not be able to do anything for her."

George looked at me as if I'd lost my mind, but to our mutual surprise, the front door opened, and Muriel burst out of the house, wrapping me in her embrace.

"I can't take it anymore," Muriel said. "This is killing me," she added as she pulled away from me.

Just behind her, Gabby looked clearly peeved as she said, "You might as well all come in. At least it's warm inside."

"The police really are coming," I said. "There was nothing we could do about that."

"Let them come," Gabby said. Though it was barely past six A.M., she was dressed as impeccably as usual, in a tailored pale-blue suit and matching shoes. "I have no reason to hide from them."

"You were harboring a person of interest," George said.

Gabby laughed as she looked at him. "I ask you, is there anything illegal about letting an old friend stay at my place, a woman who's been accused of no crime as far as we know?"

George shook his head. "No, not when you put it that way."

Gabby smiled in triumph. "Then let them come."

We all moved inside, and George asked Muriel, "Just between us, why have you been hiding?"

"Someone's trying to kill me," she said. "You used to be a police officer. Surely you can see that."

"Do you have any reason to suspect that candy cane was meant for you?" George asked. It was amazing how calm his voice had become since he started questioning her, and I could see the old cop coming out. He must have been very good at what he did when he was on the job.

Muriel said, "She was dressed like me, in my coat and wearing a wig that almost matched my hair color, though I've never had a gray hair in my life. What further proof do you need?"

"Why would someone want to kill you, Muriel?" I asked. "That's what we've all been wondering."

Muriel's lower lip began to quiver, and before she could stop it, she broke down in a crying jag that lasted until Chief Martin showed up six minutes later. Officer Grant had kept his word and discharged his favor to George, but just barely.

"I should have known I'd find you here," the chief said the second he saw me.

I didn't know how to respond to that, so for once in my life, I didn't.

After a few seconds, he shook his head, then the chief looked at Muriel. "Where have you been?"

Gabby stood between them, and I'd never seen her so fierce. "You don't have to answer that," she told Muriel as she faced the chief down.

"But I want to," Muriel said, finally getting her crying jag out of the way. "I've made such a mess of things. I never should have gotten a computer. Everything started to crumble because of that."

The chief looked at all of us in turn, and I was proud that George's gaze didn't flinch when their eyes met.

After a few moments, he said, "It's not worth the trouble getting rid of you two, so you might as well stay. Let's all hear this together." He turned back to Muriel and said, "Why is your computer to blame?"

"I got a computer because it seemed like an interesting thing to do," she said. "Then I heard everyone talking about the Internet, and that sounded like fun, too. I even opened one of those e-mail accounts, and I got the most fascinating mail from around the world, coming from people I'd never met." She stifled another crying jag, then she added softly, "And then I lost everything."

"Don't tell me," I said. "The e-mail was from Nigeria, wasn't it?"

She nodded. "He promised me riches, but he ended up taking everything."

I often got scams from foreign countries in my email inbox, but I deleted them just as quickly. The stories of scammers running rampant on the Internet were no urban legends; they were real. Unsuspecting victims kept funneling money to the thieves, whether out of greed or humanitarian reasons, or so they believed.

Muriel had grown suddenly calm. "I lost everything, and when my gentleman friend, Grayson, found out what a fool I'd been, he broke it off with me. Then, when someone tried to kill me, or someone who looked like me, I knew he'd actually come after me."

"Grayson?" I asked.

"No, Peter Exeter, the man I'd been sending money to all along."

The chief shook his head. "Muriel, if you've been sending him money, why would he want to kill you?"

"Because I ran out of things to liquidate. He's been most insistent I keep paying. He says I'm in too deep and has been threatening me. I know he's after me."

I spoke up again. "Muriel, where did you send the money? Was it somewhere in the States?"

"No, it went straight to Nigeria, of course," she said, looking at me as if I were some kind of idiot.

"You can relax, then. He's not trying to kill you. As soon as he realized you didn't have any more money, he dropped you and moved on to his next victim."

A glimmer of hope registered in her eyes. "Do you honestly think so?"

"I know it," I said, and was surprised when the chief didn't scold me for butting in again.

"Why, that's the most wonderful news I've had forever," she said. Then Muriel frowned. "But if Peter didn't try to kill me, who did?"

I almost said, "That's what we're trying to find out," but I somehow managed to keep my mouth shut, miracle of miracles.

The chief said, "We're not sure anyone did. Think hard, Muriel. There's no one who might want to see you dead, is there? No one who might benefit from your death?"

She actually laughed at that. "Why? There's nothing left to inherit, and I cashed in my life insurance policy weeks ago."

"You should make sure all your heirs know that," the chief said. "But in the meantime, you might want to find somewhere to go out of town until this blows over. Just in case."

Muriel thought about it for a few moments, then said, "I've got a cousin in West Virginia I've been dying to see. Is that far enough away?"

"It should be fine, but don't tell us anything more," he said as he looked around the room. "It's better if no one knows where you've gone."

"I'll leave as soon as I can get a bus ticket," she said. "I should be able to afford that."

To my great surprise, Gabby said, "You don't need to bother with that. I'll take you myself."

Muriel said, "Gabby, you've done enough. Whatever you think you owed me is paid in full, do you understand?"

Gabby shook her head. "Not yet, it's not."

"You don't have to do this."

Gabby smiled gently, an expression I wasn't used to seeing on her face. "That's my decision, isn't it? Now go pack your bag, we'll leave as soon as you're ready."

Muriel disappeared down the hallway, and the chief said, "Are you sure about this?"

"I am," Gabby said.

"Thanks. I'll feel better having her out of the line of fire, just in case."

"Just in case," Gabby agreed.

The chief said, "I can at least give you an escort out of town. I'll be waiting outside, but don't take too long."

Chief Martin didn't even look at us as he walked outside.

As soon as he was gone, I said, "Gabby Williams, what's going on? Why are you doing this?"

She said, "You don't know everything about me, Suzanne Hart. I'm obligated to do this, and there's nothing that anyone can do to stop me. You'll keep an eye out on the shop, won't you?"

"Of course I will," I said. This woman — normally a gossip and a bit of a shrew — was showing me a side of her personality that I'd never seen before. I couldn't have been more surprised if George had started singing opera, but I was glad I'd witnessed it myself. No matter who told me about it, I never would have believed it if I hadn't seen it with my own eyes.

"Now let's not dawdle, shall we? I've got a bag to pack myself." The brisk, cheerless Gabby was back.

As the rest of us walked outside, I saw the chief had pulled up in front of the house in his cruiser, and it was all I could do not to look around for Officer Grant.

We got back into George's car, and I said, "Thanks for calling in that favor."

"It was worth it," he said. "We can be pretty sure that Muriel's Nigerian scammer didn't travel all the way to North Carolina to kill her, and it appears no one else had a reason to want to do her harm. Now we can focus on Darlene. What did I miss? Do we have any leads that I don't know about yet?"

"I've told you everything I know," I said.

George nodded, then said, "Suzanne, I still think I should be there when you talk to Lester."

"I don't think you should," I said.

"Why not?"

"We've already gone over this. Forgive me for saying so, but you can be kind of intimidating. We need to keep Lester off balance, and if he suspects we know something, he's probably not going to cooperate."

"I'm good at questioning suspects," George said, a little sullenly.

"That's just it," I tried to explain. "It's clear you're still very good at interrogation, but I don't want Lester to realize what we're up to. He knows you were a cop, and a really good one. Do you think he's going to just open up to you? Grace and I will have more luck if we tackle him on our own."

I waited for his protest, but it didn't follow. "Okay, but you have to promise to call me if you get in over your head."

"I promise," I said.

When we got back to the donut shop, George dropped me off at the door.

As I walked inside, it was good to see Emma hadn't left her post at the register.

"Did you have any trouble while I was gone?" I asked softly.

"No, we just had two customers while you were out, and I never left the front." She opened the till, and I saw the money still there.

"Emma, I trust you, you know that."

"I just wanted to show you," she said, then turned back. "If you don't need me to watch the front anymore, I've got dishes to do."

"Thanks, Emma," I said.

She smiled softly at me, then disappeared

back into the kitchen, a place where she was clearly more comfortable.

I had a lull before more customers started coming in, so I kept thinking about Darlene, now that we'd decided to focus on her as the victim instead of Muriel. I couldn't wait to talk to Lester about that business card, and the hundred-dollar bill that matched it. Before long, business started to pick up. It was hard to believe, but it wasn't even seven yet. I'd had a busy morning, and from the sound of it, things weren't going to slow down. I was staying put. I'd already asked Emma to cover the shop too much, and I knew she was still hurting from the earlier theft. That was fine. Lester wasn't going anywhere, since he didn't go off the air until noon. Besides, I needed the next five hours to figure out exactly how Grace and I could approach him without sending him running for the nearest shelter.

A little after eight, Terri Milner and Sandy White came into the shop with their kids in tow. Terri was the mother of eight-year-old twin girls, and Sandy had a ten-year-old son.

The women put their kids in a booth, and they started squirming the minute they hit the seats.

"I want sprinkles," one of the twins said.

"We got sprinkles last time," the other twin said. "I want chocolate iced donuts this time. Four of 'em."

Their names were Mary and Jerri, and I wondered if Terri's mother was named Carey, based on the trend that was readily apparent.

"I want 'em all," Thomas said. As the alpha male, he was clearly showing off for the girls, something that made me smile.

Sandy told the kids, "If you're all good while we order, you might get something tasty to eat."

Terri leaned forward and added, "But if you're not, I'm sure we can ask Ms. Hart for some stale old donuts from yesterday."

That got their attention, and they settled down immediately.

As Sandy and Terri approached, I saw them smiling at each other.

"You two are wicked, wicked women," I said with a smile. "You realize that, don't you?"

Sandy said, "Please, that's nothing. They know we're kidding them."

I looked over at the kids, who were re-markably well behaved. "Are you sure about that?"

Terri said, "Give them two minutes, and they'll get over it. While we've got some temporary peace, could we have two large coffees, please?"

I poured their drinks, and each took healthy gulps.

Terri said, "I love my girls with all my heart, but if there's another snow day tomorrow, I'm going to go screaming mad."

"I'm with you," Sandy said. "It was fun at first, but now that the snow's melted and crusted over with ice, we can't make snowmen, the sledding is like running on rails, so we mostly stay indoors and do crafts."

Terri said, "I hope I never, ever, see another block of clay."

"We're finger-painting," Sandy said with a groan. "You should see my kitchen. It looks like Jackson Pollack had a seizure in it."

I saw that, just as they'd predicted, the kids were starting to squirm in their seats. Without being asked, I pulled out three cartons of chocolate milk and three of the requested donuts. "Here you go. The natives are getting restless."

They both nodded, and said "Thank you" almost in unison.

The kids were happy enough at first with their orders, but it soon turned into a squabble about who got what — though the donuts and cartons of milk were identical — and the women left to referee. I knew how much being with their kids meant to them, and if there were women out there who loved their children more, I hadn't met them. But I still realized that sometimes, no matter how positive the situation and how fortunate they might have felt, it helped blowing off steam. I was happy to afford them the opportunity.

I was debating whether to call home to see if Grace had made it up yet, and happily enough, she walked in before I could dial the last number.

"Good afternoon," I said with a smile.

Grace looked at her watch. "Hey, I still have half an hour before noon. I slept great last night, but I haven't been in bed the entire morning," she said as she stretched out her arms. "There's something about that guest room of yours."

"When did you move upstairs?" I asked. "When I left this morning, you were still crashing on the couch."

She smiled. "I switched right after you left. I can't believe I fell asleep out there. Your mother must think I'm some kind of bad penny, the way I keep showing up on your doorstep like this."

As I got her a cup of coffee and my latest attempt at a wheat donut that might satisfy her, I said, "Don't kid yourself. She loves having you there." I lowered my voice as I added, "Are you ready to talk to Lester?"

"Sure, but there's something else you need to hear first," Grace said. "I just found out from a friend at the bank that Darlene Higgins recently took out a certificate of deposit for one hundred thousand dollars." I nearly dropped my coffee cup. I'd seen her clothes, and the way she lived, and I couldn't imagine where she'd gotten that kind of money. "Are you sure?"

She frowned at me. "Trust me, I'm sure."

"I'm sorry, I didn't mean to sound like I doubted you," I said. "But you saw her room. Her things weren't all that nice when they were new. I have a hard time believing she would have that kind of money."

"One thing I know for sure is that she didn't steal that much from Wilma. I'm still looking into where the money came from, but I just found this out, so I haven't had time to dig any deeper."

"That's pretty deep as far as I'm concerned," I said. "But that still leaves us with the problem of how to tackle Lester."

"To be honest with you, I've been thinking about it since I woke up, but I haven't been able to come up with any subtle way to interrogate him." She took a sip of coffee, then said, "I'm still not sure what we should do about Max and Muriel."

I suddenly realized that I hadn't kept her up to date on what had been going on that morning. "That's right. You haven't heard. We found Muriel this morning, and she's fine. She was staying at Gabby's, but by now they've already left town."

"Where did they go? Has she been there the entire time?"

"I'm not exactly sure where they're off to," I said, which was the strictest truth. "Gabby owes Muriel some kind of huge favor, so she's driving her wherever she wants to go."

Grace whistled softly. "How big a favor could it be?"

"Gabby's shut down her shop until further notice," I said.

Grace shook her head in obvious disbelief. "That's hard to believe. So, does everyone think Muriel's safe, just because she turned up unharmed?"

"She's anything but in the clear." I recounted her financial woes, and Grace shook her head.

She said, "Muriel's managed to get herself into a real hole, hasn't she?"

"It sounds like it," I agreed.

"Suzanne, what if she owed more money than she admitted to you? Could she be in debt to someone close to home? If they weren't getting paid back, they might have decided to get rid of her as a warning to other deadbeats."

I hadn't thought of that, but in my defense, neither had any of the others. "I guess it's possible."

I took out my cell phone, punched in George's number, and after he answered, I said, "Grace has an idea worth considering." After I gave him the new information, he said, "I'll put it on my list," then he hung up.

I was about to tell her what he'd said when one of the twins decided to liven up my life a little. As she started to shove her tray away from her, a half-full carton of chocolate milk hit the table, bounced, and pivoted in midair, spraying milk everywhere in its wake.

There was a stunned moment of silence, and then the other twin screamed. "You doo-doo head, I'm soaked!" she shouted.

"Hang on, we can take care of this is a second," I told them as I grabbed a few clean dish towels.

I handed one to Grace and said, "Cleanup on Aisle 3."

She smiled at me, and we started attacking the spilled milk, starting on the table and then surveying the floor. How could that carton have held so much? Terri and Sandy tried to wrestle the towels from our hands, but when we wouldn't yield, they attacked the spill with napkins from the dispensers. Emma appeared a minute later with a mop, and we had it contained soon enough.

As Sandy and Terri left, dropping apologies like pennies, all three kids were miserable.

"That was fun," Grace said.

"There's always something going on at Donut Hearts." A handful of brave souls had stayed through the turmoil, though we'd lost several customers. I grabbed one of the display trays and said, "In reward for your patience and understanding, the rest of these donuts are on the house."

At first they were reticent to take any, but after Grace grabbed one, the dam was broken and in two minutes, the tray was empty.

"Hang on. Let me get the rest," I said as I made my way back to the case. It was almost closing time, and I felt they could all use a goodwill gesture. There wouldn't be any donations today, or goodwill sales calls, but that was all right. It felt nice giving some donuts away to my regular customers.

I held one dozen glazed in reserve for an idea percolating in my head, but besides that, we were wiped out seven minutes before closing.

"That's it," I said. "The shop is closed."

A few people headed for the door, but before they could get there, I added, "This didn't happen. If anyone claims it did, there won't be any more donuts for them at this shop. Are we all clear about that?"

There was a flurry of nods, but I knew it would still get out that I was giving away donuts. I just hoped nobody told the reason why.

Once the front door was locked, Grace asked, "Are we ready to tackle Lester?"

"No, I have to finish cleaning up," I said.

Emma said, "You go on. I can handle this. I appreciate you waiting until we closed before you left."

"I'm not doing that to you, Emma. You shouldn't have to do all of the work. It's my shop."

"I don't mind," she said.

"Well, you might not, but I do." I turned to Grace. "Will you grab a mop and start on the floor in here? Emma and I will tackle the kitchen, and we'll all be out of here in twenty minutes."

"Just point me in the right direction,"

Grace said. "You know I'm a whiz with a mop or a broom."

I set her up, then helped Emma tackle the last of the dirty dishes and trays that had once held donuts and other confections. It was amazing how many loads' worth of suds we went through every day. It was nearly a full-time job just keeping up with them all, and I didn't know what I'd do without Emma. I didn't have the budget to buy a dishwasher, and besides, I never thought things got clean enough in them.

As we scrubbed the last few trays, I said, "I want you to know how much I appreciate you working so hard around here."

Emma brushed a bit of her red hair out of her face with the back of her wrist. "That's a tough compliment to take, after what happened yesterday."

"Enough is enough. Emma, I don't ever want to hear you say that again. It's in the past, so let's move on."

She hugged me, and I didn't even mind the soapsuds on my back. "You're such a cool boss."

"And you're a great worker, and a good friend," I said.

Grace walked into the kitchen, then started to back out. "Sorry, I didn't mean to interrupt."

"We're just finishing," I said as Emma rinsed the last tray.

As I shut off the lights in back, I said, "Let's get out of here."

"I'm beat," Emma said. "I've been here since midnight."

"Why don't you come in a little later tomorrow?"

"Like six?" she asked, the grin clear on her face.

"I was thinking two-forty-five," I said, "but we can compromise. Let's make it two-forty-six."

She laughed as I let her out, and once the three of us were on the sidewalk, she quickly hurried to her car.

I looked at Grace and said, "It's good having Emma work here."

"She's right, you know. You are a great boss."

"Were you eavesdropping?" I asked.

"Of course I was. It's a small shop, so it's kind of tough not to hear everything that's going on. You're a pretty wonderful friend, too," she added.

"Right back at you. Now, what do you say we go talk to Lester about our little mystery? Is there a chance in the world he'll have an explanation that either one of us is going to accept as true?"

"I guess we owe it to him to at least ask," Grace said.

"Then let's go."

EASY AS PIE RAISED DONUTS

These donuts are light, airy, and have just the right touch of sweetness. When you don't have time for two rises, choose this recipe!

Ingredients

2 packages fast rising yeast (1/2 ounce total)
2 1/2 tablespoons granulated sugar
1 cup water, warm
1 egg, beaten
1/3 cup butter or margarine, melted
1 teaspoon cinnamon
1 teaspoon nutmeg
1 teaspoon vanilla extract
1/2 teaspoon salt
3–4 cups flour

Directions

Mix the yeast, water and sugar. Wait five minutes for the yeast to start working. Add egg, butter, cinnamon, nutmeg, vanilla and salt, blend thoroughly, then start adding flour until the dough is not sticky to the touch. Knead the dough for about a minute, then roll out to 1/4 to 1/2 inch and cut out donut shapes, diamonds, or ravioli cutter shapes.

Set these aside to rise for 30 minutes, then

fry in 360°F canola oil, turning once so both sides cook evenly.

Drain on paper towels, then enjoy!

CHAPTER 11

"I'll drive," Grace said. "Everybody in town can recognize that Jeep of yours, and we don't want the world to know exactly what we're up to, now do we?"

"Are you telling me that you actually risked your precious company car driving over here?" I asked. "I thought you were supposed to stay off the roads until you got approval from your boss."

"What she doesn't know won't hurt her," Grace said. "That doesn't mean I have to go back to work as soon as the roads are better. If I have to, I'll take some vacation until we find out what really happened to Darlene."

"I don't want you to miss out on anything because of me," I said.

"Suzanne, there's nothing else I'd rather be doing. Since I can't get you to leave that shop of yours for a real vacation, I'd just as soon burn my days this way."

"You know I can't just shut down, and it's not fair to dump it all on Emma and her mother. I'm sure they're fine, but then I'm not the one making the donuts, you know? Never mind. I'm sure it sounds crazy to you."

"No more than anything else you do," she said, smiling to take the bite out of her comment.

We pulled up to the radio station, a nondescript brick building with no windows that I could see from the parking lot. There was a huge tower of steel beside it, the only sign that it was a radio station and not a laundromat or a copy center.

The door had more warnings on it than a box of razor blades, and I wondered if we'd even get in. I rang the bell, then knocked, all to no avail.

"They have to eat, don't they?" I said. "I guess we'll just wait until someone comes out."

Grace shook her head. "You know, I've never been a big fan of waiting. Let me make a few calls."

"Do you honestly think you'll be able to worm your way into the station?"

"You never know. Besides, it's got to be better than standing around out here in the cold waiting for someone to come out."

"By all means, phone away," I said.

"Let me grab my cell phone. I left it in the car."

She disappeared into her vehicle just as the door to the station opened. A tall, pretty woman in her thirties rushed out, and when she saw me, a look of obvious relief spread over her face.

"It's about time," she said, obviously startled to see me. "How long have you been out here waiting?"

"I just got here," I admitted.

"Come on in, then. Lester's waiting for you. He's been tap-dancing for the last four minutes, and as much as I love seeing the man squirm, it doesn't make for a very good radio show."

She grabbed my arm and hustled me through the door before I could protest, or at least wait for Grace to catch up.

"My friend's still in the parking lot," I said.

"Then she can listen from there. No guests allowed, remember? We covered all of this on the telephone last night."

"I'm afraid there's been some kind of misunderstanding."

We stopped in front of a broad window looking into a control room, and I saw Lester sitting behind his desk, headphones on and a microphone married to his lips.

She explained, "Listen, we're a small station. Save your prima donna act for Charlotte, okay? Just go in and talk to him. It's as easy as that."

I saw the ON AIR sign go off, and the next thing I knew, the woman was shoving me through the door toward Lester. We'd met a few times, and I thought for sure he'd know who I was, but he barely looked up as I walked in.

"You're late. Sit there and put on the headset."

I started to say something when he held up a hand and said into the microphone, "Cutnip, a cut about the rest. Welcome back. Our guest has just arrived, and we're all eager to hear what she has to say about grilling salmon."

He waved frantically at me to talk, but he still didn't make eye contact. I put on the headset, then leaned into my own microphone and said, "Lester, I have no idea how to grill a salmon. I guess you keep asking it questions until it breaks down and finally tells you the truth."

That got his attention. His head jerked upwards, and after a second, he realized who I was. "That's some of our own Suzanne Hart's humor, folks. Since Chef Lisa couldn't make it today, we did the next best thing and invited our very own donut maker into the hot seat. Tell me, Suzanne, how do you justify serving food that is as dangerous to its consumers as cigarettes or machine guns? Hold that thought, we'll be back in thirty seconds while she tries to come up with an answer, folks."

I pulled the headphones from my ears as the ON AIR light went off. "What are trying to pull? That's a dirty question, and you know it."

"Why did you pretend to be someone else, just to get on the air?"

"I came to talk to you," I said. "I never claimed to be Chef Lisa, or even Chef Boyardee. Your assistant threw me in here, and you told me to talk."

"Cara, come in here," he said as he hit one of the many buttons on the panel in front of him.

"I'm busy right now, Lester."

"Make the time."

"Your commercial break is up," she said, clearly trying to buy some time.

"Then run another one," Lester said. He was a large man, with a shiny bald head and beady brown eyes that would look more at home on a ferret.

I felt bad for Cara, but she didn't seem

280

the least bit concerned when she came in. Lester pointed at me and scowled. "That's not Chef Lisa."

"I've told you before, Lester. If you insist on booking your own guests, you can't blame me when things go wrong."

"She makes donuts," he screamed.

"Bite me," she said, low enough for me to hear, but not Lester. Or so she thought.

"What did you just say?"

I stepped in before they had a blowout. "She said, 'Like me.' " I turned to Cara. "So, you make donuts, too."

She nodded, then said, "All the time."

Lester frowned, but the light came back on, and Cara escaped while she still could. I envied her the opportunity.

"Now, you were saying?" Lester said.

I was ready with my answer.

"If you eat too many donuts, I'm the first one to admit that they're bad for you," I said. "But so is ice cream. So is steak. So is watermelon. Moderation is the key to all things."

"But why make them at all?" Lester asked, still pressing me pretty hard.

"We aren't machines, Lester. Every last one of us deserves a guilty pleasure now and then. I'm sure you have a secret vice yourself. Why don't you tell your listeners what your bad habit is? I'm certain they'd all love to know."

Ignoring my counter-jab, Lester forged on. "So, you admit that what you make is poison, and yet you still sell your products to the unsuspecting public. Back for Suzanne's answer after this."

He cut the live feed, and then said, "Don't try to get in a war of words with me, especially not on the air. I'll have you tattered and crying in two minutes if you keep trying to make me look bad. Is that why you came by? To torment me?"

"No, I need to ask you some questions."

"What about?" he asked, the suspicion heavy in his voice. "I can't imagine anything the two of us have to talk about."

"Darlene Higgins is a good place to start, don't you think?"

There were no mistaking it, I'd scored a hit with that one. The ON AIR light came back on, and before Lester could say anything, I decided to jump in and defend my donuts.

"You call my donuts poison," I said. "I won't debate it. It's beneath my dignity to lower myself to your level. You're the one who needs to explain himself. Tell us all about your relationship with Darlene Higgins, Lester. Why did she have one of your business cards, and a hundred-dollar bill that matched up to it, in her apartment when she was murdered?"

I looked at him, and noticed he was smiling. "What's so funny?"

"We've been off the air for thirty seconds," he said. "Technical difficulties. Sorry about that. If you'd like to schedule a new interview time, see Cara on your way out."

"When did you cut me off?" I asked.

He fiddled with some dials, and then I heard my voice replayed saying, "You call my donuts poison. I won't debate it." And after that, there was just the hiss of dead air.

"I'll sue you for that," I said, starting to get up before I realized that I still wore his headphones. I'd have to boil my ears after I left to get his touch off me.

"For a technical difficulty? I'd love to see you prove it."

I realized pretty quickly that he was right. I didn't have a chance, and my little truncated comment was going to stand uncorrected for a long time. I was fairly sure of one thing: Lester wasn't about to extend an invitation to me on the air so I could clear my name, and my product's reputation.

"You got me, congratulations," I said. "But that still doesn't explain what that bill and your card was doing at her apartment."

"I give out cards all of the time. Anybody might have taken it and passed it on to Darlene."

"Then what about the matching hundred?" I said.

"That's my business. Suzanne, if you're going to come after me, you're going to have to have better ammunition than that. Now if you'll excuse me, I've got work to do."

"I thought you had a technical problem," I said.

"You should go. Right now."

I did as he said, not because I felt threatened by him, but because I knew he had me. I had no real proof of anything, just suspicion and conjecture, and I knew neither one of those was going to be good enough for Chief Martin.

Cara stopped me as I started to leave, and I could hear someone pounding on the outside door from the hallway. Evidently Grace wasn't about to give up until she managed to get inside.

The producer put a hand on my arm. "Thanks for covering for me. As much as I loathe working for Lester, it pays for groceries, and my kids have to eat. I lost my grip a little and snapped at him, and if you hadn't been there to cover for me, I would have gotten fired."

"It was my pleasure," I said.

She nodded. "Come here a second."

I followed her into her booth — a much smaller room that was across the hall and down ten feet — so she couldn't see Lester, and more importantly, he couldn't see her.

"I heard what you asked him, and you deserve a straight answer."

"How did you hear our conversation?" I asked. "The microphone was off."

"Just the one for the broadcast feed," Cara said. "He forgets all the time, and I get the juiciest gossip that way. Lester's nothing more than an old fishwife. He loves to spread rumors, and he gets his own pipelines in here to feed his on-air slander from his secret informants. That's why Darlene had his card and a hundred-dollar bill. There was a number on the money, wasn't there?"

I nodded.

Cara took a book out, and recited a number to me. I didn't even have to look at the bill or the card to know that it was a perfect match.

"He was paying her for rumors?" I asked. "What could she know that was worth a hundred dollars? This is April Springs, not Dallas."

"That I can't tell you," Cara said. "All I know is that she was on his payroll. Working at Cutnip must have been a great source of rumors about folks around town."

"But I just heard Lester do a spot for the salon. Isn't that kind of crazy, risking losing a sponsor like that?"

Cara leaned forward and whispered, "You don't know the half of it. Wilma's ads are the only thing keeping him on the air right now. He's lost two other sponsors in the past month. If she drops him too, his so-called career in radio will be over."

"So he had a reason to want Darlene dead, didn't he? If she threatened to tell Wilma what she knew, he could have killed her to shut her up."

Cara's face went white. "No, that couldn't be."

"It's possible," I said.

"I have to check on something, and then I'll get back to you. Is there a number where I can reach you?"

I jotted down the donut shop's number, and after a second's hesitation, added my cell phone number. "Call me anytime. I appreciate your help. Just don't do anything to get fired. I couldn't live with that on my conscience."

"And I couldn't stand by and let a murderer go free," she said.

Lester came out of the booth and started down the hall. When he saw me, his eyes narrowed to two tiny slits. "What are you doing here?"

I was at a loss for a plausible reason when Cara said, "I was just getting her a mug," she said as she slapped one into my hands. "Every guest gets one."

He tore it out of my grasp. "She wasn't a guest, she was an intruder. Now get out," he said.

"Fine, I didn't want your mug anyway," I said as I hurried toward the outside door. I nearly knocked Grace over as I darted outside.

She said, "Finally. I thought you'd forgotten all about me."

"I couldn't get you in," I said as I hurried toward her car. "Let's get out of here, and I'll explain what happened to you once we get away."

"What? Did you end up hitting him with a microphone?"

I stopped in my tracks and looked at her. "Why would you say that?"

"I heard what happened on the radio, and nobody would blame you if you took a shot at him. When I couldn't get in, I wondered if you might accuse him of something on

287

the air, so I came back to the car and tuned the station in on my radio."

"How bad was it at the end?" I asked.

"Pretty bad," she said. "Why won't you debate whether your donuts are poisonous or not? I think you should."

"It wasn't like that. He cut me off in mid-sentence."

"I figured it was something like that. Don't worry, I doubt many people heard you say it."

"Don't even pretend that you don't know that most of April Springs listens to him, no matter how bad he is at what he does. I don't know how I'm going to fix it, but whatever I come up with, it's going to have to wait."

"What's more important than saving your business?" Grace asked as we finally climbed into her car.

"Finding Darlene's killer. She was feeding Lester gossip from the beauty shop, and he was paying her for it."

"What would Wilma say about that, if she knew?" Grace asked.

"That's the question, isn't it? According to Lester's producer, if Cutnip dropped him as a sponsor, his show would go off the air. That's motive enough for murder, wouldn't you say?"

"In Lester's mind, it probably was. But how do we prove he had anything to do with Darlene's murder?"

"I'm working on it," I said, then I noticed that we were back in front of the donut shop. "Why are we here?"

"Where did you want to go, home?" she asked. "I'll take you wherever you want, but you have to give me some idea where we're going, or we're going to just sit here until it's time to eat dinner."

"I just wish I knew," I said.

We were still sitting there five minutes later when Grace's cell phone rang. Before answering it, she turned to me and said, "I could use some coffee."

"I'll make some," I said as I got out, clearly taking the hint.

I went into the shop, and before I could lock it behind me, there was a tap at the front door. A man in a heavy jacket and large hat yelled, "Are you open?"

I pointed to the sign. "Sorry, we're closed."

"Then why are you inside?"

I said the first thing that came to me. "We're doing inventory."

I hadn't done it since I'd opened the shop, though I knew I should keep better tabs on the supplies I had on hand. My operation was small enough so that if I ever ran out of anything, I just ordered more, or if it was a real pinch, I'd run to the market and pick some up myself. I knew that it wasn't the most efficient system in the world, and admittedly, sometimes it did leave me in a temporary bind, but not enough to bother with adding to my workload, when I was already open seven days a week.

Grace came in just as the coffee was ready.

"I saw a man just walk off in a huff. What was that about?" she asked as she took a mug from me.

"He wanted donuts, but I told him I was doing inventory."

"You're not, are you?"

"Of course not," I said as I poured a mug for myself, "but I had to tell him something. Are you going to share who was on the telephone, or is it none of my business?"

Grace said, "I found out where Darlene got the hundred thousand dollars, and I'm afraid it's probably just a dead end."

I put my mug down. "How could that be? That much money has to be a motive for murder."

Grace explained, "Her great-aunt Myrtle died six weeks ago in Union Square. I actually read about it in the paper. I knew the woman had money, and I remember wondering what happened to it, but then something else came up and I forgot all about it. It turns out she appointed Darlene as her executor a few days before she died. Do you want to know who had the position before that?"

"I'm guessing it was her cousin, Taylor Higgins."

Grace looked surprised. "How did you know that?"

"I didn't, not really, until you mentioned the great-aunt. Taylor's come around the shop a few times asking about Darlene, and what might have happened to her. That's why I wasn't all that surprised when you told me what you found out. Does that mean Darlene was supposed to get the money instead of Taylor?"

"No, she gets a small fee as executor, but the rest of the money gets split up into bequests to a hundred different beneficiaries."

"And they get a thousand each?" I asked.

"More like five hundred, once the rest of Myrtle's debts are paid off."

"Five hundred dollars isn't much of a motive for murder, is it?" I said.

"I'm sure people have been killed for less, but no, I wouldn't think it's an issue here. At least we can mark the money off the list as a motive."

"Just out of curiosity, who gets Darlene's share now that she's dead?"

Grace said, "It probably goes back into the pool of funds to be distributed later, but I might be wrong. I didn't think it was worth pursuing."

"It isn't, unless one of the heirs is a serial killer and is going to knock off the other ninety-eight people left, it's a dead end."

"It appears to be," Grace said.

After we finished our coffee, I poured the rest from the pot into a to-go cup, then I rinsed out the pot and mugs.

Grace asked, "What should we do now?"

"I think it's time to go home so I can take a shower and change. Do you mind? The donut smell is pretty strong today." Most days I didn't notice it, but sometimes it was all I could take to be around myself, let alone anyone else.

"Sounds good," she said.

As I locked up behind us, I looked in the parking lot and saw someone putting a note under my Jeep's windshield.

I felt my heart race at the sight of it, wondering what it meant, and what exactly someone was trying to tell me.

It was George, I was relieved to see when

he turned around.

He looked surprised to see Grace and me standing there.

As we joined him, he said, "Suzanne, I thought you would be long gone by now."

"We were, but we came back," I said. "What's going on, or do you want me to just read the note?"

He smiled as he retrieved it and balled it up into a wad before sticking it into his pocket. "I'd rather tell you. Any chance I could get a cup of coffee?"

I gave him the cup in my hand. "Here you go. I just made it."

"I can't take your coffee, Suzanne."

"If you're worried about germs, this is fresh. Grace and I already had some. Just drink it, okay?"

He nodded and pulled off the lid. "If you're sure. Thanks."

Grace's cell phone rang, and she stepped away from us to take the call.

After George killed the cup, he said, "Thanks. That was exactly what I needed."

"You were going to tell me about that note," I said, trying to keep my teeth from shivering. "What did it say?"

"Darlene's been up to something with Lester Moorefield. A few people have seen them sneaking around town together. I thought it was an odd match, you know?"

"She was selling him rumors for his show," I said.

"So you've already got what I had," he said, the disappointment heavy in his voice.

"It's always good to have confirmation," I said, trying to buck his spirits up.

"Have you learned anything else?" he asked as he chucked the empty coffee cup, along with the note he'd written for me, into the trash can near the donut shop.

"Grace said that the hundred thousand was a dead end. It's being split a hundred ways, so it's not much of a motive for murder."

"If it's being divvied up, why was it all in an account with Darlene's name on it?" George asked.

"I just assumed since she was the executor, she had control of it for now," I said.

"It should have been set up into an estate account," George said, "not one in her name. Did Grace check on that?"

"I don't know."

George frowned, then asked, "Who gets Darlene's share now that she's dead? Who takes over as executor? Are there any other assets that might be worth killing someone for? Is there a will on record, and is it the most recent one, or is there something else there we don't know about yet?"

"I don't know," I had to admit.

"Well, I'm free," George said. "Let me nose around the courthouse and see what I can come up with. While I'm checking it out, I'm going to look into her cousin, too."

"It sounds like a great deal of work," I said as a movement near my Jeep caught my eye. I kept watching it, but there was nothing else, so I finally just figured it was my imagination playing tricks on me.

"I don't mind. I'm retired, remember? Thanks again for the coffee," he said as he started off down the street. "I'll be in touch."

"You know where to find me," I said.

He turned and grinned as he pointed to the sign. "It's always time to make the donuts with you, isn't it?"

"Somebody has to do it," I said as Grace came back.

From the expression on her face, I knew it was bad news.

What I didn't know was how it would affect the investigation, and what had gone so terribly wrong.

Old Fashioned Donuts

These are a little denser than normal donut fare these days, but they might just take you back to simpler times! Absolutely worth a try!

Ingredients

1/2 cup milk
1/2 teaspoon salt
2 packages fast-rising yeast (1/2 ounce total)
1/2 cup warm water
3 eggs, yolks only
1/2 cup granulated sugar
1/2 cup butter or margarine, melted
4 cups flour

Directions

Scald the milk, then add the sugar, salt, and melted butter. While that's cooling, add the yeast to the warm water. Once it dissolves, stir it into the milk mixture. Then add the egg yolks and 2 cups of flour. Mix thoroughly, then keep adding flour until the dough is no longer sticky to the touch. Knead for one minute, then roll the dough out to 1/4 to 1/2 inch thick.

Fry the donuts in canola oil heated to 365°F, turning once as they cook. They should take 2–4 minutes total to cook.

Drain on paper towels, then dust with sugar or add your own glaze.

CHAPTER 12

"What is it?" I asked. "Did someone else die?"

"No, it's nothing like that," she said.

"Grace, it's got to be bad; don't try to tell me it's not. I can take it, go ahead and tell me."

"I have a meeting with my boss in Charlotte this afternoon," Grace said softly. "I've got two hours to get there, and I was told to pack an overnight bag. She said that I'd be staying overnight at the Stansbury Hotel."

"That doesn't sound like the end of the world to me," I said. "That's a really nice hotel. Or so I've heard. I've never been able to afford to stay there, myself."

Grace looked as though she wanted to cry. "The roads are still slick, but she didn't care. She said this couldn't wait. Add to that the fact that we never meet at the Stansbury. It's where my boss takes people she's about to fire or promote, and I've got a feeling I'm not climbing the corporate ladder."

I did my best to cheer her up. "But it could be good news, right?"

"Sure, I suppose it's possible. I think I'll get a lottery ticket on the way over. It's possible I'll win that too, maybe even more likely, if I know my boss. I know I'm going to get sacked, I just know it."

"I'm so sorry," I said, "but Grace, you're a terrific saleswoman. You'll get another job soon enough."

"I don't want another one," she said. "I like the flexibility of this one."

I wasn't about to tell her that maybe her flexibility in the past was what was going to get her fired tonight, but I couldn't stop myself from thinking it.

I patted her shoulder. "It's going to be all right. I just know it. Would you like me to come home with you to help you pack a bag for tonight?" I asked. "I know you're not crazy about going back there alone."

"Thanks, but this is something I'm going to have to do sooner or later, so why not now? Besides, I hate crying in front of you, and if I time things right, I can get a good jag in before I meet her."

"At least call me tonight and let me know what happens," I said.

"I promise, but it's probably going to be the shortest telephone conversation in the history of the world."

"Don't forget. I mean it."

"I know, I know."

I could see tears starting to form in the corners of her eyes, and suddenly I said, "I'm going with you. You shouldn't have to deal with this by yourself."

"What about your donut shop?" Grace asked.

"What about it? If Emma and her mom can't run it tomorrow, I'll just shut it down. Let me make one quick call while we're here, and then I need to pack something for myself."

She put a hand on my shoulder, and I could see the tears receding. "Suzanne, I can't tell you how much that would mean to me, but I have to say no."

"I don't mind," I said, being a little more insistent than I probably should have.

"I know that, but I have to do this by myself. Thank you so much for offering, though. That really means the world to me."

She was gone before I could try to convince her again to let me come with her, and I finally decided that was probably for the best after all. I knew Grace, and one of the things she prided herself on was her calm demeanor. If she wanted to put on a brave face for me, I knew I shouldn't try to stop her. Let her have privacy when she cried the tears she needed to.

I got into the Jeep, not sure where to go next now that I was alone, when I heard a voice coming from the back seat under a blanket I kept there in winter.

He said, "It's about time. I nearly peed my pants when George walked up to the windshield. Could you turn on the heater? I'm freezing."

It was Max — my errant ex-husband — and probably the last person in the world I expected to find hiding in the back of my Jeep waiting for me.

"Max, have you lost your mind?" I said. "Chief Martin's been looking everywhere for you."

"Would you do me a favor and turn around and drive?" he said. "I don't want anyone to know I'm back here."

I thought about it a few seconds, then said, "You know, what I should do is take you straight to the police station."

"But you're not going to, are you?" There was a real edge of fear in his voice, something I had never heard before.

I didn't move a muscle. "I'm not sure yet.

Before I do anything, I have to know one thing. Did you have anything to do with Darlene's murder?"

He nearly sat up before remembering he was supposed to be in hiding. "How can you even ask me something like that? Don't you know me well enough to believe I wouldn't kill anyone? Suzanne, I'm really disappointed with you."

"Well, I'm not too happy with you either, so I guess we're even. Answer the question, Max. You can either tell me, or you can tell the police."

"I didn't kill her," he said. His words were flat and barely had any emotion in them at all. Oddly enough, in most people I would have naturally assumed they were lying. But with Max, I'd learned long ago that the more he protested, the greater his histrionics, the more chance he wasn't telling me the truth.

"Fine," I said as I started the Jeep and pulled away from the shop. "Where do you want to go?"

"Could we drive around a little?" he asked. "I've got to talk to you about a few things, and then I need to ask you a huge favor."

"Why should I help you at all?"

His head bobbed up for a second before it

302

disappeared again. "Don't the years we had together mean anything to you?"

"I could ask you the same thing," I said. "Go on, I'm waiting for an answer."

Max paused, then said, "Because deep in your heart, where you might not even admit it yourself, you're hoping we'll get back together some day."

I nearly wrecked when I heard his line of reasoning. "That's the craziest thing I've ever heard you say since I've known you."

"Crazy, or completely true?" he asked.

"Trust me, it's the crazy option." I drove down Springs Drive, toward Union Square and away from home. I guess I made my decision without realizing it. Max tensed as we drove by City Hall, and I wondered if he really thought I was going to turn him in at the police station after all.

I saw him peeking out, and took my foot off the gas as the building neared to give him a good scare.

"Suzanne, what are you doing?" He was on the edge of panic, and I realized that I'd been a little too cruel to him.

"My foot slipped," I lied, as we sped on past. He didn't look out again, even after we went past the town clock where Darlene had been murdered.

Once we were headed out of town, Max

asked, "Do you think I could sit up front with you now?"

"Sure, if you're willing to risk someone spotting you in my Jeep. I won't try to outrun the police for you, Max, so you'd better be ready to turn yourself in if they stop us."

He must have thought about that for a full thirty seconds before he replied a little sullenly, "Okay, I'll stay back here. Just take it easy on the turns, would you? I don't have any warning they're coming, and it's making me a little sick."

"I guess that depends on what you have to say," I said. "I won't punish you as long as I think you're being honest with me. Max, you wanted to talk. So talk."

He was silent for a few seconds, then he said, "Some of the things I'm going to tell you are probably going to upset you, but I want you to promise you won't go ballistic until I'm finished. Can you do that for me?"

"It depends on how bad it is," I said, after mulling over his question.

"Suzanne, give me a break here, okay? I've been going out of mind worrying that the chief is going to try to pin this murder on me. You know how he is. He's got a one-track mind, and the easiest solution is always his favorite." Max laughed softly, but there was no amusement in it. "And let's face it. I'm the easiest answer he's got right now."

"I didn't turn you in, did I?" I asked. "I'm getting impatient, Max. It's been a long day for me, remember? I'm worn out. What is it?"

"First things first. Don't blame Emma for losing your money at the donut shop. It wasn't her fault."

"How did you know about that?" A split second later, I screamed out, "It was *you*. I can't believe you stole from me!"

"I needed money, and I knew if I tapped into my own accounts, the chief would find out. I had no choice. I'd been keeping an eye out on the donut shop, hoping to get a chance to talk to you, but every time I was there, someone was with you. When you left, I had no choice but to wait across the street until you came back. I saw Emma slip in back, so I rushed over, cleaned out the till, and got away before she even knew I'd been there."

"You stole from me," I repeated, feeling the anger boil up inside me.

"I borrowed from you," he corrected me. "And I have every intention of paying you back. I know exactly how much I took."

"Believe me, so do I," I said.

I felt a little better knowing that Max had been watching the place and had merely seized an opportunity to take advantage of us.

"Do you forgive me?" he asked after a few minutes of stony silence.

"Why did you rob me?"

"Suzanne, you've got to understand my situation. I had no money on me. I was going to run away and lay low until this thing was over, but that took money."

I looked at him in the rearview mirror. "Then why didn't you do us both a favor and do exactly that once you robbed me?"

"Borrowed from you," he corrected me.

"So you say. I'm still waiting for an answer, Max."

"It wasn't enough," he said. "I needed more."

"What were you going to do, wait until I built up the cash in my register again before you took more?"

"I'd never do that," he said. "I'm sorry, but I was desperate. I don't know what else to say."

"I don't, either," I said.

After a few seconds, I said, "You said some of the things you said were going to make me mad. What else do you have to confess? Have you changed your story about you and

Darlene?"

"Of course not," he said. "This next part doesn't involve her at all. This is about Grace."

I didn't need a playbill to tell me what was next on the horizon. "I should have figured that out on my own. You're the one who broke into her place."

"I needed a place to stay," he said shrilly. "I knew she was staying with you, so no one would be there. I never dreamed you two would come back when you did. I had to race out the back as that cop was coming in the front door. Another second of hesitation and he would have had me."

"You violated my best friend's sense of security," I said. "She's shattered about the break-in. Max, she won't even go back home by herself."

With a hint of regret in his voice, he said, "I can apologize to her right now, if you want me to."

"I doubt it would do much good," I said. "She was pretty rattled by it. Besides, Grace isn't even in town. She's on her way to Charlotte by now."

His voice was tired and beaten as he said, "I said I was sorry, and I meant it. I'll do whatever I can to make it right."

"I'm not sure there's anything you can

do," I said. "So, why are you here? I'm sure there's more to it than your desire to confess your sins to me."

"I need help, Suzanne. I'm running out of options. I know you are investigating the murder, and I need to know what you've uncovered so far."

I couldn't see what it would hurt telling him what we'd found, but there was a part of me that didn't want to ease his mind at all. "Why should I tell you?"

"Because I'm going crazy with worry," he said, his voice cracking as he spoke.

I decided I might as well tell him what we'd found. "Muriel is in the clear as a possible victim. She has problems of her own, but she's out of the picture for now. Gabby Williams drove her out of state, so she'll be safe."

"Where did she go?"

That was an odd question. "Why do you care, Max?"

"Curious, I guess," he said.

"Sorry, I wasn't privy to their plans," I lied. I didn't even feel bad about withholding the truth from him. Goodness knows he'd done it enough with me when we were married.

"Fine, I don't need to know. I'm just glad she's safe. What else is going on?"

"There are some connections we're still looking into," I said as I pulled into Union Square. "Where do you want to go now? I should warn you, I'm not driving you to Tennessee, no matter how nice you ask."

"Could we just head back to April Springs?" he asked.

I was surprised by the request. "I figured that was the last place you'd want to be. It's a little small to find a good hiding place, isn't it?"

"I can't do anything about that. Without much money, I have to depend on my friends to help me. There's a way I could leave, though."

"Go on, I'm listening."

"If you could loan me a thousand bucks, I could take off until this mess blows over."

I turned around and started back to April Springs.

Max said, "Does that mean you'll do it?"

I laughed, despite my ill-tempered mood. "What makes you think I have that kind of money? I own a donut shop, Max, I'm not printing money there."

"Suzanne, remember who you're talking to. I know you've kept ten hundred-dollar-bills in the Bible on your nightstand ever since you could afford it. It's your rainy-day money, and believe me, from where I'm sitting, it's pouring."

"Max, that's my security blanket, and you know it."

"I'll pay you back," he said, lifting off his chair. "You know if I tell you something, you can believe it."

"Like the marriage vows you made to me that you broke?"

"That's low, even for you," Max said. "I made a mistake, and I've been paying for it ever since. When are we going to ever be square?"

"Mister, you haven't even touched the interest you owe me yet. Forget about the principal."

"So, that's how it's going to be? You won't help me?"

"I never said that," I said. "But don't expect to get it without jumping through some hoops first."

"Then you'll do it?" he asked, the hope starting to surface in his voice.

"Probably."

"That's fantastic, Suzanne. I appreciate it so much, I can't even tell you."

"Just make sure you pay it back," I said. "And I don't mean a year from now, either, Max."

"Consider it done, Suzanne. The second I get my hands on my bank account, I'll pay you back."

As we drove back toward town, I looked back at Max and saw there was a gun tucked into his jacket.

"Please tell me that's from your prop department at the community theater," I said.

"It's real enough. As long as there's a killer on the loose, I'm going to protect myself."

"Do you even know how to use it?"

He nodded. "I played a part in a regional production in Raleigh, and the director was a method man. He took me to a firing range and made me practice until I was comfortable enough to shoot it without flinching."

"I don't like the idea of you being armed," I said.

"Well, I don't like the idea of dying, so we're even."

A few minutes later, Max asked, "Have you found anything else out about Darlene?"

"We have," I admitted. "Though I'm not sure how much I should share with you."

"You know you can trust me," he said.

My laughter echoed in the tight confines of the Jeep.

"Suzanne," he said, the scolding in his voice evident.

"Be very careful right now," I said.

311

"You're right. I'm sorry," he said. "Seriously though, did you find anything else? I might be able to help you, if I know what you've found out so far."

I had to admit that Max might have some insights that could help our investigation. "Okay, here's what we've got so far. Wilma claims Darlene stole from her at Cutnip, and we all know what kind of temper Wilma has. Lester Moorefield was paying her an informant's fee for dirty gossip around town, and we think she might have threatened to tell Wilma about the arrangement. Since she was Lester's last sponsor, that could be a motive for murder."

"Anybody else make your list?" Max asked. He hesitated, then added, "Besides me, I mean."

I let that one go. "There's her cousin Taylor, but I'm not sure how viable a suspect he is. To be honest with you, I don't have much information about him, but he's been hanging around April Springs a lot lately, and from what we've heard, he was the executor of his great-aunt's estate until she changed it to Darlene at the last second."

"Wow, I'm not sure I even want to know what you and your friends have on me."

"Believe me, your name has come up in our discussions of suspects several times."

"George and Grace never liked me," he said.

I swerved the Jeep — though nothing was in the road — nearly dumping Max onto the floor.

"Hey, take it easy."

"Sorry, there was a dog in the road."

He didn't believe me, and I didn't care.

After a few moments, Max said, "Who else made your list?"

"There are a few people we haven't talked about much yet. Darlene's roommate could have done it."

"Kimmi? You're kidding, aren't you? She wouldn't hurt a charging bull if she had a stick of lit dynamite in her hand."

"You know her, do you?"

"We've met," Max said, a little too cryptically for my taste. "Who else is on your list?"

"That's it," I admitted. "If someone else did it, they're flying under the radar."

"I might have a few ideas of my own," he said.

"Go on. I'm willing to listen."

"We can talk after I get the money," Max said.

"What's the matter, Max? Don't you trust me?"

"Of course I do. Would I have come to you if I didn't?"

I shook my head. "From the sound of it, you didn't really have much choice, did you? You were running out of options, and fast."

"I had other people I could ask for help," he said. "But I chose you."

"Then tell me who else you suspect," I said as I pulled back into town.

"Let me get my thoughts in order a little first," he said.

We drove through April Springs in silence. As I neared my driveway, I slowed down to a crawl as I spotted a squad car through the evergreen trees.

"Max, I think Chief Martin's at my house."

Without a word, the back flap opened and Max slipped out.

"What about the money?" I called out.

But it was too late.

Max was gone.

Again.

"Where have you been?" my mother asked me as I walked into the house. "I've been calling your cell phone for the last two hours. Suzanne, why do you even have one if you're not going to answer it?"

I pulled my phone out of my purse, ignoring Chief Martin for the moment. "The battery's dead. I'm having a hard time holding a charge lately. Sorry, I'll get it fixed tomor-row."

"Phillip wants to speak with you," Momma said.

"Hello, Chief," I said as I turned toward him. "What can I do for you?"

"You can start by telling me why you drove to Union Square, then turned around and came back without stopping anywhere along the way."

Had someone seen Max with me, despite his precautions? No, if they had, the chief would have led off with a very different question for me.

"Are you actually following me?"

"I'm the one asking questions here," Martin said.

My mother stared hard at him. "I'd like to know the answer to that question myself. You're here by my favor. The only thing you told me was that it was important that you speak with Suzanne."

"Pardon me, Dorothy, but I don't need your blessing to talk to your daughter any time I want to."

My mother was openly glaring at him now, and I was glad her gaze wasn't point-ing at me. She said, "Perhaps not, but if you wish to remain on good terms with me, you might want to appease our curiosity and answer Suzanne's question. Do you have an officer following her?"

He seemed to chew the question over in his mind, and I knew the fact that the chief's yearning for my mother hadn't lessened any over the years was weighing heavily in his response. He was going to answer, and all three of us knew it.

Finally, he shrugged and said, "One of my officers was in Union Square, and he spotted Suzanne's odd behavior."

"How did he happen to be there in the first place?" I asked.

"He wasn't following you, and I told him not to tail you when you turned around and came straight back here. I don't work that way, and you know it. My officer called me out of curiosity, but he was there with his family, not there to watch you."

I had to believe that, since Max hadn't been apprehended the second he'd left my Jeep. At least I hadn't heard of it happening, and I figured the chief would have mentioned that particular turn of events with real pride in his voice.

"Now, it's your turn," he said. "What happened?"

It was time to lie, and this time, I didn't feel bad about doing it at all. "I was going to eat at Napoli's, but then I changed my

316

mind at the last second."

"Why?"

"I didn't feel like eating alone," I said.

He scratched his chin. "Okay, we'll leave that for now. What are you and your friends up to? I heard you and Grace were at Darlene's house the other day. You're not snooping into my murder investigation, are you?"

"We were looking for a place to live," I said, recalling Grace's excuse to search Darlene's room.

"You're not leaving here, are you?" my mother asked, with more than a hint of hurt in her voice as she spoke.

"It's for Grace," I explained. "She's tired of living alone."

My mother looked relieved by the admission. "That's fine, then." She frowned, then said, "She could always come live with us on a permanent basis. It's been lovely having her around."

"The point may be moot," I said. "There might be a big change in her life soon."

The chief cleared his throat. "Ladies, can we get back to the subject?"

"I wasn't aware there was one," I said.

"We both know better than that. How did you find out where Muriel Stevens was hiding before my men did? And why didn't you come to me straight away as soon as you knew, instead of going there yourself."

I looked out the window, wondering if Max was out there, watching. I was getting tired of the chief's questions, but I wasn't at all sure I could refuse to answer. "I have hunches myself, you know," I said. "It's as simple as that."

"Now why don't I believe you?" the chief asked.

My mother had finally had enough. "That's it, Phillip. I'm afraid I'm going to have to ask you to leave."

He looked surprised by the request. "Dorothy, you told me I could talk to her when I came to the house."

"You may talk, but so far, you've refused to accept a single answer she's given you as the truth. We're finished here."

As she stood, so did the chief, albeit reluctantly.

I tried not to look at him, and diverted my gaze back to the window. I don't know what kind of look might have passed between them, and frankly, I didn't want to see it.

I didn't turn around again until the door closed, and I saw Chief Martin walking down the steps, an angry scowl on his face.

"Thanks, Momma, I owe you one. I love

the way you stood up to him."

"You are my daughter, my only child. Of course I'm going to take up for you." She paused, then added softly, "What exactly were you hiding from him?"

"What makes you think I wasn't telling the truth?" I asked.

"Oh, please. I can tell when you're lying from twenty miles away. There are a set of signals you give off that are like flares to me."

"I'll have to work on that then, won't I?" I said with a smile.

"I'm still waiting for an answer."

I thought about lying to her — I honestly did — but suddenly I found myself telling her about Max, and all he'd said to me.

After I was finished, she merely nodded. "As you know, I'm not Max's biggest fan, but if you believe he was telling the truth, then I'm willing to give him the benefit of the doubt when he says he didn't kill that woman."

"Why should you?"

"What?" she asked, obviously startled by the question.

I looked hard at her. "You said it yourself, you're not a big Max supporter. So why do you believe him?"

She took my hands in hers. "Because you

do, my dear. I trust your instincts."

I was so flabbergasted, I didn't know what to say. At least I was saved from an awkward response when the house phone rang.

"I'll get that," I said.

Momma beat me to it. "Nonsense. I've been expecting a call all afternoon."

She spoke to the caller, then handed the phone to me. "It's for you."

"Is it Grace?" I was dying to hear from her, and I'd have to charge my telephone as soon as I could so she wouldn't have to call the landline.

"I don't think so," she said. "Why don't you ask her yourself?"

I took the phone and said, "Hello?"

"Suzanne, this is Cara, from the radio station. I tried calling your cell phone, but it put me straight through to voice mail. Is it on?"

"The battery's dead."

"That makes sense. I looked up your home number, because this couldn't wait. I've got something I need to tell you."

"Go ahead, I'm listening."

She hesitated, and I could see that Momma was watching me curiously. I shrugged, and she shook her head as she walked into the kitchen, giving me some privacy for my conversation.

"I'm not sure if I should do it over the phone," she said.

"Nobody's bugging my place," I said. "So, unless your phone's tapped, we should be fine. You're not calling from the radio station, are you?"

"No, I'm on my cell phone in my car. Listen, I know I'm being paranoid, but Lester's been acting strange ever since you left, and I'm getting a little worried."

"Then perhaps you'd better tell me right now," I said. I didn't want anything to happen to Cara — I'd liked her from the start — but if she knew something, I wanted to hear it before anything could.

"You're right. Here goes. I lied to you."

"You wouldn't be the first person to do that, even today," I said. "What was it about in particular?"

"I told the police that Lester was broadcasting from the Winter Carnival, but that's only partially true. He started his broadcast from there, but something happened to the live feed, and we had to go to the Best of Lest, his reruns we keep cued up just in case."

"When did he go off the air?" I asked. "And where was the booth?"

"We set it up across the street from the newspaper. You know how he likes to goad

Ray Blake."

That would have put him within two hundred yards of the crime scene, which meant he had the opportunity to slip away and commit the murder.

"When did the broadcast break down?" This was a crucial bit of information. The timing was everything.

"I've got it right here," she said. I could hear her flipping through pages, then she came back on the line and said, "I checked with a friend at the police department, so I was able to match his absence up with the time of the murder. The feed stopped nine minutes before the murder, and picked back up six minutes after the body was discovered."

"So he could have easily done it," I said, more to myself than to Cara.

She said, "That's not all."

"There's more?"

Cara said, "I sent one of my techs out to check the equipment, and there was nothing wrong with any of it. The only way we could lose the feed like that is if Lester did it deliberately himself."

CHAPTER 13

"Who was that?" Momma asked the second Cara and I hung up.

"It was just a friend of mine," I said, not wanting to get into it all with my mother.

"I know all your friends, and that voice didn't sound familiar," she said. "Does she have a name?"

"She sure does," I said, trying my best to ignore the direct question. "I'm starving. Is there anything to eat?"

My mother frowned at me. "That's why I first started calling you this afternoon. I wanted to tell you that I was having dinner with Betty Mathis tonight, and that you'd be on your own. I suppose I can cancel, if you'd like me to."

"Don't be silly, Momma. Go eat with Betty. I know how much fun you two have when you're together."

"But what are you going to do for dinner?"

I laughed. "Momma, I've cooked for myself before. Don't worry, I'll be fine."

She patted my shoulder lightly. "I wish I could believe it."

"You can," I said, trying my best to re-assure her that I was all right, though we both probably knew otherwise. I couldn't stop thinking about Max, and what he'd said, and not just about the case, but about our relationship. It was clear Momma could sense that I was troubled, but I prayed she'd drop it.

I could tell she wanted to say something, but at that moment, we both heard a car horn out front. "That has to be Betty."

She started for the door, then turned back to me. "You're welcome to join us, you know."

I would have rather taken a beating from two ugly men than go with them, but it would have been impolite to say so. "Thanks anyway, but it's been a long day. I'm going to grab a quick bite, then go to sleep. I've been missing out on it lately."

Momma paused at the door and said, "It's been fun having Grace here with us though, hasn't it?"

I nodded as the car horn sounded again.

Momma said, "She's rather impatient tonight, isn't she? I'm going to have to teach

Betty a lesson one day about blowing her horn."

"I just bet you will," I said. "Good night, Momma. I'll see you tomorrow."

She kissed my cheek softly. "Good night, Suzanne. I love you."

"I love you, too."

After a quick sandwich and a glass of milk, I headed off to bed. It was barely seven, but I was exhausted, and I knew I needed my sleep if I was going to cope with things tomorrow.

I don't know how long I'd slept when my cell phone rang. It startled me, since I'd docked it in its charger before I'd eaten and then promptly forgotten all about it. I almost always turn the ringer off when I go to bed, since my schedule is not like anyone else's I knew except Emma.

"Hello," I said, barely able to keep the yawn out of my voice as I spoke. I looked blearily at the clock and saw that it was nearly one AM.

"Suzanne, I woke you up."

It was Grace, and I was suddenly wide awake.

"That's okay, I have to get up in a few minutes anyway. I've been hoping you'd call."

"I said I would, didn't I?" She sounded happy, something I doubted she'd be able to do if her boss had just fired her.

"Don't keep me in suspense. What happened today?"

"It turns out I was all wrong. It looks like I've got a good shot at a promotion," she said, almost squealing into the phone. "They've had their eyes on me for a while, so when a supervisor's position came open, my name was mentioned. I had a dinner interview this evening, and my final interview's tomorrow morning."

"They don't waste any time, do they? Congratulations."

"I haven't got the job yet," she said, and I could hear a hitch in her voice. "There's something else, though."

"Isn't there always?" Suddenly, something struck me. "You're not moving to Charlotte, are you?" Charlotte was almost two hours away from April Springs, and if Grace moved there, she might as well be moving across the country.

"No, it's not in Charlotte."

"That's a relief," I said. "I'd hate it if you were so far away."

"The position that's open is in San Francisco," she said, and I felt my hands go numb. "That's where I am right now."

"You're all the way across the country?"

"The woman who'll be my new boss is going on vacation in two days, and they want to fill the position before she's gone."

When I didn't say anything in response, Grace said, "Suzanne, are you still there?"

"I'm here," I said. "It sounds wonderful. I'm really happy for you."

Grace said almost apologetically, "I'm not sure I'm going to get the final offer, and even if I do, I might not take it."

"Nonsense," I said, trying to pump my voice up with false bravado. "They'll offer you the job, and you can't turn it down, can you? You've been complaining for years about not moving up. This is your chance."

"I know it is, and don't think I'm not tempted," she said. "I'm just not sure I can leave April Springs."

"You have to at least try, don't you think? You'll never be able to forgive yourself if you turn this down. Grace, you have to take it if they offer you the job." It broke my heart to give her that particular advice, but she was my friend, and I wanted what was best for her, not for me.

There was a pause, and then she said in a meek voice, "Funny, I was kind of hoping you'd talk me out of it."

"I'd love to, believe me, but I can't. This

is what you've been waiting for. I'll miss you more than anything in the world, but you shouldn't let that stop you. Besides, planes fly all the time, don't they? And we can talk on the phone every day."

"You really think I should do this?" she asked.

"I do, if it's what you really want. The only thing in the world I want is what's best for you."

There was a long pause, then Grace said, "But how do I know what that is?"

"Trust me, you'll know. Now get some sleep. You have a big day tomorrow, and you need to be at your best."

"Yes, you're right. Good night, Suzanne. And thanks for understanding."

"What are friends for? Call me tomorrow, no matter what time it is."

She laughed. "As if our chatting schedule wasn't mixed up enough as it is, I'm throwing time zones into the mix." Grace paused, then said, "Oh no. It's one in the morning there, isn't it?"

"Almost time to wake up," I said, trying to sound as cheerful as I could.

"I can't believe I didn't even think of that. Do you forgive me?"

"You're a lot of trouble, but you're worth it."

"So are you," she said, then hung up.

I had such little time before my alarm clock was due to go off that there was no reason to try to go back to sleep, even if I could; Grace's news had jolted me awake. Everything I'd told her had been true. She deserved a chance to spread her wings, and I was behind her all the way. My friend was about to start a new chapter in her life, one without me in it. The selfish part of me wanted her to blow that interview, but fortunately, it was a tiny part.

She was moving on, and I realized that, in a very real way, so was I. Earlier that day, Max had been genuinely shocked when I told him we were through, and I wasn't really certain until that moment that it was true myself, but as I lay there in bed, I realized that it was as honest as I'd ever been with him. I wasn't sure what my own future held, but wherever it led me, I knew it wouldn't be with Max.

I knew where I'd thought I'd wanted it to go, but that wasn't an option anymore. I could see myself falling in love with Jake Bishop, but unfortunately, it appeared that there wasn't enough room in his heart for me and his late wife. It stung when I realized that he didn't want me.

I wasn't about to let that keep me from

living, though. If I grew old and died running a donut shop and living at home with my mother, it would be my choice, and not someone else's.

And honestly, what more could I ask of life?

At three the next morning, Emma said, "Let's turn on the radio. I want to hear the weather forecast."

"I can save you the trouble," I said as I mixed the dough for the yeast donuts in the big floor-stand mixer. "Cold today, cold tonight, and cold tomorrow."

"I heard we might be getting more snow," she said.

I shook my head. "I don't think so. It's three days from Christmas, and I'm guessing we've already had our big snowstorm for the season. It will probably be February before we even see another flurry." That seemed to be the pattern for our part of North Carolina. We either had one big snow in December, or a spattering of smaller snowfalls spread out after Valentine's Day. The exception was one year when I'd been growing up, where it had snowed every Tuesday for a month, and we missed school for that long, too. The downside to all that white was that we had to go to school on

Saturdays until we made up the days we'd missed, which was pure misery.

"I'm still going to check. Hang on a second," Emma said as she walked out of the kitchen to the front.

I didn't need her for that stage of the donut making, but I did like the company.

She came back thirty seconds later. "You should see this."

"What is it?" I said as I measured out the flour. I'd made a mistake once at this stage and had been forced to start over, so I was always particularly careful so it didn't happen again. I prided myself on rarely making the same mistake twice, but I'd still found new, creative ways to mess up over the last few years.

"I'm not saying a word, so take your time," she said. "You have to see this for yourself."

I finished adding the flour, turned the mixer on and set the timer, tucked the portable alarm into my apron pocket, then said, "What's so important?"

"Follow me."

As I walked out into the front section of the shop, I could see heavy snow coming down outside, visible in the light from our place where it underwent a mysterious transformation from gray to bright white as the light hit it.

Emma grinned at me. "Now, what were you saying about the weather forecast?"

I laughed. "I said I thought it was going to snow a bunch, and soon, too."

"It looks like you were right, then," she said.

"Don't get too excited," I said. "It will probably all be over by the time we open in a few hours."

"And you're so good at predicting the weather, I should believe you, right?"

"I don't see why not," I said with a smile. "You could at least pretend to think I'm right."

"What fun would that be? We're still taking our break outside, aren't we? It's really beautiful."

I looked through the window at the swirling mass of white. "You can go outside if you'd like to, but the way the wind's blowing and the snow's coming down, I think I'll have my coffee on the couch and watch where it's warm."

She shook her head. "You can stay inside if you'd like, but I'm going out."

"Have fun," I said, as the timer in my pocket went off. "But we have work to do before you get your break."

"Spoilsport," she said with a smile.

"That's me, one big killjoy," I said.

After the yeast dough was finished mixing, I turned the machine off, pulled out the dough hook, and covered the big bowl with a towel, and it was the official beginning of our early-morning break.

"Are you sure you don't want to come outside with me?" Emma asked as she started to bundle up in her heavy coat and mittens.

"I'm positive. You have fun, though."

She unlocked the door and walked outside, while I poured myself a nice mug of coffee and settled in on our best sofa where I could watch the snow falling in steady waves of white. The town had added a streetlight across the way a month ago — part of the mayor's new downtown revitalization plan — and I'd had mixed emotions about it. It did make me feel safer having nearby illumination, particularly given my odd nocturnal hours, but it also killed one of the things I liked about working so early in the donut shop every morning. Before, it had felt like we were up before the rest of the world, toiling to make other people's days a little better. The light killed part of that feeling, but I had to admit that as I watched the snow swirling down into the cone of light under the lamp and jumping to life, it was a pretty spectacular sight.

Emma came in three minutes later, covered in snow.

"That didn't last very long, did it?" I said, then sipped more coffee.

"It's coming down hard," she said as she shook her jacket off before hanging it up.

I stood and got some newspapers we'd been saving, just in case we got more snow. "Put your boots on these," I said as I handed the stack to her.

"Wow, I don't believe I've ever seen it snow this hard. Do you think anybody will be able to get to us this morning?"

"It shouldn't be a problem today," I said. "The snow's not that hard to drive on. It's ice that will kill us."

"Then let's hope it keeps snowing," Emma said.

I watched it cover the parking area in front of the shop. "I don't know if I'm going to wish for that, either."

Emma grabbed a mug of coffee, and took a seat beside me. After taking a healthy swallow, she said, "This is so good."

"It's nice," I agreed.

She looked at me carefully, then asked, "Suzanne, is there something on your mind? You seem kind of distant today."

I hadn't said a word about Grace or Max,

but it was foolish thinking Emma wouldn't notice. We worked too closely together for there to be many secrets.

"I'm sorry. I've got a lot on my mind this morning."

"If you want to talk about it, I'm a good listener."

I stood, then patted her shoulder. "I know you are. I just have to digest it all before I'm ready to talk about it. Thanks for offering, though."

"I'm here if you need me," she said.

That's when the timer went off, ending our break.

"Time to make the donuts," I said, grinning at her, emulating the old donut commercial I'd loved as a kid.

"Suzanne, if there's one thing I've learned about this business, it's always time to make the donuts."

We got back to work, and by the time we opened at five-thirty, we had display cases full of donuts, but from the way the snow was still pelting down outside, nobody was going to be able to make it in to eat any.

Or so I thought.

As I looked out the window, I heard a rumbling coming down Springs Drive, and I looked outside to see a plow lumbering up the road.

It appeared that my two favorite plowmen were back.

Bob and Earl came in, shook the snow from their hats, then walked up to the counter together.

Bob, the big, gregarious one of the two, said, "Man alive, it's coming down out there. We had trouble getting our plow out of the garage this morning, didn't we, Earl?"

His slightly-built partner merely nodded, which was his preferred method of communication. Working so closely with Bob, Earl probably found it an easy habit to acquire, since Bob enjoyed talking so much, whether he had anything in particular to say or not.

"Let's see," he said as he rubbed his hands together. "What looks good? You know what? It all looks great. What do you think, Earl?"

His coworker smiled. "Hmm."

I got them two coffees, then grabbed a tray for their orders. "Another dozen donuts this morning, gentlemen?"

Bob patted his expanding waistline. "I'd better start with five. My overalls are getting a little snug."

He slapped his partner on the back, and I half-expected the happy blow to send Earl to his knees, but he didn't even rock from the impact. It was pretty clear that Earl was stronger than he looked.

He held up three fingers, and said, "Pumpkin."

I got his donuts, then turned to Bob. "And you?"

"Surprise me," he said.

As I grabbed some of my best donuts, I asked, "Is it as bad as it looks out there?"

He shook his head. "No, not yet, but the National Weather Service is saying that this one's going to get worse before it gets better. By noon, we're supposed to have eight inches, and then it's really going to start cranking up. They're saying we could have two feet by nightfall."

"You're kidding," I said. We hadn't had two feet of snow since I'd been a little girl, and that was long ago.

"No, ma'am, I never joke about snow accumulations, not in my line of work." He looked outside at the falling snow, then added, "We're going to get these to go, if you don't mind. I've got a feeling it's going to be a long day."

I did as he asked, then said, "As long as it keeps snowing, I'll keep refilling your coffee cups on the house. How's that sound?"

"Like you're going to lose money on us," Bob said as he frowned.

"Are you kidding me? I'm counting on you two to keep the roads open so my customers can get here." I smiled at them both, then added, "Besides, I figure I'll more than make up for it with all the donuts you're going to buy."

He laughed, a sound that rattled the windows. "You will at that. I can always get bigger coveralls," Bob said.

He looked over at Earl, who was standing patiently by, and asked, "Are you going to stand there all morning gabbing, buddy, or are we going to go plow some snow?"

"Snow," Earl said, and the men left with their orders, back to their jobs making the roads safe for the rest of us.

By seven, we'd had no other customers, and I'd pitched in to help Emma with the dishes. I left the dividing door between the kitchen and the front open in case someone came in, but I wasn't worried about the money in the till. Max knew if he pulled that trick again, I'd skewer him with one of my long wooden donut turners.

We did all we could in back, and as I threw a dish towel over my shoulder, I said, "You can go home, if you want to. It looks like nobody's going to make it in today."

"If you don't mind, I'd just as soon stay here with you."

"You know you're welcome to, but I thought I'd offer."

"If I go home, Dad will find something for me to do, but if I stay, he'll think I'm working hard." She shrugged, then added, "It hasn't exactly been easy around the house lately."

"Is he still giving you a hard time about what happened here?"

Emma nodded, the sadness easy to see in her eyes.

I'd promised to help Max, but not to the point of hurting Emma. "Can you keep a secret?" I asked.

"I don't know, I guess it depends on the secret."

"It's one that will make you feel better, but you can't tell anyone else. At least not until later."

She looked at me and arched one eyebrow. "Okay, I'll admit it. You've got me curious."

"We weren't robbed the other day," I said.

"You took the money?" she asked, a hint of hurt in her voice.

"Don't be silly. Max did. He was watching the store, and the second you disappeared, he rushed over and cleaned us out."

"How do you know that?" Emma asked.

"He told me yesterday."

She looked startled by that declaration as well. "You've talked to him? I thought the police were looking for him."

"They are. He hid in the back of my Jeep yesterday when we closed up shop, but then he took off again. I honestly don't have a clue where he's hiding now." As I looked outside at the snow, I added, "But I hope it's someplace warm."

She shook her head. "I appreciate you telling me that, but it still doesn't help."

"We're getting the money back," I said, not understanding her attitude. "It's not lost after all."

"I left my post," she said. "That's what matters."

"We're not in the military," I said. "You didn't desert in the face of enemy fire or anything."

"Try telling my dad that," she said.

Well, at least I'd tried to make her feel better.

I was surprised to see Wilma come trudging through the snow to get to my shop, since she wasn't exactly a regular customer of mine.

As she took off her heavy parka and put it on the rack up front, I said, "Good morning. You're a brave soul facing this kind of weather for a donut."

She barely glanced at me as she said, "I thought my customers deserved a treat this morning. Would you get me two dozen donuts, any assortment? I figure if they're willing to face this snow to get their hair done, they're entitled to something special."

As I grabbed two boxes from under the counter, I said, "It's nice of you to think my donuts are special."

Wilma smiled at me, then I saw her eyes go to the counter where I had some of my Christmas decorations. When she saw my nativity scene, the stand-up forest of snow covered mountains, the mini-tree lit with small lights, my fully-stocked gumdrop tree, the carolers, and the stuffed snowmen, she did a double take and stared openly at the display until she saw me notice her fixation.

I said, "I know it's a bit much, but Christmas only comes around once a year."

"And you're taking full advantage of it, aren't you?"

"Why not?" I asked. "If you don't mind my asking, I heard something around town that disturbed me. Were you and Darlene fighting around the time when she was murdered? I'm not saying you killed her. I'm just wondering if everything was okay between the two of you when she died."

"They were fine," Wilma said, "and any-one who says otherwise is a liar." She eased her tone a little as she added, "I never really had anything to do with her outside of work, but we didn't have to be best friends to work together. As a matter of fact, I've never even been to her place, and she's certainly never stepped foot in mine. That didn't make us enemies, though. You'd be amazed how many of the girls who work for me have no idea what my house looks like. I like to keep things that way, too. It gives us a kind of distance, you know? I learned early on that it doesn't pay to get too overly familiar with your employees."

"I don't know, Emma and I are pretty close," I said.

"Has she been to your house?"

I thought about it, and realized that I didn't know. "I can't say," I admitted.

"Thanks, you just made my point."

I got her donuts, took her twenty, then made change. "Do you have a lot of ap-pointments scheduled for today?"

"Suzanne, it's three days before Christ-mas. Everyone wants to look good for the holidays." She stared at my ponytail, then added, "But I could squeeze you in if you'd like. Why don't you lock up and come to the shop with me this morning? It won't

342

take long, I promise."

"No thanks," I said. There was no way I was going under her scissors. "I'm afraid my customers are just as hungry for what I do as yours are for you. Everybody likes donuts at the holidays."

She shrugged. "If you change your mind, let me know."

"Oh, you can bet on that," I said.

Half an hour later, a few brave souls started making their way through the snow to Donut Hearts.

George came in, and shook the snow off his hat.

"Why didn't you answer your cell phone?" he asked accusingly.

I patted my pockets, then I remembered where I'd left it. "Because it's still at home. I was recharging it last night, and I forgot to bring it with me this morning."

"That explains it. Try your phone."

"I just told you, it's at home."

He frowned as he pointed to the wall behind me. "I mean that one."

I picked it up, and instead of the dial tone I'd been expecting, all I heard was a hissing and crackling on the other end.

"It's dead," I said.

"That's why I came trudging through the snow. I was worried about you."

343

"I'm fine," I said. "You didn't have to come all this way."

"Are you kidding me? I've been going crazy with worry."

"Is that what brought you out in this mess? I'm touched, I truly am."

George shrugged. "Man, do I have a blockbuster for you."

"I could use some new information," I said. I remembered my conversation with Cara, and said, "I've got some news myself."

"Go ahead, let's hear it."

"I found out Lester Moorefield lost his feed the day of the murder and was off the air long enough to kill Darlene and get back to the remote station."

"Didn't someone from the station notice he was gone?" George asked.

"He worked the location alone," I said. "Lester is still on our list, stronger than ever." I looked at George, then said, "Go on. I can tell you're about to burst. What did you find out?"

"It turns out that Darlene's cousin, Taylor — the one who was executor of their great-aunt's estate — has a dirty little secret of his own."

"What is it?" I asked.

"He's got a record as long as my arm, and

344

I'm pretty sure he had more of a reason to kill Darlene than any of us realized."

PILLA BITES

These are very loosely based on a Mexican dessert, but I've changed it quite a bit over the years. These aren't as sweet as most donuts, but they're still tasty.

Ingredients

1 cup flour
1/2 teaspoon baking powder
1/2 teaspoon baking soda
1/4 teaspoon salt
1/2 teaspoon granulated sugar
1 tablespoon butter, soft
Water, warm (as needed)

Directions

Sift the flour, baking powder, baking soda, salt, and sugar, then add the butter until it's absorbed into the dough. Add warm water to the dough until it reaches the consistency of pie crust. Set it aside for 20–30 minutes, then roll the dough out to 1/8 inch. Cut diamonds, rounds, or donut shapes out of the dough, then fry in 360°F canola oil. They cook very quickly so keep watch, and flip when one side browns.

Drain on paper towels, dust with a little sugar or dab on a touch of honey, and enjoy!

CHAPTER 14

"What has he been arrested for?" I asked.

"The list is pretty long, but it's mostly centered on fraud. The man's a con man, and one of his scams was robbing widows out of their inheritances. You'll never believe how he did it."

"You've got my attention," I said. "Stop holding back."

George nodded. "Good old Taylor found new widows without anyone else in their lives, and he stepped in and offered to take over as executor for their late husbands' estates. By the time he was done milking them, there wasn't much left. I have a feeling that if he got his hands on that money, there wouldn't have been anything left to distribute."

"And a hundred thousand dollars is a motive for murder, even if a thousand isn't," I said. "That's good work, George."

"It wasn't too tough, once I figured out

his real name, and some of the aliases he was using."

"What do we do now?" I asked as I topped off his coffee.

George said, "I told the chief what I suspected this morning, and he's looking for Taylor right now." He looked at me as he added, "Suzanne, I owed him that, after what happened with Muriel. I had to get back in his good graces."

I patted his hand. "I don't care who catches the killer, just as long as he's caught. You really think he did it?"

"I think there's a good chance of it," George said. He took another drink of coffee, then said, "If you'll excuse me, I'm going to help them look. I'll let you know when we find him."

Once he was gone, Emma walked back out front. "Was that George?"

"As a matter of fact, it was. He thinks Darlene's cousin Taylor killed her, and he's out looking for him now, along with the police."

"I don't know how you do it," Emma said.

"Do what?" I asked as I cleaned one of our tables. The snow was still coming down outside at a furious pace.

"Deal with murderers," she said. "At one point I thought I was cut out for digging into people's lives, but deep down, I realize that I'm not."

"It's not like I go out looking for trouble," I said. "It just seems to have a way of finding me."

By eleven-thirty that morning, we'd sold a great many more donuts than I'd ever expected, and I was glad we'd braved the elements and come to work.

Emma kept looking outside, until I finally said, "Why don't you just go on home. I can handle it till closing."

"Are you sure?" she said as she grabbed her coat. Emma had learned early on that whenever an escape route was offered, it made sense to jump on it, since things could change so quickly.

"I'm sure," I said before she was halfway out the door. I got out my mop and touched up the floor where newspapers didn't quite cover it, and was just putting it away when the front door opened.

From the look on his face, Lester Moorefield hadn't come by Donut Hearts for a morning treat.

He looked angry, and I suddenly realized that I was at the donut shop all alone.

"Good morning, Lester," I said. "Shouldn't

you still be on the air?"

"We're running the Best of Lest for the last hour." He didn't even offer me a greeting back. "Suzanne, you need to stop what you're doing, or someone's going to get hurt."

"What are you talking about?" I said as I eased myself back toward the mop. It wasn't much of a weapon, but it had to be better than facing him down barehanded.

He kept approaching, and in a few seconds he cut off my route to the back. "You're sticking your nose somewhere it doesn't belong."

"I'm sure I don't know what you're talking about," I said. Why on earth had I sent Emma home early? Not that she would be much help if something happened, but it would be nice if there was a witness to whatever Lester had in mind for me.

"You know exactly what I mean," he said, and I could smell a trace of alcohol on his breath.

We held the stare for a few seconds when the front door opened. A burly man bundled up for the weather came in, and Lester stepped away from me and left the donut shop without another word.

The man stared at his retreating form, then asked me, "Is everything all right?"

"It's fine," I said, collecting myself and waiting on him. Lester's behavior had shaken me more than I cared to admit. I'd known all along that I was vulnerable working at the donut shop, and I wondered if perhaps Emma was right. Maybe I should step out of the way and let Chief Martin handle the criminals. I would be a lot safer if I just stuck to donuts.

But I couldn't do it. If I, or someone I cared about, was under suspicion when I knew in my heart they were innocent, I couldn't stand idly by. I wasn't wired that way.

No matter what the risk, I had to help my friends, or what was I? And that circle included Max. Though my love for him was finished, there was still an element of caring there. It mattered to me what happened to him, and if I could help him, I would.

That didn't mean I had to set myself up, though. I decided to close up early, and locked the front door ten minutes before noon. I wished I could leave, but I still had some cleaning to do. If I didn't, Emma and I would face twice the work tomorrow morning. But it felt good latching the deadbolt in place, and as I did, I saw that it was still snowing at a rapid pace, coming down in sheets of white. What was going on with the weather?

There were barely a dozen donuts left as I cleaned the trays, so I put them in a box to take home with me. All I wanted to do was clean up and get out of there.

As I collected the soiled newspapers on the floor, something on the counter caught my attention, and I nearly fell over when I realized a connection I'd been missing all morning.

I knew who the murderer was, and the clue had been staring at me even before Darlene was murdered.

I put on my boots and grabbed my jacket, then almost as an afterthought, grabbed the clue that had finally struck home and headed out into the blizzard. I knew Chief Martin was out there looking for Taylor, but suddenly, I realized he was going after the wrong suspect.

The storm was fierce, and I'd just made it three steps out my door when a voice came from around the corner. "Get back inside."

"Hi, Wilma. I was just on my way home."

"With that?" she said as she gestured to the gumdrop tree in my hands.

"I thought it would look better on our fireplace mantle at home."

"Do as I say and get inside, Suzanne."

And that's when I saw the gun in her hand.

Once we were back in the shop, I knew I was lost, but that didn't mean I was ready to give up. If I could stall her long enough, maybe someone would come by. George could return, or I might find an opening to stop her from killing me. One thing was certain; if I just submitted to her will, I was dead.

Wilma said, "You're smarter than I thought you were. That was a pretty clever trap you set." She motioned toward the gumdrop tree. "Pretty bold of you, sneaking it out of her apartment like that."

"Believe it or not, this isn't Darlene's. We must have the only two in town. I thought my eyes were playing tricks on me when I saw it at her place a few days ago."

Wilma's expression faltered. "Why should I believe you?"

I said, "Why shouldn't you? You're the one with the gun, and it just happens to be the truth."

"Then how did you know I killed her?"

I started working my way toward the mop. Maybe I could knock the gun out of her hand with it. At least I'd die trying to save myself, and not be shot like some tin can in a shooting gallery.

"I saw the way you reacted when you spotted it on my counter. You told me yourself that you'd never been in Darlene's apartment, but why would you lie about it, unless you had something to hide? It's the only way it all made sense. But honestly, why kill her, Wilma? Did the money mean that much to you?"

"It wasn't the money, you idiot," she said. "It was the betrayal. I could have lived with her stealing from me, but when she took money from Lester Moorefield to spread rumors about me and my shop, she went too far. My business is my sanctuary, and she soiled it. I had no choice. I thought a stake through the heart was an appropriate response for a traitor, even if it was on the other end of a candy cane."

"How is it that no one saw you do it?" I had to keep her talking. I was nearly at the mop, and if I could just get a little closer, I could make my move.

Wilma laughed, like a child getting a special Christmas present. "Trust me, no one could be more surprised than I was. I kept expecting someone to wrestle me to the ground, but when I realized that no one had noticed what I'd done, I simply walked away."

"And you can do that again right now. You don't have to kill me," I said. "I won't tell a soul."

"We both know better than that," she said.

"People are going to realize you had to be the one who shot me. It's pretty clear you're tied up into this mess, and Chief Martin's no fool."

"This is going to look like a botched robbery. You were already hit once this week, weren't you? It's not hard to believe that whoever robbed you the first time came back for what was left."

I realized that she was probably right. No one but Emma knew Max had robbed the shop himself. She'd come forward after I was dead, so at least I had hope that it wouldn't go unsolved.

But I never wanted it to get that far. "Wilma, we can work something out."

She shook her head. "I'm afraid you're just a loose end I need to tie off, Suzanne. I'm sorry, I truly am." She stared at my ponytail, then said, "You really should have let me do your hair. Tell you what. I'll talk to the funeral home and volunteer my services. When everybody in town sees my hairstyle on you in that open coffin, they'll be amazed at how lovely you look."

That was even more incentive to stop her.

I'd rather die than have her touch my hair, and I was about to prove it.

As my hand lunged for the mop, a shot filled the shop with explosive noise, and I could swear I felt the wind from the bullet.

"Stand still," she commanded me as she took aim for another try.

Just as she spoke, the front window of the donut shop shattered into a thousand tiny glistening fragments. Wilma turned toward the street, and I grabbed the mop and swung it with all my might. I missed her head, hitting her shoulder instead as another shot rang out. The gun went flying, and we both dove for it.

But not before Max could get there first. He plucked it out of the mess and pointed it at Wilma.

"Get up," he ordered. "I'm inclined to go ahead and shoot you after what I just saw, so don't give me any reason to follow through with it."

She stood up meekly, and I did as well, moving toward Max.

"Great timing," I said as I heard a police siren in the distance.

"I saw her force you inside, but I stopped to call the cops before I did anything else. Suzanne, are you all right?"

"I'm a little shaky," I admitted. "How

about you?"

"Me? I'm on top of the world."

That's when I noticed the blood seeping high out of his chest.

"Max," I said, my voice full of terror. "She shot you."

"Yeah, I noticed that too," he said. "Maybe you'd better take the gun."

I did as he asked, and felt him start to collapse beside me. I did my best to hold him up, and as I looked away, Wilma lunged toward me.

"One more step, and I'll shoot you," I told my captive as I let Max slump to the ground.

"You don't have the nerve," Wilma said.

I put a shot into the clock just over her head, and it shattered splendidly.

"That almost hit me," she said indignantly.

"Let me try again. I'm sure my aim will get better with a little practice."

I didn't have any more trouble with Wilma after that.

Chief Martin showed up a minute later, and as he glanced at Max, he asked quickly, "Is he dead?"

"I hope not," I said.

He took the gun from my hands. "What happened?"

"Wilma killed Darlene, and then she tried to kill me."

"Looks like her aim was a little off," the chief said.

Max came around, looked up at him, and said, "I don't know, she didn't have any trouble hitting me." While I'd been watching Wilma, Max had taken a bandana out of his pocket and was pressing it to his chest. The bullet must have hit higher up and to the right than I'd first thought from the way he was applying pressure to it.

"You all right?" the chief asked him.

"I've been better," he said as the EMS crew finally showed up.

I knelt down beside Max and kissed his forehead. "Thank you."

"You're welcome. I'll bet you'll take me back now, won't you?"

I looked deep into his eyes, then said, "Not on your life."

Max looked hurt for a second, then I could see he finally got it.

We were finished.

"I'm still glad I saved you."

"So am I," I said.

The chief whistled above us. "Man, you're even tougher than I thought."

Max said, "You'd better believe it."

"I was talking to her."

"Thanks," I said.

"I didn't mean it as a compliment."

And then the med techs were working on Max. The chief took Wilma away, and I was left with a donut shop in ruins. Snow started to drift in through the gaping front window, but I realized that I just didn't care.

Without another glance backward — the day's proceeds still in the cash register and the shop filling with snow — I walked away, and wondered as I did if I'd ever be able to come back.

CHAPTER 15

"Can I see her?" I heard George ask my mother as he came to the front door of our house.

I'd been cocooning there on the couch for the last three days, hiding out from the rest of the world while my wounds healed. Wilma hadn't done anything physically to me — as much as she'd tried — but the injuries I'd sustained had been just as bad as if her errant shot had struck home. Since my divorce from Max, I seemed to be a magnet for trouble, and I had to wonder if April Springs was really the place for me after all. With the prospect of Grace leaving and everything that had happened at Donut Hearts, maybe it was time to make a clean sweep of things and find somewhere I could start over. Momma had been shielding me ferociously since I'd come home, and it was time I'd needed to think long and serious thoughts.

But I had to face my friends sooner or later, and at least now, I thought I was ready for it.

"It's okay, Momma," I called out. "Let him in."

"Are you positive?"

"It's all right," I said. "But thank you for protecting me."

"It's what a mother does," she said as she stepped aside.

George came in and offered me a smile as he took a seat opposite mine in front of the fireplace. He had a present in his hands, which surprised me, since we'd never exchanged them before. The snow was finally starting to melt, just in time to give us a slushy Christmas. That's when I realized that it was indeed Christmas day.

"Hang on one second, George," I said.

I walked over to Momma, who was watching from the edge of the room, and hugged her.

"Merry Christmas," I said. "I'm so sorry. I've been so wrapped up in what's been happening with me, I forgot all about you."

She hugged me for another second as she stroked my hair. "Suzanne, there's nothing to apologize for. As long as I get to spend the holidays with you, that's all I care about."

"I love you, Momma," I said.

"And I love you, too." We didn't say it much — probably not nearly enough — but today, it was the best gift I could get, or receive.

George had been watching us. It was easy to tell by the way he diverted his eyes when I came back to the couch.

"Suzanne, if you're not ready to talk, I understand. Just say the word, and I'm out of here."

"I have to face the world sooner or later," I said. "Merry Christmas."

He nodded, then thrust the present toward me.

I didn't accept it, though.

"George, I didn't get you anything."

"This is from me, and a lot of your other friends and customers in town," he said. "Emma pitched in, too."

As I tore the paper off, I realized that it was a photo frame. "It's lovely," I said as I flipped it over, and then noticed the picture inside.

"It's my donut shop the way it used to be," I said.

George shook his head. "No, it's the way it is now. We took that picture yesterday."

I studied it more carefully. "But the window's back in place, and the decorations are all up. How did you manage it during the holidays on such short notice?"

"We all pitched in, and a few of us called in favors, too. It's ready for you whenever you want to come back," he said.

"I appreciate that," I said, putting the frame on the coffee table between us, face down so I didn't have to look at the picture.

"When are you coming to open Donut Hearts back up?" he asked.

I looked over at Momma, who was clearly about to say something, and shook my head. "I don't know," I said.

"We all miss you," George said.

"That's sweet of you. Please thank everyone for me, would you? Now if you don't mind, I'm a little worn out."

He got the hint. "I understand. Thanks for seeing me. I hope you have a merry Christmas, Suzanne."

"Merry Christmas," I said, the words sounding hollow on my lips. What my friends had done touched me, but I wasn't sure it was enough to ever get me back to my shop.

What would I do instead, though? I'd held several different jobs over the years, but if I was being honest about it, none of them had mattered to me, except the last one. It wasn't that donuts were my life — I didn't care if I ever made another one at the moment — but they were a gateway to friends I never would have met otherwise, and that made them more precious than gold. I stared at the back of the frame for ten minutes, then turned it over and looked at my shop again. It was beautiful, even I could see that. The converted train depot had been transformed into a place that was every bit as much my home as my mother's house.

And I realized I could never walk away from it. Sure, things would be different with Grace gone, but that was life. Change was always bound to happen. No matter what might have happened at my shop before, I had to go back. Donut Hearts was where my heart belonged, and suddenly, all the angst I'd been going through, the mourning for giving up my shop, fell away like an old coat I'd just thrown off, and I had hope again.

The phone rang, and I grabbed it before Momma could. I'd been shielded long enough.

I was overjoyed when I realized that it was Grace.

"Merry Christmas, my friend," she said.

"You sound absolutely chipper," I said, a

little sad that she could be so happy about leaving town.

"Why shouldn't I? Everything's worked out better than I could have hoped."

"So, you liked San Francisco," I said.

"I loved it," she said. "But I'm back in April Springs, still waiting to see you. Are you ever going to let me come over?"

I decided to ignore her question. Honestly, I hadn't been able to face her until I could accept the fact that she'd be gone soon. "When do you have to move?" I asked, trying to keep the tears out of my voice.

"That's what's so wonderful. If you won't let me tell you in person, I'll do it over the phone. Suzanne, I don't have to go."

Did I just hear that right? "What do you mean?"

"I turned the promotion down," Grace said. So why did she sound so happy about it?

"Why on earth did you do that? You've been coveting that job for years."

Grace laughed. "Apparently I wasn't the only one. When my boss found out I said no, she and her boss came up with a counterproposal. My boss gets the San Francisco position, and I get North Carolina. Suzanne, I don't have to move after all. I can work right here from April Springs most of the time."

"Outstanding," I screamed into the phone loud enough for Momma to come running into the room.

"Are you all right?" she asked.

"I just got the best present ever," I explained. "Grace isn't moving to California after all."

"That's wonderful," she said.

"Hello. I'm still here," I heard Grace's voice say over the telephone.

"Then come on over. We'll celebrate."

"I'm on the front porch, you nit."

I jumped up from the couch, and we met at the door.

"Welcome home," I said.

"I can say the same thing to you, can't I?"

I nodded. "I'd say that's just about the perfect thing to say right now."

Grace, Momma, and I were just getting ready to eat the Christmas feast my mother had prepared when the front door rang.

Momma said, "Suzanne, would you get that? I've got my hands full."

"Who on earth comes calling on Christmas day?" I asked.

"I suppose you'll have to go to the door and see."

When I opened it, I'd been expecting one

of my friends, or even a band of carolers. What I didn't expect was to find Jake Bishop standing there, his hat literally in his hands.

"Jake? What are you doing here?"

He looked like he was about to cry, and then he said, "I'm transporting Wilma Jackson to Raleigh."

"They don't usually make you do that, do they?"

I could see the vulnerability in his eyes. "They don't, but I requested this assignment. I wanted to see you."

I shook my head. "We've said all we need to say to each other," I said. "Good-bye, Jake."

"What if I'm not ready to say that?" he said as he put a hand on the door, holding it open.

"You aren't ready to say anything else," I said. "It's okay, Jake, I understand."

"Suzanne, I know I've been a complete fool, but I'm trying here, okay? At least give me a chance."

"You had your chance," I said. I was still hurt by the way he'd thrown me away, like a wrapper he was finished with, no matter what his reasons had been.

"You're with *him,* aren't you?" he asked,

as he tried to look past me, inside the house.

"Him? Who are you talking about?"

"Max. He's in there. I just know it."

I laughed, despite the way I felt seeing him again. "Jake, Max and I are ancient history, and he's finally gotten the message. I'm tired of looking back. It's time to focus on what's ahead."

He looked relieved by my admission, then said, "If there's room for me, I'd like to be a part of that."

"I can't," I said. "Or more importantly, you can't. You live in the past, and I'm not saying I blame you, but I can't compete with your dead wife."

"I don't want you to," he said, and I could see tears forming in his eyes. "I need a chance to start over."

"I just wish it was that easy," I said. "Maybe if we were just meeting for the first time, if we could wipe everything that's happened between us away, things could be different. Good-bye, Jake."

"Good-bye," he said.

I closed the door, not even daring to allow myself to watch him drive away. Turning Jake down was the hardest thing I'd ever done, but it was for the best. I'd meant what I'd said. If we could start fresh, maybe things would work out between us, but too much had happened.

Maybe there were no do-overs in life.

I started back to the kitchen when there was another knock on the door.

Despite my attempt to slow myself to a sedate pace, I ran toward it, suddenly hoping against hope that he wasn't giving up after all.

Jake was there again, and I started to say something when he said, "Hi, my name's Jake Bishop, and my car seems to be stuck in the slush. Would you mind if I use your phone?"

I raised one eyebrow, and he continued, "What's your name?"

"Suzanne Hart," I said hesitantly.

He offered his hand, and I took it. "Suzanne, it's a pleasure to meet you." Jake paused, then said, "Pardon me for saying so, but that smells delightful."

I couldn't help myself. I'd meant everything I'd said to him, and yet he'd been willing to put himself out there.

The least I could do was meet him halfway.

"We're having Christmas dinner," I said. "Would you like to stay? I'm sure my mother wouldn't mind."

"I'd hate to impose," he said, his smile still bright.

I tugged on his arm and pulled him inside. "Okay, enough with the role playing. Now, are you going to kiss me, or am I going to have to throw you out again?"

He stepped forward and took me in his arms as he said, "Well, if you put it that way . . ."

And then it was very good being me again.

We hope you have enjoyed this Large Print book. Other Thorndike, Wheeler, Kennebec, and Chivers Press Large Print books are available at your library or directly from the publishers.

For information about current and upcoming titles, please call or write, without obligation, to:

Publisher
Thorndike Press
295 Kennedy Memorial Drive
Waterville, ME 04901
Tel. (800) 223-1244

or visit our Web site at:

http://gale.cengage.com/thorndike

OR

Chivers Large Print
published by AudioGO Ltd
St James House, The Square
Lower Bristol Road
Bath BA2 3SB
England
Tel. +44(0) 800 136919
email: info@audiogo.co.uk
www.audiogo.co.uk

All our Large Print titles are designed for easy reading, and all our books are made to last.